ORBIT 4

"This is a choice collection of haunting tales collected by the founder of the Science Fiction Writers of America. Most of the stories typify the emerging new domain of science fiction, with its emphasis less on the 'out-there' than on the 'right-here, right-now.' Harlan Ellison, for example, in 'Shattered Like a Glass Goblin,' paints a picture of a houseful of hippies in the thrall of drugs and bestiality that is much too believable for comfort. In 'Probable Cause,' Charles Harness cites the use of clairvoyance in a case before the Supreme Court; and Kate Wilhelm portrays the agonizing problems of a computer analyst working on a robot weapon which requires the minds of dead geniuses to operate effectively. These are only a few of the many celebrated science fiction writers whose stories are included in the anthology, 'Orbit 4.' "

—*Publishers' Weekly*

Nine New SF Stories Especially Written For

ORBIT 4

EDITED BY

DAMON KNIGHT

A BERKLEY MEDALLION BOOK
PUBLISHED BY
BERKLEY PUBLISHING CORPORATION

Published by arrangement with the author's agent

Originally published by G. P. Putnam's Sons

BERKLEY MEDALLION EDITION, AUGUST, 1969

BERKLEY MEDALLION BOOKS are published by
Berkley Publishing Corporation
200 Madison Avenue
New York, N.Y. 10016

BERKLEY MEDALLION BOOKS ® TM 757,375

Printed in the United States of America

CONTENTS

Kate Wilhelm, who appeared in ORBIT 1 *with "Staras Flonderans," in* ORBIT 2 *with "Baby, You Were Great," in* ORBIT 3 *with "The Planners," offers another complex and fascinating story, in which fantasy and reality so intermingle that they can no longer be distinguished· When asked why she writes this way, the author suggests a look at the front page of the daily newspapers.*

WINDSONG

By Kate Wilhelm

We are three. We drive along the coast slowly until Paula says, "This one." Then we get out of the car and walk around the house nonchalantly, wade through the dunes to the ocean and swim there alone, away from the crowds that form a solid crust like soiled snow up and down the public beaches. How Paula knows this house is empty, but not that one, we don't know. She is never wrong. Subliminal signs that only she can perceive? A shade drawn wrong, a chair outside that should have been moved from the sun, a garment, long since dried, sun-bleached even, still flapping in the wind? We never know, and she can't tell us.

Paula is the windsong, quick, nimble, restless, long hair salt-dulled most of the time, too thin, sharp elbows, knees, cheekbones, collarbones. No makeup; she is in too

7

much of a hurry. A nail breaks and she bites it even again. She never pauses to examine anything; her restless gaze flicks here and there, noting perhaps, not lingering, and she says, "We have to go back. A storm is coming." How does she know?

Gregory says she noticed the grey in the water far out near the horizon. That and the feel of the wind on her skin, and the way the clouds scudded now, all were clues for her. But he can't tell when a storm is coming. Gregory is her twin brother. Both are fifteen this summer. Gregory is the rock around which the wind sings and flutters, departing to pry into this and that, but always whirling back again. Gregory can give reasons for most of her conclusions, but he can't reach the conclusions intuitively as she can.

Dan Thornton stirred in his seat and opened his eyes slowly. There was no sound that had roused him, nothing out of the ordinary. He listened for a moment to the familiar soft humming of the computer at his right side and before his gaze turned to it he knew the rippling play of lights would be normal. The instrument panel before him showed nothing abnormal either, no flashing amber light, or worse, the steady throbbing of the red light. Systems okay. He yawned and stretched. Time to make the routine checks. He opened and closed relays, turned the television camera on and studied the passengers, all piled in boxes like rows of frozen goods on a supermarket shelf; he turned the camera off again. Readings on his instruments, all normal. He got out the food capsules carefully, and put them on a sectioned dish and slid it into the recon unit. He waited until the light went on, killing two more minutes, then slowly drew out the dish of scrambled eggs and bacon, toast and honey. He dropped another capsule into a cup and slid it in, then sat down with his breakfast. Presently he had coffee and his first cigarette. He looked over the book titles on the spools. He dropped the spool he selected and some of the thread-tape unwound as it rolled across the cabin. He kicked it hard and abruptly sat down. The computer was calling him.

The alarm clock hummed, and Thornton woke up groggily, feeling the ache of unrested muscles. He turned off the clock before it could start its second phase: a raucous buzz that sounded like fifty men with fifty saws clearing a swath through a forest. His hand left the clock and groped for his notebook and he wrote down the dream details before they began to flit away. He paused and tried to remember something: a dream within the dream? Nothing came of it, and he wrote about the cabin he had seen, and the books on spools like thread. The reconstituter for food struck him as a particularly good idea, one he had never encountered before. He finished the dream sequence and only then stretched and felt each muscle protest again.

He padded in bare feet across the room to the bathroom and stood under a hot shower for ten minutes. The icy follow-up failed to revive him and he knew that his efficiency would be at about 60% of normal unless he took his zoom-wowie pills. He looked at the small bottle disdainfully, but swallowed two capsules and only then looked at his face.

"This is the way we start most of our days, old man," he said to the face. "Aches, try to shock the system into awareness, then the pep pills and a gallon of coffee. It's no good, old man. You know it's no good."

The old man in the mirror didn't answer, and he was almost sorry. The day the image did answer, he'd quit, just walk out and never come back, and that would be nice. Shaving, he repeated to himself, emphasizing each syllable of it, "That would be nice!"

At the office he was met by his secretary who handed a memo to him. Meeting for nine sharp. The Secretary would be present. End. He crumpled it and nodded to Jeanne. It was 8:45.

"Coffee?" he asked.

The girl nodded as he started through the doorway to

his inner office, a cubicle ten by ten. "I poured a cup, and there's more in the pot," Jeanne said. "Shall I start on the mail?"

"Sure, honey. And, Jeanne, try to winnow it way down, huh?"

She smiled sympathetically and he started on the coffee. He tried not to look at his desk, which Jeanne had cleaned up as much as possible, but which still was a jumble of plans, memoes, doodles, slide rules, schematics . . . The coffee was blistering hot, strong, black. The day began to seem less infernal. When he left for the conference in ten minutes he was carrying his third coffee with him. He grinned at Jeanne, and his stride was purposeful and his back straight.

There were fifteen men at the conference that morning, and all of them looked as bad as Thornton, or worse. They had all been driving on twelve-to-eighteen-hour days for seven months now, and the end was not in sight. Thornton could almost envy the union-protected maintenance men. He nodded to others and there were low greetings and hurried conversations in the shorthand that passed for talk. He thought, one bomb right here, right now, and poof, there goes the Special Institute for Applied Research.

He saw that the Secretary was already in the room, cloistered by several bodies near the window, speaking in his low monotone to Halvern, the Director of the Institute. The clock chimed softly and Halvern moved toward the long table, the Secretary following, still talking, like a priest mumbling incomprehensible prayers.

Introductions were unnecessary since the Secretary had been there before. Thornton thought of his bomb and enlarged it a bit in his mind, still not The Bomb, of course, but slightly bigger than the one he had contemplated earlier. Would the war stop then? He knew it would not, but there would be those on the outside who would sanctify him. He grinned at the thought, and for a moment he was afraid the grin had reached the outside of his face. But there were no looks askance, and deliberately he turned his thoughts from that line and became attentive to what the Secretary was saying:

". . . imperative that we solve this final problem before negotiations are finalized. When the talks begin, our activities in the field will be curtailed . . ."

Thornton added: *and we have stalled the Secretary-General about as long as possible.*

"Naturally we are trying to bring about peace talks as rapidly as possible *on the surface anyway where we can point to our efforts,* but it is difficult to negotiate with an enemy that is so xenophobic. *You mean he hates our guts, with reason, and he doesn't believe a word we say.* I repeat, the President has informed me that it is imperative that we complete our plans for the Phalanx and try it out under battle conditions so that we will better be able to assess its potential in the event we are faced with a major land war. . . ."

Thornton turned him off then, letting his gaze slide from the Secretary's hand-tooled-leather face to the window that framed a vista of Tennessee hills touched with early spring. Dogwoods and redbuds were in bloom, and a strong wind whipped them unmercifully. Kite wind. Sailing wind. Sailing . . . He smiled inside and wished he could go sailing along the coast on the curious flat-bottomed skiff Gregory had picked up somewhere in the distant, almost forgotten past. Twenty-five years ago, by God! For a moment the thought of his boyhood friend stirred something, and his hand toying with a pencil tightened its grip painfully.

He wrenched his attention back to the Secretary who had left the familiar rah, rah, team talk, and was on something new finally. "I am scheduling the first simulated battle test for one month from today, and the first actual battle test for sixty days subsequent to that date." There was more of it, but Thornton perversely blocked it out. So they should all work for twenty hours a day instead of eighteen. He shrugged inwardly and decided that he didn't care. With wow-zooie pills and coffee they would all stay on their feet until they collapsed, and it didn't matter what shape they would be in when the year was over. One year in the Institute, one year off resting, then back to the university to pick up the threads of classwork, lectures on Advanced Programming Theory, and his own small quiet lab. And back to his family, of course.

Thornton returned to his office after the meeting and was confronted with the meaningless garble from other departments that he had to translate into a program. Very deliberately he didn't try to understand most of the problems that he worked with. He didn't want to know what the Phalanx would be able to do and what it would not.

He divided his day into thirds: the first third, from 8:45 until 1:00, he worked on the advanced programming that was his to do: after lunch, 1:30 until 5:30, he went over the papers prepared by others, sometimes accepting them, often sending them back; from 7:30 until exhaustion stopped him he worked with the computer searching for errors. Then dream-laden sleep until 7:30 the next morning. At 5:30, three days a week, he spent half an hour with his analyst, and it was to him that he reported any interesting ideas that had come to him during his dreams, awake or asleep. His analyst, Dr. Feldman, believed implicitly in the creative ability of the unconscious to serve up workable ideas which generally were brushed aside because they were far afield of the patient's area of interest. Now that he was aware of the sort of things that Feldman was looking for, Thornton also searched his dreams and his reveries for those ideas, and was surprised to find how many of them there were. Surprised and excited. This was something that he planned to take from the Institute with him when he left. Most of it he planned, swore he would leave behind him forever.

He told Feldman the dream without consulting his notes: "I was in the cabin of a spaceship, carrying cryo-

passengers to a distant star system. I was responsible for
them. Everything was functioning smoothly." He told in
detail how he had prepared his breakfast, and then went
on to the book incident. "It was a variation of the micro-
film process, I suppose, simplified somewhat. I read the
title the way you would read the label on a spool of
thread; it even had the feel and texture of a spool of
thread. I dropped it, though, and woke up then. My clock
went off."

Feldman didn't interrupt him, simply nodded when
Thornton came to the end of it. When Thornton pulled
out his notebook and read from his notes, he was cha-
grined to find that he had omitted parts of the dream.

Feldman said, "The dream that you remember, what
kind of a dream was it?"

"Kind? Oh, I see. I think it was black-and-white. I
don't remember any color. I didn't feel it particularly, I
don't think."

"Yes. Could you come out of it at any time? Did you
realize that you were dreaming?"

"I don't think so. I have done that, and noted it afterward, but not this time."

Feldman worked on the dream within a dream, but
Thornton couldn't remember if there had been one or
not. Short of hypnosis, Feldman decided, it would stay
repressed for the time being. Thornton and Feldman had
discussed dreams in the past, and he knew that Feldman
believed there were three major types of dreams: the hyp-
nagogic dreams that float in and out of awareness on falling asleep, and on awakening, the kind that fade in and
out of a short nap when you know you are dreaming
and even take a hand in directing the dream sometimes.
Then there was the next stage where the dreamer had no
control, but was really more an observer than a partici-
pant, although he could be both at the same time, watching himself from a distance. The third kind was the sort
that Thornton rarely had, or if he had, seldom remembered: the dream that is a reality in itself, the dream that

can result in a heart attack if it is a nightmare, or in orgasm if it is sexual, the dream that exists, that can change the dreamer just as a living experience can.

Feldman was smiling happily when Thornton looked at him at the end of the questioning, and Thornton knew that finally he was proving interesting to the psychiatrist. After seven months of unshakable normalcy, he had done something interesting. He felt a stab of fear and wished he hadn't told the dream completely, had let it go at the remembered version, but even as he thought it, he knew that it would have been impossible. Feldman would have known, and resistance would have delighted him even more than mere repression. For a moment he hated the smiling man, but it passed, and he grinned back briefly.

"You think I'm going to earn my keep after all?" he asked.

"When you have something come up after this length of time, I must assume that there is the possibility that it can be connected with the work here, yes. We shall see. I am scheduling you for an hour tomorrow, starting at five. Is that convenient?"

The question was rhetorical.

"You should give thought to the spool of thread that you tried to rid yourself of," Feldman said. "As you fall asleep, think to yourself, spool of thread, spool of thread. Who knows, perhaps it will come to you." He held open the door and Thornton left.

Thornton knew that early in their dealings Feldman had had him in deep hypnosis, that he had few secrets from the man, that probably Feldman had left him with some posthypnotic cues, and he wondered if it had been a suggestion, or an order, that he should think of a spool of thread, and even as he wondered about it, he knew that coming from Feldman a suggestion could have the force of an order given at gunpoint. His smile was without mirth as he remembered what Feldman had said once when asked why he didn't merely hypnotize all his patients and have them recite their dreams and fears to him.

"Ah, but the associations, the meanings would be lost then, perhaps. Why do you repress this and not that? This is what is interesting, not what you repress particularly, although it can be. No, I might nudge you from time to time, but I want you to bring them out with the proper associations, the associations that only you can make."

Spool of thread, spool of thread . . .

He remembered, dreamed, of losing his first tooth, and the thread his mother had tied around it, her gentle insistence that he pull it himself, and her promise, after a look of surprise and amusement that, yes, they would send it to his father. He drifted out of the dream-reverie and was wide awake thinking about his father who had been a good man, kind and wise, a colonel in the army. He got out of bed and paced his tiny room smoking furiously, but the image of his father naked and bruised, shaved clean, dragging one foot, being pulled hobbling down a street crowded with Oriental faces that were grimaces of hate, the image remained, just as he had watched it on television. A good man, he repeated soberly. But he might have done the things they accused him of doing. He might have.

He swallowed a pill and returned to bed and found himself repeating: spool of thread, spool of thread. He wanted to get up again, but the pill was quick and he felt lethargy stealing over him. He would be achy in the morning, always was achy when he resorted to sleeping pills. Spool of thread . . .

He dreamed discordant, meaningless dreams, fantasies without basis in reality. And slept deeper, and was less restless on the single bed.

We walk through the museum arm in arm and it is Paula who is leading us, although she is in the middle. Her steps are light and quick, and she talks incessantly. She pauses before the paintings of the new artist, Stern,

and she squints and cocks her head this way and that,
then she pulls us on to the next one. She is changed now,
her hair still long and straight, but shining clean, and she
has done something to her face, something so subtle that
I can't decide what it is. I find myself staring at her again
and again, and she smiles at me, and for an instant I find
the wild girl who lived for the ocean only five years ago.
Then it is gone and she is saying, "It's such a joke! He's
wonderful! Don't you see it?" There are fifty paintings,
arranged in aisles that meet and interconnect so that it is
hard not to repeat an aisle. There is no arrow pointing
this way, no numbers on the paintings, but Paula has led
us through them to the end, and she is laughing with delight. The artist is there, regarding Paula with deep and
penetrating interest. She runs to him and kisses him on
his bearded cheek and says, "Thank you. I won't tell."
And she doesn't tell. Gregory goes back to the beginning
and works his way slowly to us once more, and when he
comes back, his eyes share her mirth, but he won't tell
either. I know that he can explain it although she can't,
but he needed her to tell him there was something to explain. I return later and study the paintings alone for a
long time, and I don't know what they found. I am lost
there. The paintings are grotesque, hideous and meaningless, and the arrangement is meant to befuddle, not to en-
lighten.

Paula loves the city as she loved the beaches. She runs
and dances through the streets joyously, tasting what no
one else tastes, smelling what no one else smells, seeing
what is not there for my eyes to see. She sings in the city
like a fresh breeze from the ocean.

Paula plans to leave school in the spring. She
wants. . . she doesn't know what she wants, but it is not
in school. She will travel, perhaps marry. I feel tightness
in my throat and I ask if she will marry me and she stops,
frozen, and finally after a long time she says no. I am
angry with her and stalk away. Gregory says that she is
like a bird now, she must fly here and there before she

stops and love would stop her. I hate them both, their closeness, their awareness of each other. I want to kill them both. Especially Paula. My hands are fists when she comes near me and the smothering waves of love-hate immobilize me at a place where the pain is unendurable.

She knows. Paula is like a spring wind then, gentle and soothing, and I am filled with her presence. For two weeks we are together and she is in every cell of me, deep in me where she can never escape now. Then she is gone. Gregory knows where, I think, but he doesn't tell me. He plods with his books, getting every detail of every subject letter-perfect, but he never originates anything, never offers anything and he is like a shadow without the wind. I know his loss is greater than my own, but I don't care about that. I return to California where I am still in school, and the jet is my scream of anguish that I cannot utter for myself. I want her out of my life. I want never to see her again. I want her dead so that no one else can have her.

Dan Thornton strode across his mammoth office and began pushing buttons on a four-by-eight-foot console on one side of his desk. Three doors flew open from other rooms, and shaking men entered; he waved them to seats and waited for the Secretary.

"I have your answer," he said to the Secretary on his arrival. "It is simply this . . ." He was dying, his throat tightening and choking him, his heart pounding harder and harder. . . .

He sat up shivering. He reached for the notebook and the light, and wrote quickly and lay down again. He thought he had been wakeful off and on most of the night, and now the sky was lightening, a pale grey touched with peach tones. He squeezed his eyes tighter, desperately wanting sleep to return, deep, untroubled sleep, and he knew that it would not.

Feldman said slowly, "You are aware of what the

Phalanx is, yet you consistently deny any real knowledge of it to yourself. Why is that?"

Thornton shrugged. He thought of his wife and three children and talked of them for a few minutes until Feldman stopped him.

"I know about them. You told me early about them, and it is on your file. Tell me about the spool of thread."

He free-associated for a while; he had learned to do it quite well, but privately he thought it was nonsense. He paid little attention to his own voice when he free-associated. It wasn't as if he were being analyzed for a medical purpose, he had told himself early in the business. Feldman was paid to keep tabs, that was all. He had nothing to hide, nothing of interest to learn about himself, so he cooperated, but didn't pay much attention.

Feldman said, "Maze," and he answered, "Art Museum." He sat straight up on the couch. He was shivering. Feldman nodded to him when he swung around to look. "So that is that," Feldman said. "What it is actually I don't know, but you do now, don't you?"

Thornton shook his head violently, shivering hard. He remembered the feeling of being lost at an art exhibit years ago. "It was so meaningless," he said. "This exhibit was arranged like a maze and the artist came over to me while I was standing there feeling stupid, and he told me that it meant nothing. I had worked hard trying to puzzle it out, and he said it had no meaning. It was arranged like a maze."

Feldman looked disappointed. His silence invited Thornton to keep talking, but there was nothing more to say about it. Thornton said, "The Phalanx is the final solution to the problem of modern warfare. It is an armored computer bank designed to control at least twenty-five subunits at this time, and it will have the capacity to control n subunits when it is completed. The subunits to this point have been built to scout jungle trails, and go through undergrowth where there are no trails searching out the enemy. They come equipped with flame throwers, grenade launchers, rocket launchers, communications units, infrared sensors, mass sensors, mine laying, or mine detection devices, chemical analysis labs, still and movie cameras, audio sensors and transmitters . . ."

He became aware of Feldman's bright, unblinking gaze and he paused and grinned at the analyst. Softly he added, "But the main problem with the Phalanx is that it doesn't know what a smile is on a friendly face. It can't distinguish between friend and enemy. It can't tell if the metal it senses is a gun or a hoe. It has no way of knowing if the mass-burdened heat source is a man with a howitzer or an ass with a load of firewood. And no matter how many changes the psycho-cybernetics lab sends to me, I can't program those things into it."

Thornton stood up and stretched. His gaze followed a low, long shaft of sunlight coming through the venetian blind where a slat was crooked. "I'm going for a walk," he said. He sensed that Feldman made a motion toward him, but there was no effort to stop him, or to force him to complete his hour.

"Tomorrow at five," Feldman said, and that was all.

His thighs burned as he climbed. He had wanted to climb the hill ever since the first tracery of white blossom had appeared high on its side, but no time, no time. And now his thighs burned. He should write to Ethel tonight. Hadn't even opened her last letter yet. He had put it down somewhere and had forgotten it. On the dresser in his room? On his desk? He groaned to himself at the thought of his desk, and he slipped on a moss-covered rock and banged his knee. Sitting on the damp pungent ground he rocked back and forth nursing the knee for a few minutes, catching his breath. He had come farther than he realized. Below him, almost hidden, he could see the Institute building. It had started as a low, long simple two-story building, but had been extended in three directions, like dominoes, and at the end of one of the newer additions there was construction going on. He had a vi-

sion of it worming its way over the hills, growing like a
snake through the mountains, creeping through valleys,
over crests, following watercourses . . . He closed his
eyes and composed part of the letter to Ethel. It would be
dull, he decided, faltering after the initial hope-you-are-
well bit. Ethel was a good woman, but dull. God, she was
dull. He remembered the shock he had felt the day he understood that Ethel had settled in on herself, that she`
would change no more, only become more what she was,
more dogmatic, less malleable to change of any sort,
more picture-pretty and smug. Ethel was forty. She had
been forty on her twenty-fifth birthday, would be forty on
her eightieth. But she was good, kind, considerate, a good
mother, a faithful and helpful wife, good social
animal. . .

They could say that about him. A good man. Plodding
maybe, but a good man. Wouldn't hurt a fly. Good to his
kids, a real father.

He leaned back against a treetrunk and watched the
sunset without thinking.

A good man.

The breeze on his cheek was warm and fragrant with
spring. Gradually he forgot about the cold, damp ground
beneath him. He thought about the three kids. Bang,
bang, bang, three years, three kids. That was the way
they had wanted it. Have them all together, raise them together and be done with that part of it. By the time we're
both forty, they'll be almost grown and we'll still be
young. Well, he was forty-four, and they were all grown.
But he wasn't young. Ethel wasn't young. Both of them
were good, good, good, but they were not young. He
dreamed of romping with the kids, and he knew the
romping was wrong. They were glad when he tired of it
and left them. He dreamed of his daughter's soft cheek
against his, as she whispered secrets to him, and his yawn
that had driven her away. Yet, he did love her with an
intensity that sometimes had startled and frightened him.
Perhaps that was why he had driven her away. He re-

membered her flying past him on her bicycle, hair streaming behind her, thin legs pumping harder and harder . . .

We go down the coast in the skiff with the wind
driving us hard. Feeling of fear, exhilaration, alertness,
watching for the sudden wave that could topple us. Paula's hair streaming out in the wind, hitting my face, stirring something in me, making me look at her through different eyes for a moment. And the intolerable ache that
was Paula. The searing, burning, unbearable pain that
meant Paula, and the release that was just as sudden and
even more intense.

He jerked from the tree and was on his feet. He shud-
dered once and started down the hill. He had been dreaming of his wife and the kids. Of his daughter . . . A flush
of deep shame swept over him and he stumbled blindly
back to the Institute.

"Dr. Thornton, there has to be a way to program these
abstracts, as you call them." Melvin Jorgenson paced. He
was a restless man. Even pacing failed to satisfy his need
to move, and in his hands he carried and played with a
pen whose point he extended and retracted over and
over, each time making an audible click. Thornton noticed that he was pacing in time to the click, or was he
clicking in time to his tread? He said nothing, and waited.
Maybe they were going to fire him.

The Director was there also, and it was to him Jorgenson was addressing himself, although he prefaced his re-
marks with Thornton's name. The Director looked unhappy.

"You know that we have been experimenting with various techniques," Jorgenson said, glancing at Thornton,
but still talking to the Director. "We have a simple psycho-modular unit in operation now, much like the one
you described in your book of several years ago. That
gave us the necessary line to follow, but as I say, this is a
simple unit."

He continued to talk and pace and by listening to him

very carefully, and ignoring the clicks as much as possible, Thornton finally understood that there was to be a major revision in the Phalanx, and he was to program the revised version with all the data that already had gone into the obsolete model. He started to laugh and continued to laugh until someone, the Director himself, brought him water. He said that he had strangled on a smothered cough, that he had caught cold when he had fallen asleep out in the woods a few nights ago. He allowed Jorgenson to lead him to the new unit ready to be connected to the Phalanx, and he asked the right questions, intelligent questions, and he made intelligent notes and finally said, sure, why not?

"The Phalanx," he wrote in his diary (because writing it, even though he would have to destroy what he had written afterward, set it in his mind: once written, never forgotten, he had learned early in his school career, and so had gone through school laboriously copying passages, notes, sometimes almost whole textbooks; he had remembered all of it, still remembered all of it), "is apparently a small building, and only on close approach can you see that there are treads under it, hidden by sides that come almost to the ground. There are pseudo-windows, a pseudo-exterior that can be made to conform to any local style of building. Inside . . ." He put the pen down and walked to the window. It was raining hard. He was slightly feverish; he really had caught a cold, and he had taken the afternoon off on the instructions of the infirmary doctor. He was supposed to be sleeping now, but the sound of the rain was unsettling instead of soothing, and he wanted to be out in it, walking bareheaded under the driving, stinging sheets of water. He thought yearningly of the pneumonia that would almost certainly follow, and the discharge from present duties, and the long rest afterward. Rest, travel, sunbathing, reading, being conducted through the computer laboratories of major countries throughout the world. His name would be magic after a year on the project, even if they hadn't brought it off yet. Eventually they would, and then everyone connected with it would be known, not to the public, but to their peers, where it mattered. He pulled the blind over the window and returned to the diary.

"Inside the 'house' are the computer, its weapons and sensors, with a monitor board in the center. Here it is that we are forced to maintain human surveillance. A man has to oversee the data that are brought in, has to be able to jump over intervening bits of data to connect those things that have no apparent reason for being linked together. For instance, if a fire is to be started to clean out an area, the man has to note the weather—a fire during a thunderstorm is a futile gesture. He has to note the wind, the placement of other units, the relative value of migratory birds in the area, for example. Or the possibility of livestock that will be killed by smoke downwind from the area. All of these we can program in, if we can formulate them in clear, unambiguous language. We don't dare let the Phalanx get confused."

His dropped his pen again and went to the bathroom and took his temperature. It was up, 102.6. He lay down. He was thinking of the statements that could confuse the Phalanx unless all parts were satisfied: A.B, A+B, A/B, A→B, A≡B . . . They couldn't do it. How describe a smile in clear and unambiguous language? The Phalanx couldn't be unmanned. Nor could it be manned in the usual sense. The Phalanx and its offspring were to be the call boxes, like the police telephones that were spaced all over cities. Imagine, he told himself, what it would be like if the call box on the corner not only alerted the precinct station, but watched suspicious characters, measured and weighed them, analyzed them, noted what weapons they carried, made countless other observations about them, came to a decision that they were okay, or not okay, and if not, then apprehended them, or killed them. Imagine that. What if it made a mistake and burned down a city block in error? *Sorry 'bout that.*

But if they could make it work, wouldn't it be good? Wouldn't it be better than armies over the face of the earth? Good, good, good . . .

Dan Thornton couldn't lift his arm because they had pinned gold braid on it. Real gold. They got the other arm and he wanted to beg off, but they insisted, refusing to hear his pleas. With the fastening of the braid on his other arm all he could do was stand, trying not to sway, knowing the weight would topple him if he swayed. He was paralyzed from goodness, he thought.

They had this old brain hanging around, see. The guy died on the operating table, abdominal surgery, and his head was intact, going to waste. So they put the brain in this jar of nice warm nutrients and fed it now and then and it went on ticking away, thinking its own thoughts. Then they put electrodes in it, this is the sight center, this the kinesthetic . . . And they put return wires and hooked them to an EEG and they watched the pens go up and down, up and down, and they kept getting cuter with it until they could get that little old brain to tell them what was on its mind. Not much, as it turned out. You see, that little old brain had gone crazy as a bedbug from the various things they had done to it, but still those pens went up and down, up and down, and it couldn't stop, couldn't refuse to cooperate, couldn't do anything but soak up the nutrients and sit there ticking away.

"Doesn't he look natural, like he might get up and talk to us any minute."

But don't look behind that eyeball, ma'am. Empty behind it. That one too, and that.

Most of them go mad, if not immediately, then as soon as they are hooked to the computer that is sending messages at the rate of a million bits a second. They had time, and psycho-modular units to work with. They found a unit that did not go mad when they linked it to a computer. It was a simple computer, however.

If chips are black and white, and this object is green, then this object is not a chip. If tiles are red and blue, and this object is green, then this object is not a tile. And so on, and on, and on, at the rate of one million bits a second. The brain ticked away and did not go mad. They made it more complex. The object was green and round. Then more complex: green, round, and weighs n grams . . . The brain did not go mad. Yet. They hooked it to the Phalanx, and the brain went mad.

Dan Thornton stood with his arms dangling, paralyzed by his own goodness and the heavy gold braid that testified to the goodness and watched the brain go mad. How they could tell it was going mad was by the way it made the pens go up and down, up and down. It was drawing paper dolls, all joined at feet and hands.

We stare at each other across a roomful of people and somehow we come together without either of us moving. I hold her tight against me and murmur into her hair that smells of sea winds and sunshine, and my murmur has no words, but says that I love her. "It's been a long time, Dan," she says. Her eyes are shining and I feel that she is happy to see me. Again she is different. The wild girl is deeper, harder to find now, but still there. She says, "Let's go somewhere else." We walk the streets, her hand in mine, our steps matched, even though she has to take long strides to keep up. We walk for hours, see the night out, watch silently when the last star is lost in a lightening sky.

We talk and I find myself defending my father. She stops me with cool fingers pressed against my lips. "You are shocked that you can love someone who is capable of evil," she says, as if surprised at me. "We are all capable, it's just that most of us never get the chance to do more than small evil things." I argue that he wasn't evil, that he never hurt anyone in his life. She is skipping at my side, not listening, and I know she thinks I am foolish. I am angry with her, almost as angry as when she said she would not marry me. I ask her again and she shakes her head. I ask her what she is doing, how she is living and she is amused that I don't know of her. She puts a slim book into my hand, says I should not open it until she is gone again, and that won't be until Monday.

The weekend is an agony of pleasure, and on Monday she is gone. The book is poetry that I cannot understand. They say she is brilliant, a genius, that she is the eyes and ears of the world. And I can't understand her poetry.

Two weeks later I marry Ethel and we plan to have three children right away.

"Doctor Thornton, if you'll just raise your hips a bit. That's right."

He was being taken somewhere on a stretcher on wheels. It was too hard to try to understand, so he let himself be carried and cared for, and sometime later he knew that he had the pneumonia that was to release him and send him home. After the serious part of it passed and he was told to take it easy and soak up sun on the wind-protected sunporch, he thought about the project, and he knew he wouldn't ask to be relieved from it. The Institute brought in Carl Brundage, an old friend of his to substitute for him until he was well enough to resume a full schedule. Carl stopped in to talk when he had time, and that helped the slow days along.

"The major mistake is in the lack of selectivity in the psycho-modular units they are forced to use. Most of them belong to enlisted men, untrained minds that probably never used a tenth of their potential. You have to think of that one unit as pre-programmed, you see. It can accept no new training, can't learn anything, can't develop any of its potential; it is the coordinator, that's all. The mistake lies in thinking that it is more than that. But that's all it needs to be," he added, deep thought furrows aging his face for a moment. Something . . . ? Whatever the thought had been, it had not come to consciousness, however, and he shrugged. It would. He knew the workings of his own brain, knew that he might feel twinges of this sort off and on for a while, then a new idea would hit him and the twinges would go away until another new idea was born.

"Are you going to be allowed to watch the first test on Monday?" Carl asked.

"Sure. But it will be a failure." Moodily he repeated that to himself after Carl had left to do the work that he, Thornton, was supposed to be doing.

He rested over the weekend, sleeping deeply and heavily under massive sedation. Monday was clear and warm with high cirrus clouds forming milky streaks in a perfect sky. The wind velocity was five to ten miles an hour, air temperature a mild 71. Thornton rode in a jeep to the demonstration site, twelve miles from the Institute building, in a narrow gouged-out valley, where spring was arriving later than on the more exposed hillsides. Pale green spears of unfolded leaves tipped the trees and the dogwoods still bore tiers of snowy flat blossoms.

The Phalanx sat in the center of the small valley, looking like a miner's cabin. At the signal given by the Director the sides of the Phalanx rose slightly, enough for ten small, rounded subunits to roll out from the interior. The subunits were called the bugs. They were painted randomly in browns and greens, and when they moved away from the Phalanx, they merged with the earth and the undergrowth and were invisible. The test was to be in two parts; the first was without the psycho-modular unit hooked in, the second with it.

Scattered in the valley and on three sides of the surrounding hills were Institute men, taking the part of the enemy. Thornton had expected to be one of them, and he was grateful for the pneumonia that had turned him into a spectator. The ten bugs were only part of the force the Phalanx could control. Two of them carried sprays that threw out an arc of a water-dye mixture; in battle that would be fire. Two others recorded on film and soundtrack everything in a radius of up to ten miles, terrain permitting. Another moved along with a radar antenna

spinning, homing in on a helicopter that thundered overhead, while its companion followed a flight of birds, then
picked up a jet making a pencil-thin contrail.

Each bug apparently functioned as planned. Thornton
waited. The sun heated his thighs and he remembered
how they had burned on the climb up the hill the day he
had caught the cold. His driver, one of the junior pro-
grammers, shifted excitedly and pointed to one of the
bugs that was leaving the ground, skimming over the top
of bushes, over a runoff stream. The Phalanx had everything under control. It didn't fall apart until three rabbits
were flushed from the bushes and ran straight at the mine
detecting bug. The dye thrower swung around and
sprayed the rabbits, and with them the mine detector that
was immediately frozen in its tracks. The Phalanx had
been programmed to put out of commission any of the
subunits that were scored on. Following the rabbits the
dye-thrower rolled over a "mine," and it also was immo-
bilized.

One by one the subunits proved vulnerable to the unexpected, and within half an hour the Phalanx sat alone,
unprotected, and the men moved in and "captured" it.

Thornton watched the slumping figure of the Secretary
and the unbowed figure of the Director who was gesturing
expansively. The second session would take place after
lunch, after the psycho-modular unit was hooked in and
the men resumed their positions.

With the psycho-modular unit in place, the test was
more impressive. Some of the men on the hills were
"killed" by the dye-throwers, others were "gassed," but
none were taken prisoner. The Phalanx was not equipped
to take prisoners. This time the Phalanx refused to be
fooled by rabbits deliberately introduced by the men, and
it sent a unit after the men themselves. It shot down three
crows and two jets, and a hawk. When it went mad in
less than an hour it had the subunits destroy each other,
and turn on the Phalanx itself.

While technically a failure, the second session of the test gave great satisfaction.

There was a rally that night, conducted by the Secretary himself.

Thornton's son was of draft age, or would be in a month. He could understand the tenor of the country that clamored for an end to the draft, an end to the endless wars, an end to the frustrations that dulled the young men and made them restless in school, made them marry too young, drive too hard and fast, experiment with drugs and danger wherever it was presented to them. He didn't need or want the Secretary to outline this for him, but the Secretary did. His voice was sad and rousing by turns. Thornton used his illness as an excuse and left early.

The work continued. The psycho-modular units continued to go mad. Thornton convalesced without incident and discontinued the heavy sedation, and went back to a shortened work-day. He also went back to his sessions with Dr. Feldman.

There was an air of excitement at the Institute now. Success was in the smell of the spring air turning into summer, and the scientists and technicians were light-headed. Thornton too. Carl was almost embarrassingly grateful to him for having become ill so that he had been called in. He worked like a man possessed, trying to spare Thornton all he could. Thornton knew that other departments were working even harder than his own. The psycho-cyberneticist and the perception psychologist must not sleep at all, he thought one night when he met them both in the hall. He had returned for his notebook, after napping for three hours. He would return to sleep, but they seemed prepared for an all-night stint.

How does man know what he sees? How does the brain communicate with itself; with the hormonal system; with the autonomic nervous system . . . ? He didn't envy them their work. When they found another answer, he got it in the language of formulae and symbols that he

then translated to binary digital language and put in the
Phalanx. This was tested, and if it was wrong, he took it
out again, and they went back to the original problem.

Thornton dreamed often of the Phalanx and its bugs
now. "Are the others reporting dreams about it?" he
asked Feldman.

"They dream of everything," the analyst said.

Thornton wondered if Feldman were curious about why
his dreams seemed never to concern sex. "When I was
young," he said, "I was as horny as anyone, I guess. But
now . . . After I got married and settled down, it seemed
less important. I guess I'm one of those fortunate people
who isn't driven by sex so much. I've hardly missed Ethel
at all," he added. It surprised him to say it and know that
it was true. Of course, when he had been ill, he had
missed her. She would have been good to have around
then. She had a way with sick people, soothing, gentle,
comforting. But normally his work was enough, and the
momentary pangs of longing seemed almost directionless,
certainly not aimed specifically for her. Or anyone else.

"Were you ever in love?" Feldman asked when the silence lengthened.

"Sure. A couple of times. High-school stuff; then, of
course there was Ethel."

"What about the high-school stuff? Any particular girl
who stands out now?"

He couldn't remember the name of any one girl he had
admired in high school.

That night he had three programs to check. Carl had
admitted mistakes in them. "Garbage in, garbage out,"
Carl had said, flinging the papers down on Thornton's
desk. "And I can't find the garbage." He had been dis-
gusted with himself for letting the error slip past in the
first place, and even more so for not finding the error
after it was known to be there.

The three programs comprised a whole; the error could
be in the first of them, throwing off the next two; or it

could be in the last step of the third program. There were over fifteen hundred steps involved.

Thornton worked on it until 1 A.M., knocked off half an hour to stretch and have a sandwich, then went back to it again. At 3 A.M. he realized that Feldman was pushing him for some reason that he couldn't fathom. For months his relationship with Feldman had been casual, in the line of duty, but now it was different. The difference in Feldman was like the change that came over a cat that had been playing with a ball and was presented with a mouse. The same gestures, but with a new intensity, a new concentration. He wandered out into the night to smoke and let his room clear of the smoke there. He was coughing badly with each cigarette, the after-effect of pneumonia, he guessed.

He had talked to the psycho-cyberneticist about the selection of the psycho-modular unit, and Jorgenson had been in bitter agreement with his theory that they could expect no great strides forward until they were allowed to select for themselves. He knew the Director had brought it up with the Secretary, but no word had filtered down as yet about the outcome. Meanwhile the units continued to go mad and the Phalanx tried to commit suicide periodically.

He didn't like the phrase, "tried to commit suicide," but it was how they all talked about it. He remembered his mother and her suicide that followed the execution of his father. He remembered the pictures of the mangled children that had arrived in the mail, and the letters, and phone calls, and his mother's anguish and final surrender. He would not have got through that period without Paula and Gregory. His hand froze in the process of lifting his cigarette to his lips.

Paula! He hadn't thought about Paula for twenty years. Not since he had gone to hear her speak and read her poetry. Ethel had been so bored by it. They hadn't stayed for all the program, but later he had gone back and met Paula at the reception that followed. She never appeared surprised to find him, he had thought then when her face lighted with pleasure at his approach. Never surprise, only pleasure to see him again. He almost asked her if she loved him then, but he didn't. Again she seemed different, wiser, but not only that. In touch with something that he couldn't grasp, perhaps. Tuned in, the students said of her, adoring her and what she wrote for them.

He inhaled deeply, coughed hard and held onto a tree until he had his breath back. Coughing made him dizzy, made his head swell and throb. He thought fleetingly of himself dying, dead, and Paula coming to the funeral, weeping over his lifeless body, pleading for another chance with him. A bitter smile twisted his face and he pulled hard on the cigarette, finishing it, not caring if he coughed or not. Another paroxysm, and he knew that he did care. He waited for it to pass and then returned to his room and the programs that had to be corrected.

Toward dawn he threw himself down on his bed and fell asleep instantly.

We pull ourselves up the steep rocks of the cliff and when we get to the top we have no breath left for talking. Paula is sweating, and she rubs the back of her hand over her face carelessly, leaving a smudge of dirt there from her forehead to her chin. I lie back with my eyes closed, trying not to cry yet. Hoping never to cry over my mother. Paula says, "Mom and Dad say you can live with us until you go to school in the fall. Okay?"

It isn't really a question. I can go with them or I can go with my aunt and uncle who came from Ohio for the funeral. The state won't let me stay alone yet because I am only seventeen. My aunt told me that much. She is angry because my mother, her sister, killed herself. It was irreligious of her. It was selfish of her. I despise my aunt.

I feel Paula's toe digging my side and I squirm, wanting not to cry. She giggles and the bare toe prods again, digs and wiggles against my side. I look at her and I know that I won't cry now. I jump up and grab her, meaning to shake her, but I just hold her, and she stops giggling. We

don't move for a long time until Gregory interrupts us.
He hasn't noticed anything so maybe it wasn't so long,
but that moment goes on and on.

When we go back to my house my aunt is angry with
me. She says I am selfish for leaving now when people
have been coming by to pay respects. She is going to lec-
ture me, but Paula goes to her and puts her dirty hand on
my aunt's smooth, clean sleeve, and Paula says something
I can't hear. Then she says, "It's going to be all right.
We'll take care of him." My aunt bursts into tears and
falls down in a chair crying like that, shaking, ugly with
crying, and Paula, Gregory and I leave her there.

Thornton woke up, remembering the dream in detail.
He made notes of it for Feldman's benefit. He rolled over
again and went back to sleep.

The work went slowly, and badly. They had plateaued
and apparently could go no further. But all of them could
see the next step so clearly, and all of them knew that
without the next step the project was a failure. The Secretary returned and huddled with the Director and several
other top men, and following this meeting there was
something not so open, something uglier about the Project. No leaks came from the meeting, and there was a
dearth of rumors for once. A new brain was installed,
and hope rose as it continued to function after twenty-
four hours, then thirty-six hours. A field test was scheduled, but before it could be held, the brain went mad.

Gloom settled heavier over the men, and mistakes were
made that would have been unthinkable four months in
the past. They analyzed the results of the last psycho-
modular unit and its stresses and the final breaking point,
and it was then that Thornton learned that this brain had
been especially selected. He knew vaguely who Lester Ferris
had been, but he didn't know how he had died, or
when, or how his brain had come into the possession of
the Institute. Ferris had been a child prodigy, a brilliant
mathematical physicist who had shaken up the world of

physics at the age of fifteen. Crippled in body, with a mind that sang, he had drawn the attention of the entire world with theories that might be proven in some distant future, or might never be proven, but were unmistakably original and brilliant. He had settled down at the Institute for Advanced Study at the age of twenty-five, and as far as Thornton knew no more had been heard from him.

Thornton began reading the daily papers that were brought to the Institute, and every time they had a brain that was more successful than the previous ones, he searched the obituaries, but he didn't ask anyone any questions. No one was asking questions.

He and Feldman went over the incident of his mother's suicide several times, and slowly he found that he was remembering things about Paula that he had forgotten completely. Feldman knew her work and was impressed that Thornton had been her lover. Thornton found that he could talk of it freely, as if it had happened to someone else.

Sometimes Thornton went for walks in the woods, now dark green and summery, harboring snakes behind rocks and logs, alive with rabbits, birds, insects that sang and whirred and buzzed. He didn't do it as often as he would have liked because there was no time. His year was running out. The second test was due within weeks, and although the idea of a battle test had been abandoned, the field test was still on the schedule. They were learning what kinds of brains were best suited for the symbiotic relationship with the computer that was called Phalanx, but they were unable to find just the right one. The brains continued to go mad.

They had a Delphi session, with each man answering questions about the sort of mind, the kind of mentality that would work with the Phalanx. Thornton bit his pencil and slowly filled in the answers to the printed questions. Afterward they read them aloud and talked about them. The papers were gathered by the Director.

"What do you think now of Paula Whitfield?" Feldman asked.

"Oh, she's a promiscuous bitch. Exciting, probably very beautiful still. She was, you know, but in a wild, unpremeditated way. Not the cover-girl look of studied loveliness."

Feldman nodded. "Your wife is very lovely," he said after a moment. He was making idle talk now that the hour was almost over and Thornton had been wrung out.

"Ethel is beautiful," Thornton said. It surprised him. She really was. He had a letter from her in his pocket then. She would meet him and they would drive to Florida and go from there to Nassau. She was excited about the trip. She was lonesome for him.

"Is Paula Whitfield really promiscuous?" Feldman asked curiously. "There's no hint of that in her work."

"She sleeps around," Thornton said, hearing the contempt in his voice. "She's got a couple of illegitimate kids, you know." He shrugged and got up. "I guess that's unfair. I don't really know what she's like now. It's been twenty years since I saw her. A genius with the morals of an alley cat. That's what she was then."

He opened the door. Feldman said, "Tomorrow, five, one hour. Okay?" Thornton looked back and nodded, and Feldman added, "Why did you put her down as the one mind that could exist with the Phalanx?"

He ate little dinner, and walked afterward. He hadn't. He knew he hadn't. He visualized the sheet of questions and his answers, and he knew that his memory would reproduce it faithfully for him. He hadn't put her name down. The questions had all led to that one, of course: Can you name anyone who you think would qualify as a psycho-modular unit?

He had left it blank.

He saw it again in his mind, and it was blank.

He felt a stab of fear. What was Feldman after?

He wouldn't recommend Paula, even if the thought had occurred to him. When Gregory died, eighteen years ago, she had written that crazy poem about the boy who chose death rather than killing. Gregory had died under enemy fire. He had mailed her the firing pin of his rifle, then had walked upright until he was felled. Stupid act of insanity. It had made all the papers, his death, and the bitter poetry that had flowed from Paula afterward. She was practically a traitor, as Gregory certainly had been. Again he wondered what Feldman was trying to do. He returned to his desk and worked until midnight.

He dreamed that night of the psycho-modular unit fixed in the island inside the house that was the Phalanx. It was a sealed tank that looked very much like an incubator, with rubber gloves built into it so that the operators could push their hands into them and handle the thing inside. There were six pairs of the gloves. To one side of the tank a screen, not activated now, had been placed to show electroencephalograph tracings. Thick clusters of wires led to desks close by, and on them were screens that showed chemical actions, enzymic changes, temperature of the nutrient solution and any fluctuations in its composition. Inside the tank were wires that ended in electrodes in the brain, the input and output wires, and they too were tapped so that men at desks could know exactly what was going in and out.

The Phalanx had been in steady operation for seven days and nights. The lights twinkled steadily, and in the back the EEG tracings were steady. The technicians had replaced the walls about the computer so that it was a house within a room, a tank within the house, a brain within the tank. There was still work to be done, still many programs to plan and translate and feed to the Phalanx, but any good programmer could do them now. They were talking about increasing the number of bugs to an even four dozen, and no one doubted that the computer could keep them all under control.

Thornton stood in the doorway looking at it for the last time. His work was done, his year over. Others would be interviewed now, or already had been, and they would feel the excitement coursing through them at the chance to work at the Institute for a year. He turned and left, picking up his bag at the main door. A car was outside to take him to the gate where Ethel would meet him. Feldman was on the steps waiting. He thrust a book into Thornton's hand.

"A goodbye present," he said. Thornton wondered if he had seen tears in the analyst's eyes, and decided no. It had been the wind. The wind was blowing hard. He rode to the main gate, and when he left the car and walked through, he dropped the book. He got in his own car and drew Ethel to him.

"I was so afraid you'd be different," she said after a moment. "I didn't know what to expect after your year among geniuses. I thought you might not want to come out at all." She laughed and squeezed his hand. "I am so proud of you! And you haven't changed, not at all."

He laughed with her. "You too," he said. He wondered if there had always been that emptiness behind her eyes. She pressed on the accelerator and they sped down the road away from the Institute.

Behind them the wind riffled through the book until the guard noticed it lying in the dust and picked it up and tossed it in a trashcan.

Charles L. Harness was born in 1915 in "an area of West Texas noted mostly for cactus, mesquite, and sandstorms." As a young man, while attending a theological seminary, he worked in a business establishment which happened to be located in the red-light district of Fort Worth. This stimulating double life ended, and he became a policeman in the identification bureau of the Fort Worth police department. "In this capacity I had the melancholy duty of fingerprinting many of my friends, both from the 'District' and from the Seminary. They were a lively lot, and did not seem to mind." Later, in Washington, D.C., he took a degree in chemistry, then another in law; married, and became a father.

He started writing in 1947 to clear up the obstetrical bills that followed his daughter's entrance into the world. He stopped, a few years later, "because she would stand in the hallway under my attic studio and cry for me to come down and play." When she left for college in 1964, he began writing again. Now a patent attorney for a large corporation, he lives in Maryland with his wife, daughter, and 13-year-old son.

Harness's early stories—thirteen of them, including the novel Flight Into Yesterday and the short novel The Rose—were vanVogtian melodramas, exuberantly inventive, cracking with paranoid tension, intricately plotted. The new ones he has been producing since 1964 are more mature, more contemplative, more realistic in tone, but they are constructed in the same complex mosaic fashion. "Probable Cause" is

*about clairvoyance, the Constitution of the United
States, thoughtography, the U.S. Supreme Court,
feminine intuition, and the assassination of a President, among other things. Nobody but Harness could
have woven all this into so symmetrical and satisfying
a pattern—or made it mean so much.*

PROBABLE CAUSE

By Charles L. Harness

*The right of the people to be secure in their per-
sons, houses, papers, and effects, against unreasonable searches and seizures, shall not be violated, and
no Warrants shall issue, but upon probable cause . . .*

*Nor shall any person be compelled to be a vitness
against himself . . .*

—Constitution of the United States,
excerpts, Fourth and Fifth Amendments

Benjamin Edmonds turned the film advance knob
on the self-developing camera in slow rhythmic motions of
hand and wrist. When the mechanism locked, he placed
the camera on its side next to the bronze casting on the
wall table. He flipped off the ceiling light and turned on
the faint red darkroom lamp over the developing trays.
He sat for a moment, studying the casting and waiting for
his eyes to adjust to the near darkness.

The replica was a plain, almost homely thing: a hand
clasping a piece of broomstick. Even after a century and
a quarter it still radiated the immense strength and supra-
human compassion of its great model, and it would surely
help to waken the distant sleeping shadows. Edmonds

laid his own big hand over it softly; the metal seemed oddly warm.

It was time to begin.

He turned off the red light and let the blackness flow over him.

The images began almost immediately. At first they flickered vaguely, seemingly trapped within the plane of his eyelids. Then they gathered clarity and stereoscopic dimension, and moved out, and away. They were real, and he was there, in the crowded theater, looking up at the flag-draped presidential box, occupied by the three smaller figures and the tall bearded man in the rocking chair. And now, from behind, a fifth. The arm surely rising. The deadly glint of metal. The shot. The man leaping out of the box to the stage below. And pandemonium. Fluttering scenes. They were carrying the tall man across the street in the wavering paschal moonlight. And finally, in that far time, Edmonds permitted the strange hours to pass, until the right moment came, and the right image came.

It was the critical instant. This last scene, this static vision in time, must now be captured on the emulsion waiting inside the camera. As always, the mental process of transfer was sharp, burning. And then it was done.

He stood up and turned on the ceiling light again. He was breathing heavily. He felt cold, but his face was dripping with sweat. He pushed the bronze casting aside, rubbed at his eyes with a couple of paper towels, then pulled the film out of the camera. He studied the positive print briefly, but with approval. He rubbed the negative carefully with a hypo-stick and placed it between the carrier plates of the enlarger.

Why, of all the transcendent possibilities, did he think Helen would want this simple thing of hands? Why not the gangling young man, brooding at the grave of Ann Rutledge? Or the poignant farewell from the rear of the train just before it pulled out of Springfield? No, none of these. For Helen Nord, it had to be the hands.

For a bachelor in his fifties, thought Edmonds, I am a fool. And if Helen only knew what I have been doing here, she would certainly agree. I'm worse than Tom Sawyer, walking the picket fence to show off in front of his young lady friend.

He smiled wryly as he turned off the ceiling light once more and reached for the 8×11 bromide paper.

The secretary in the outer office looked up from her typewriter and smiled. "Good morning, Madam Nord. The Justice is expecting you. Please go right in."

"Thank you." Mrs. Nord returned the smile and walked through into the inner office.

Benjamin Edmonds stood up gravely and motioned her to the chair by the great oak desk.

Helen Strachey Nord of Virginia, once known only as the widow of John Nord and the mother of three sons (all now launched in professional careers) was a handsome woman in her late forties. The tragic death of John Nord in the first Mars landings had brought her initially to the public eye, but her own remarkable abilities had kept her there. After working several years at NASA and taking her law degree at night, she had been appointed to the U.S.-Soviet Arbitration Commission to settle the Lunar Disputes of the late seventies. War had been averted. She was the obvious choice for the next appointment of a United States delegate to the U.N. And finally, when old Justice Fauquier died, President Cromway submitted her name to the Senate as the first female Justice of the United States Supreme Court. The ensuing senatorial debates and hearings made the long forgotten Cardozo and Black appointments seem exercises in benevolence. But for Cromway's assassination, she would never have made it. As a courtesy to the late President, enough votes were collected. Just barely.

How strange, thought Edmonds, that this woman, who has known passion, and who has nourished three fine sons, can yet bring such intricate insights into bankruptcy, space law, admiralty . . . the whole gamut. He said: "Glad you could drop by, Helen. I have something for you." He opened the attaché case, took the picture out and handed it to her. "It's only an eight by eleven, but if you like it I can make you a bigger blowup for framing."

The woman walked over to the window and studied the picture.

Edmonds asked: "Do you know what it is?"

"Yes—that is, I know what it would be, if it were possible. The hand of Charles Leale holding the hand of the dying Lincoln in the dawn hours of April fifteenth, eighteen sixty-five." She looked back at him, pondering. "But it can't be, because I also know that no photographs were taken. Not on that terrible night. But no matter. It is superb." She continued, sorting it out in her own mind. "It was the crowning, exquisite irony of the Civil War. You know the story, of course. Dr. Leale was a young army surgeon. He had come to Ford's Theatre that night just to see Lincoln. It was the great ambition of his young life to shake the hand of the President, but he scarcely dared hope for this. And so he was the first doctor in the presidential box after Booth leaped down to the stage. Leale had the President moved across the street, and endured the last hours with him. And, it being his army experience that a dying man will sometimes regain consciousness in the moments just before the end, and wanting Lincoln to know he was among friends, he came around to his right side, and took him by the hand, with the tip of the forefinger on the fading pulse, just as you see here." She looked back at Edmonds thoughtfully. "It is certainly pertinent, considering the case we'll have at conference today."

His eyes searched her face uneasily. "Poor timing, wasn't it? I'm truly sorry. But you'll have to learn not to let a case get to you, Helen. Not even *Tyson* v. *New York*. Especially not *Tyson*."

"Ben, do *you* think Frank Tyson shot President Cromway?"

"What *I* think about it personally is irrelevant. I can think about it only as a judge. And being a judge, even on this Court, is a job like any other. We get paid for interpreting laws made by other people. Our personal feelings of right and wrong are supposed to be irrelevant." How could he explain to her that he himself had never learned how to deal with that bitterest judicial duty—to decide whether a man lives or dies—and that he was reconciled to the knowledge he would never learn how to deal with it? He had never understood the rationale of capital punishment. After a history of six thousand years, it did not deter murders that led to further capital punishment. Maybe it had reduced the number? There was no way to tell. There was no control experiment. He shrugged. "The only thing that you and I and our seven brothers will have to think about is whether New York violated Tyson's constitutional rights in convicting him. As a Lincolnian, you must appreciate that."

"I know. Poor Dr. Mudd—his only crime was to set the broken leg of a stranger—who later turned out to be John Wilkes Booth. For which he was sentenced to life imprisonment."

"And Mrs. Surratt, in whose house the conspirators met."

"Yes. Even when the hangman pulled the black bag over her head, she did not understand."

They both looked around. Edmonds' secretary was standing in the doorway. "Excuse me, sir. The five-minute buzzer."

Edmonds nodded.

Helen Nord took a last puzzled look at the photograph before she put it away in her briefcase. Edmonds followed her out into the corridor.

Subtler and more far-reaching means of invading privacy have become available to the government. The prog-

*ress of science in furnishing the government with means
of espionage is not likely to stop with wiretapping. Ways
may someday be developed by which the government,
without removing papers from secret drawers, can reproduce them in court, and by which it will be enabled to
expose to a jury the most intimate occurrences of the
home. Advances in the psychic and related sciences may
bring means of exploring unexpressed beliefs, thoughts,
and emotions.*

—Justice Brandeis, dissenting in *Olmstead v.
United States* (1928)

At his first Friday conference, Edmonds had thought
the custom rather silly: each of the nine justices of the
United States Supreme Court, the most prestigious body
in the world, had to shake hands with the eight others before they could take their seats around the long table. But
now, after several years on the high court, he could understand why Chief Justice Fuller had instituted the practice nearly a hundred years ago. It softened long-standing
frictions and differences that might otherwise prevent nine
totally divergent minds from meshing together as a court.
He thought wryly of analogies from the ring: "Shake
hands and come out fighting." Thirty-six handshakes. It
was possible now, at eleven o'clock in the morning. When
they adjourned at six, it might not be.

And now they took their places around the long black
table, Chief Justice Shelley Pendleton at the south end,
Senior Associate Justice Oliver Godwin at the north end,
and the other associate justices, in order of seniority,
around the sides. The great John Marshall gave them his
blessing from his portrait over the ornate marble fireplace.

The face of Chief Justice Shelley Pendleton was a paradox—almost ugly in its craggy, masklike impassivity, yet
capable of dissolving into a strangely beautiful humanity,
warm, humorous, even humble. It was whispered that he
had retired to his office and wept after his first affirmation

of a death penalty, and that the widow was still receiving a pension from the manager of his immense personal estate. Before his appointment, he had been a well-known figure on Wall Street. Edmonds admired the man. He found it incredible that such lucid opinions could flow from such a complicated intellect. It used to bother him, until he finally concluded that the Chief Justice considered *all* possible angles, sifted out the major controlling aspects, weighed them against each other in a multi-dimensional balance, and accepted the answer. The Pendleton technique involved all factors of legal precedent . . . *stare decisis* . . . logic . . . the common law . . . social needs . . . and a fine prophetic grasp of the impact of a given decision on future similar cases. Marshall had been a constitutionalist, Holmes a historian, Brandeis a sociologist, Cardozo a liberal, and Warren a humanist—but Pendleton was none of these; for he was all.

The Chief Justice spoke rapidly and concisely. "The first case on our agenda is *Frank Tyson, petitioner,* v. *New York.* Petition for certiorari to the Court of Appeals of New York. All of you know what this one is about, so I need restate the facts but briefly. Tyson was indicted, tried, and convicted of killing our late President Cromway in the entrance of the United Nations Building, with one bullet from a telescopic-sighted rifle, from a window in an empty room in a nearby building. Tyson's palmprint was found on the rifle, and ballistics tests showed that the bullet taken from the President's body was fired from the rifle. An elevator operator named Philip Dopher testified that he saw Tyson leave the room, carrying something, and hurry down the stairs. Tyson, a porter in the building, contends that he was supervising a shipment of files to a warehouse for storage, that he heard a shot in the empty room, went in to investigate, found the rifle, picked it up, then looked out the window, took in the scene instantly, and realized that he was holding the weapon that had just killed a President of the United States. He panicked, thinking only to get rid of the rifle.

He ran down the side stairs with it and hid it, unobserved, in a crate of files standing by the freight elevator. Seconds later, the movers took the crate down the elevator to the van waiting on the other side of the building. And there, in that warehouse, it was eventually—found."

He paused and looked around at the intent faces.

"Thus far, the case does not present a federal question. I want you to ignore the enormity of the crime and the fact that a President of the United States was murdered. All of us knew him personally, and we all have an abiding respect and affection for his memory; some of us are here by his appointment. These aspects standing alone cannot possibly warrant our review. The sole issue of relevance to us, and indeed, the sole ground urged as basis for reversal, is the alleged violation of the Fourth Amendment to the Constitution by officers of the State of New York, in that their warrant to search the warehouse was not issued 'upon probable cause.' Specifically, petitioner contends that the officers hired a clairvoyant, one Dr. Drago, to read petitioner's mind, without his consent, thereby to visualize the location of the rifle, and that the New York magistrate issued the warrant to search the warehouse on this so-called information, and on nothing else. The primary question therefore seems to be, can clairvoyance adequately substitute for the routine and legally sufficient visual and aural observations as basis for a sworn statement on which a search warrant may validly issue? If we accept this as the heart of the matter, we may have to consider ancillary questions. For example, is there actually such a thing as clairvoyance? If we can satisfy ourselves here and now that there is not, then we would of course have some basis for deciding that the warrant was not issued on probable cause: and Tyson might be freed. On the other hand, if we can decide here and now that clairvoyance does exist, we have no escape from the next question: Was the exercise of this power an unconstitutional invasion of Tyson's right of privacy? If it was not, then he was properly convicted. But if it was an improper invasion, then of course the evidence developed by it—the rifle, and his fingerprints on the rifle, would be inadmissible under the Fifth Amendment, and again he would go free."

He shifted restlessly in his chair. "There is more. Mrs. Nord, will you please step to the door and ask the marshal to bring in Exhibit Q?"

For over a century, no clerks, messengers, or secretaries had been permitted in the room during conference. The duty of doorman fell to the juniormost appointee.

Helen Nord stepped to the door, waited until the marshal and his assistant had placed the object on the felt pad in the center of the great table, and closed the door after they left.

"As you know," resumed the Chief Justice, "this is *the* safe. And you know what it is said to contain. During Tyson's trial, the so-called clairvoyant, Dr. Drago, testified that he had placed a suitably cushioned auto-developing camera inside, then locked the safe, and delivered it into the custody of the trial court—but without the combination. So far as the record goes, Drago is the only one who knows the combination. If we grant certiorari, he will provide the combination. In fact, he is waiting in my outer office at the moment. He refuses to give the combination to anyone but me. But back to the facts. At the trial, New York put Drago on the stand to prove the existence of clairvoyance, and hence that the warrant was validly issued. Drago testified that his clairvoyant power—he called it 'psi'—was erratic, that it comes and goes, and could not always be called up at will. But he said he could prove it existed. He then predicted, over petitioner's objection, that New York would convict Tyson, that we would grant certiorari, and that the majority of us would reverse Tyson's conviction, holding that the warrant was not issued upon probable cause. He further predicted that most of us would deny the existence of psi. His proof to the contrary is supposed to be inside Exhibit Q, which we are invited to open after handing down our predicted decision."

"What colossal impertinence!" roared Oliver Godwin. His white handlebar mustache trembled indignantly.

"Mr. Godwin," said Justice Roland Burke coldly, "since the days of John Marshall it has been the custom at these conferences that each of us will be heard in turn without interruption, starting with the Chief Justice and proceeding down the line in order of seniority. I will ask you to await your turn."

The hard blue eyes of the Senior Associate Justice crackled. He said gravely, "Sorry, Roly. Sometimes I forget you're no longer barely passing my course in torts, back at Harvard Law. Ah, what a time you had with proximate cause, and those prolix, tautological so-called briefs. In fact, you still do. You used nearly fifty words just to tell me to shut up."

The ample cheeks of Justice Burke turned pink. "I'd resent that, if you weren't a senile old man, who should have retired long ago." He concluded primly, "You confuse tautology with logic."

Godwin grinned evilly. "Do I? 'Senile' is from *senex*, Latin for 'old man'. I'm an 'old-man old man.'" He laughed. "Well, perhaps I am. But age is a relative thing, Roly. If you leave me out, the average age on this court would be about sixty. And you're well over *that*. If it weren't for me, Roly, *you'd* be an old man."

Pendleton's mouth twitched faintly. "If we can defer the actuarial comparisons for a moment, I think I can finish. I don't want us to grant certiorari and then find we have to decide whether there is or is not such a thing as psi. And I want to ignore Exhibit Q altogether. Its contents—or at least the eventual contents of the camera—if any—are not of record. Drago's insistence to the contrary, we can give it no consideration. Certainly, we cannot open it. Another point: petitioner urges an analogy to wiretapping. What has been done to him, if clairvoyance was in fact used, he calls 'clairtapping.' We have held that evidence obtained by wiretapping or by any other unlawful means is inadmissible, in both federal and state courts. *Mapp* v. *Ohio, Berger* v. *New York*. The contention is therefore made that 'clairtapping' is a violation of privacy as bad as, if not worse than, wiretapping, and that evidence so obtained must be similarly excluded. I think that there is merit in this contention. In summary, if the rifle was located by clairvoyance, the search may well have been unconstitutional in analogy to wiretapping. If clairvoyance does not exist, then there was no basis on which a valid warrant could have issued at all. Thus there is a possibility that we could decide the case without deciding anything about psi." He paused and looked down the table. "Mr. Godwin, I yield to you."

"Thank you, Shelley. It was about time. Several things bother me. *Can* we decide on the merits without deciding about psi? It's rather like that Kidd will case in Arizona, back in the sixties, where the testator gave all his money to anybody who could prove the existence of the soul. The judge *had* to decide whether human beings have souls. Pity we didn't grant cert on that one. Always wondered whether I'd get a soul out of a 5–4 decision. Sorry, brothers—and sister. An old man likes to ramble. So I'll just ask a question: why don't we just open that safe right now and see what's on the film? Might save a lot of argument and embarrassment later on."

"You read the testimony," said Pendleton. "At the moment there's supposed to be nothing on the film."

"Then what in tarnation is the good of it?"

"Some kind of image—and don't ask me what—is eventually supposed to appear on it."

"When?"

"On Decision Day."

The Senior Associate Justice snorted. "You expect us to believe that?"

"No."

"I should think not. Let's get back to reality. As I view this thing, we're on the horns of a real dilemma. If we take the case and reverse Tyson's conviction because there was an unconstitutional invasion of privacy, then we have probably ruled that clairvoyance is a real and functional phenomenon. Science arises in anguish. On the other hand, if we rule that clairvoyance doesn't exist, and that, therefore, there was no invasion of privacy, then the bleeding-heart liberals arise in howling dismay at the official blessing we have now given police use of clairvoyance. Who needs wiretaps anymore? Psi is easier, and the cops will be welcome to use all the psi techniques they can dig up: telepathy, clairvoyance, hexing, prekenners . . ."

"What's a 'prekenner,' Judge?" asked Edmonds, fascinated.

"Somebody who *pre*viously *kens* what's going to happen, so as to set up police traps to catch criminals in the act. I just made up the word. But if Roly can use two words when he means one, surely I can use one word when I mean two. That's all I wanted to say. You take it, Roly."

"Thank you, Mr. Godwin," said Burke coldly. He paused a moment, looking at the chandeliers overhead, as though simplifying and tailoring his thoughts for certain of the less disciplined minds around him.

Edmonds awaited the dissertation with interest. Somehow, of course, it would turn on logic.

In Burke's early days as a judge on the New Jersey bench, Frankfurter had been his model. But this had changed over the years. Burke (like Cervantes) had finally recognized that every man was the product of his own work. But where Cervantes had been content to permit the process to operate subconsciously, Burke went to the final logical limit. He found in his own past works his best inspiration. As he shaved in the morning, he listened to tapes of his previous decisions. And he listened to the same tapes in his car as he drove to court, and at night put himself to sleep with them.

He had founded the Burke Chair in Logic at Harvard.

His famous text, *Logic in Appellate Decisions* (dedicated to himself) consisted largely of annotated excerpts from his own decisions. He was both ignorant of and indifferent to what others thought of his magnificent narcissism. In fact, he considered himself modest, and sought out situations where his modesty might be displayed, noticed, and commented on. Roland Burke's long love affair with himself had not dimmed with the passing of time: it was a serene thing, unmarred by lovers' quarrels. He had no portraits hanging in his office; only mirrors.

Edmonds sometimes wondered at his own reaction to Burke. Far from feeling contempt or derision, he found he envied the famous jurist's confident, self-centered, doubt-free integration into his codified environment, and his system of logic that so easily resolved all questions into black and white, with no plaguing shades of gray left over.

"Psi," began Burke, "is hogwash—illogical by its very definition. Yet, as I shall demonstrate, logic requires that we take the case. There are only two possibilities: a) to deny the petition, and b) to grant. If we deny, this sets a precedent that the Supreme Court will refuse to review constitutional questions involving psi. Our refusal would be interpreted by the lower courts as endorsing warrants issuing on clairvoyant information. Such a consequence is clearly unthinkable. This leaves us, therefore, only with the second alternate, b), to grant. Logically, we must grant."

"Quod erat demonstrandum," murmured Godwin.

Burke ignored him loftily.

"Thank you, Mr. Burke," said the Chief Justice. "Mr. Moore?"

Nicholas Moore of Louisiana spoke with a soft drawl. "I disagree. This is not the kind of case this court should take. Even if there *is* a federal question—which I doubt —we can turn it down. Since the revision of the Judiciary Act in the twenties, we have been free to turn down practically any case we wish—excepting issues between the

states, or the states and the United States government. It's
a question of policy. We can handle no more than a hundred to a hundred fifty cases a year—less than ten percent of the appeals that come to us. Our every decision
should throw light on some current judicial problem and
state principles for the guidance of the lower courts in
thousands of similar cases. We did this with the wiretapping cases, the desegregation cases, the school-prayer
cases. But how many cases involving this psi thing are
currently pending in the lower courts? None at all, that
I've heard about."

"Mr. Blandford?"

"I agree with Moore," said the Massachusetts justice
thoughtfully. "We took considerable interest in this kind
of thing in Salem three hundred years ago. We burned
people at the stake for less. We weren't too sure about
God, but we certainly believed in the Devil. I hope this
isn't evidence of a trend. We're not an ecclesiastical court
of the middle ages. We can't go back. I don't think we
should get involved. No, never again."

"Thank you. Mr. Lovsky?"

Justice Lovsky stared suspiciously at the safe. "The
whole thing smells. But I agree with Mr. Burke, *supra*.
We ought to take it. If we deny the cert, you'll have every
J.P. in the country issuing warrants on psi. *Cf*. Godwin.
It's a return to the general warrants of eighteenth-century
Britain, *q.v*. We had a little revolution about *that*. Madison, *Federalist Papers*. The Bill of Rights, Madison, *op.
cit.*, would be down the drain. In a few years we'll get a
hundred petes for cert on the same point. *Ibid*. The time
to stop it is now."

"Mr. Randolph?"

Justice Randolph spoke on all occasions with slow inci-
sion, as though dictating, direct to the stone cutter, immortal inscriptions for the entablature of a majestic new
federal building. He clipped:

● CONSTITVTIONAL ● QVESTION ●

and then was gloomy because the first word, under the

circumstances, was possibly superfluous. His law clerks always conferred with those of Justice Lovsky, fitting, with consummate artistry, Lovsky's footnotes to Randolph's headnotes. The result read like pages in *Corpus Juris Tertium*. This procedure required that the justices always agree; they found this a small price to pay for the exquisite result.

"Mr. Edmonds?"

."Isn't it a strange coincidence? Here we are in the opening months of nineteen eighty-four." He tossed a book on the table. "It's Orwell's *Nineteen Eighty-Four*—the ultimate regimented state. All citizens under police surveillance twenty-four hours a day. No privacy at any time. The police have even installed closed-circuit TV in homes and apartments. When this book was popular, forty years ago, many people laughed. It was absurd. It couldn't happen in America. Well, it *has* happened. It's here now—except clairtapping is even worse than spy TV. It penetrates the privacy of our minds. We must deny its use to the police."

"You sound as though you really believe in this stuff," said Godwin.

Edmonds shrugged.

"Thank you, Mr. Edmonds. Madam Nord?"

"*My* argument for granting certiorari will, I think, seem totally incompetent and irrelevant to most of you. And I expect that my distinguished brother, the Senior Associate Justice, may have a stroke. In a word, I think Tyson is innocent. Also, I think we ought to open the safe."

There was an embarrassed silence.

Then came Oliver Godwin's stage whisper: "Don't knock it, boys. Never forget, we're the only high court in the world with our own Madam."

Helen Nord led the laughter.

The Chief Justice rapped the table with his knuckles. "We will vote. Madam Nord?"

"To grant."

The vote went backwards, in inverse order of seniority. The theory, which seemed utterly fallacious to Edmonds, was that the junior justices would thereby not be influenced by their seniors. In this group, he thought, nobody influences anybody. Nine sovereign independent republics.

"Mr. Edmonds?"

"Grant."

Two more votes were needed.

"Mr. Randolph?"

● GRANT ●

"Mr. Lovsky?"

"To grant."

"That's it. And now we can accept the combination to the safe. Madam Nord, will you please ask the deputy to summon Dr. Drago?"

"Most irregular," grumbled Justice Burke.

"Possibly," admitted Pendleton. "But at least it's by stipulation of counsel. All we permit him to do is hand me the combination in a sealed envelope. We ask him nothing, and we must silence him if he attempts to speak. Ah, here they come."

Edmonds was mildly surprised. Drago was a tall, dignified young man with smooth, pale cheeks. He might have been the desk clerk at the local YMCA, or a bank teller, or a deacon at Edmonds' own church.

Drago's eyes opened a little wider as he exchanged glances with Edmonds. And then his searching stare passed quickly around the table, next resting momentarily on Helen Nord . . . then Moore . . . Blandford . . . Godwin . . . and finally Pendleton. His mouth opened slightly, as though he were whispering to himself. Edmonds strained to hear. Was it, "Oh no"? He could not be sure.

Pendleton said gently, "We thank you for coming, Dr. Drago. I am Pendleton. I understand you wish to give me the combination to the safe."

Like an automaton, Drago walked to the end of the

table, and without a word handed the envelope to the Chief Justice.

Edmonds was leaning forward intently. There was suddenly something very strange about Drago's face. The cheeks were no longer smooth. And the man's hair . . . seemed *bushier*. And then Edmonds knew: Drago's face and scalp were rough with goose bumps. The thought sent a chill along his own spine. He looked rapidly around the table. No one else had noticed.

But *why?* And *what,* in this, the law's inmost, most austere sanctum, could possibly terrify any man, be he clairvoyant or not? He watched uneasily as Helen Nord led Drago outside and closed the door behind him. It required an effort of will to return to the business at hand.

Pendleton was dictating into the transcriber: "Frank Tyson, petitioner, *v.* New York. Petition for writ of certiorari to the Court of Appeals of New York, granted, limited to the single question presented by the petition as follows: 1. Whether the search warrant used by the State Officers in the instant case violated the Fourth Amendment to the United States Constitution in that said warrant was not founded upon probable cause."

Eavesdroppers, or such as listen under walls or windows, or the eaves of a house, to hearken after discourse, and thereupon to frame slanderous and mischievous tales, are a common nuisance and presentable at the court-leet.

—Blackstone, *Commentaries*

Edmonds paused at the door to Godwin's office, and, as was his habit, stared across at the portrait of Laura Godwin hanging on the opposite wall.

The room was full of reminders of the old justice's dead wife. Actually, three portraits of Laura hung from the walls. The last, the one that now held Edmonds, was a brilliant, haunting thing, painted by the younger Wyeth

just before her last illness. It still showed the elfin eyes
that had conquered presidents. On her right wrist she
wore Godwin's wedding gift, a bracelet of green laurel
leaves, clustered with pink pearls representing the little
flowers. In death, as in life, the great court left her un-
awed, and she looked out upon the justices, individually
and collectively, with the tolerant respect due precocious
children.

Godwin sought out anything that spoke her name. On
a stand by the window grew a tiny bonsai laurel, a *Kal-
mia latifolia* transplanted from the Blue Ridge Mountains.
Like the ancients, Godwin believed that this living symbol
of his wife had the power to ward off lightning and similar disasters.

In the burdened bookshelves behind his desk was an
illustrated edition of Petrarch. Godwin had learned Ital-
ian just to be able to read of the poet's Laura in the original. Next to Petrarch was a volume of Goethe's poems.
Edmonds had once pulled it out, and it had fallen open
automatically to the marvelous *Mignon: "Die Myrte still
und hoch der Lorbeer steht*. The myrtle silent, and high
the laurel stands."

The clock on the fireplace mantel had been stopped
years ago, at the moment of Laura's death. Godwin had
never since permitted it to be wound. On his credenza sat
a small silver casket engraved in laurel leaves. Edmonds
knew its contents: a shining black plastic ink-blot; a box
of matches that would not light; a deceptive fiberglass
cigar; a cement egg—all paraphernalia that Laura had used
in years past in perpetrating her famous April Fool jokes
on her famous husband.

The room seemed warm to Edmonds. A log fire was
burning with steady cheerfulness in the handsome fireplace. He knew that Godwin's chief secretary got to the
office thirty minutes early to start the fire, after the old
man had once complained of being cold.

"Ben! Come in, my boy." Oliver Godwin peered up at
Edmonds from behind the stacks of books, files, and doc-

uments cluttering his big oak desk. "We'll have a full house at argument today. Have you seen the headlines? Here's the *Daily News:* High Court Hears Mindreading Case. And the *Post:* Assassination Case to Supreme Court. And the *Star:* Supreme Court Questions Tyson Evidence. Well, I think we're ready for 'em. I've dug up a little wiretap chronology. History, dear boy, that's the modern touchstone. Bah! Holmes said it first, nearly a hundred years ago. 'One page of history is worth a volume of logic.' " His hands began fluttering like pink mice through the debris covering his desk. "Strange, very strange. I had it here just yesterday, right next to the nineteen eighty-three *Annual Index.*"

Edmonds had seen this a hundred times. It always fascinated him. He knew that Godwin made valiant efforts to keep all his papers and files on his desk. Godwin never knowingly filed anything. And although his desk was the largest in the Marble Palace, it had become buried years ago, soon after his appointment to the Court. Thereafter, the heaps could grow only vertically. Still, legend stated that the system had actually worked in the early years. Nothing could possibly get lost; it had to be there, somewhere. And knowing that it was there, Godwin did not mind digging until he found it. He developed the skill, intuition, and patience of a trained geologist in excavating for the exact stratum. Stooping, he could peer at the side of a stack of papers and read them, edgewise, as an archaeologist would read tree-rings, or varve-layers in an ancient lakeside. At one time, Edmonds had wondered whether Godwin would be driven to rediscover carbon-dating. But then came the day when Godwin had mislaid his famous dissent in the double jeopardy case. Laura Godwin had to drive in with his "house copy," just at robing time. And then and there she had forced his clerks and secretaries to swear an oath in blood, the old man's wrath notwithstanding, that they would start a decent filing system.

And now Godwin pounded the stacks on his desk and

shouted through the rising clouds of dust: "GUS!" Although monosyllabic, it was a long, wailing cry, fully orchestrated, a blend of supplication, outrage, entreaty, and indignation.

His senior law clerk, Miss Augusta Eubanks, a lady of indeterminate years, walked in quietly, holding a paper cup in each hand and a file under her arm. "The Tyson file, Mr. Godwin?"

"What else?" he roared. "I'll bet it was lost in that metal junkheap you keep out there to curse and torment my declining years. Well, hand it over!"

"First, your pills, Mr. Godwin. And we will not have a scene in front of Mr. Edmonds."

Edmonds took all of this philosophically. He happened to know that Laura Godwin had called Augusta to her deathbed and had extracted her promise to stay with the judge until he retired. He also knew that the old gentleman had set up a sizable trust in Augusta's name.

The old man meekly tossed down the pills and water. She gave him the file.

"You have to be firm with them," he whispered as she left. "Patient, but firm. *They're* the ones the Senate ought to confirm. They think they run the place. And maybe they do." He flipped the folder open. "Ah, here we are. First wiretapping, California, eighteen sixty-two, after they strung the telegraph across the Rockies. And California was the first state to make wiretapping a crime. But General Jeb Stuart of the Confederate Cavalry couldn't care less. He had his own personal wiretapper in the field. Doesn't say how they did it. Shunt tap, maybe. And then Alexander Graham Bell invented the telephone in eighteen seventy-six, and the real fun began. The New York police had already been actively tapping for several years when the first tapping litigation hit the courts and the newspapers, in eighteen ninety-five. And here's a note on the nineteen twenty-eight Supreme Court case, *Olmstead* v. *United States*. The feds tapped the phone of four indignant rum runners." He leaned back in happy contemplation. "Prohibition, Ben. Before you were born. Everyone had his personal bootlegger. Speakeasies. The eye at the peephole. The raids. But the bathtub gin—ugh! That's why they smuggled it in."

"So what happened to the four rum runners?"

"The Supreme Court said their constitutional rights hadn't been violated by the wiretap, and that the evidence obtained by tapping was admissible. Holmes dissented, of course. 'A dirty business . . . the government played an ignoble part.' And do you know, it took us thirty years, but we gradually came around to Holmes's view. Ten years after *Olmstead,* in *Nardone* v. *United States,* we conceded that maybe Holmes was partly right, but only for evidence offered in federal courts. We still didn't think the Fourth and Fifth Amendments applied to the state courts. And then finally, in *Mapp* v. *Ohio,* we extended the doctrine to apply to the states. In those early days, when we finally did get around to finding a few instances of illegal wiretapping, we made it turn on trespass. Some of the early distinctions were fabulous. If you drilled a hole in a wall and pushed a mike through, that was trespass, and it was illegal. But merely hanging a mike on the outside of the wall was still okay. And if you drove a spike mike into the wall, it was legal if it didn't go all the way through, provided it didn't touch a ventilating duct. But of course all these nice distinctions are buried in the footnotes now. Today, any kind of electronic pickup is illegal, and evidence obtained by wiretapping can be excluded in any court in the country, even if the cops wiretapped by a court order. *Berger* v. *New York.* But do you think our rulings have stopped wiretapping?"

"I'm sure they haven't."

"Indeed not, my boy. In fact, we redoubled it. The police now have to wiretap twice as much to get evidence that they can prove they didn't get by wiretapping. And telephone wiretapping is the simplest trick in the world. Ex-employees of big city phone companies do it best. They call a clerk in the repair section and ask for the terminal box and location of the 'pairs'—the two electrodes for a specific telephone. There're several pairs in each terminal box, in a nearby underground utility conduit. They run a line from the pairs, attach a hand-set, and they're in business. They might run a dozen lines from a dozen different terminal boxes to an empty room in a nearby building, and have one man monitor all the lines, with automatic tape recorders that start whenever a number is dialed. I think at one time or another every important phone in Washington has been tapped."

"Surely not *our* phones."

"Of course, my boy. We were tapped liberally in nineteen thirty-five and thirty-six, in the *Ashwander* v. *T.V.A.* case. And maybe at other times that we never found out about."

"Holmes was right. It *is* a dirty business."

Godwin was thoughtful. "Dirty, ignoble . . . but very possibly necessary. Three-quarters of the racketeers and dope peddlers convicted in New York before the *Berger* case were caught with wiretapping. Ben, I just don't know. Surely there are instances where it is justified, say to recover a kidnapped child, or to save the life of an innocent man. Maybe we're going to have to figure out a way to let the police keep up with the criminal. Telephone tapping is passé, anyhow. The criminals are afraid to use a telephone. The police use bugs, hidden mikes, parabolic microphone pickups, light beams reflected from a windowpane vibrating from voices in the room."

Edmonds looked toward the window, and beyond to the white dreary innocence of the Library of Congress. "Do you think somebody out there is reading *your* window?"

"Who knows?" said Godwin genially. "The point is, you can't find the heading 'Wiretapping' in the *Index to Legal Periodicals* anymore. They started grouping everything under 'Eavesdropping' long ago—a broader term, of course. I imagine the rash of law journal articles that *Tyson* will generate will all show up under 'Eavesdropping,' not 'Clairvoyance' or 'Psi.' And we'll be back to the old common law misdemeanor. A dirty business? I suppose. But let's fit our reports together. What did your clerk turn up on clairvoyance?"

"Very little. Only two cases, in fact—both criminal." Edmonds opened his file. "Here's *Delon* v. *Massachusetts,* nineteen fourteen. A so-called clairvoyant was arrested for practicing medicine without a license. It seems she went into a trance, and the spirits gave her the diagnosis and what medicine to prescribe. She had a license to practice clairvoyance, but not to practice medicine. Went to jail."

"Seems reasonable. What's the other case?"

"New York vs. *MacDonald,* eighteen ninety-six. MacDonald was absolutely identified as a would-be burglar in an apartment on Second Avenue in Manhattan. But he produced several hundred alibi witnesses who swore that at that very moment, he was on the stage of a Brooklyn theater, under hypnosis by the famous Professor Wein. The professor explained to the court that MacDonald's astral projection had simply got loose temporarily and had unwittingly materialized miles away in Manhattan. The judge let MacDonald off with a warning not to get hypnotized, ever again. But there's the bell. Time to robe."

They walked around to the robing corridor together.

The last demand upon him—to make some forecast of the consequences of his action—is perhaps the heaviest. To pierce the curtain of the future, to give shape and visage to mysteries still in the womb of time, is the gift of imagination. It requires poetic sensibilities with which judges are rarely endowed and which their education does not normally develop.

—Justice Felix Frankfurter

Lawyers on a Supreme Court case for the first (and

generally the only) time describe the experience in hushed tones. They compare the long walk up the marble steps and through the towering white columns as a thing of horror, like mounting the guillotine, and the wait in the great boxlike courtroom until their case is called, a refinement of hell. And to wear tails, rented the day before from a Washington haberdashery, uncomfortable and occasionally not a perfect fit, when before they have never even worn a tux, with the certain knowledge that every mouth in the packed room is curled in scorn at their naivete and gaucherie, is an experience not voluntarily repeated.

It is thus for the petitioner's lawyer, even though he knows that over half the cases heard by the high court result in reversals in his favor. And it is even worse for the attorney for the state. He is full of gloomy forebodings. Back home, with all the power of his state behind him, he got a conviction. Here, he has to start all over again. And now immense forces are arrayed against him. The tables are turned. He is now the defendant.

Guy Winters, Assistant Attorney General for the State of New York, ran his finger halfway around his collar, then folded his hands self-consciously on the table in front of him. His eye wandered over the long bench of Honduras mahogany, extending almost the width of the courtroom, and then one by one to the nine faces behind it, and finally to the back of his opponent, Walter Sickles, representing Frank Tyson. Sickles was already at the lectern and was about to begin.

Edmonds was not surprised to find the courtroom packed. Some of these people, he guessed, had stood in line all night to get in. A triple quota of reporters was present. The oldtimers of the press could frequently forecast how the vote would go just by listening to the questions asked by the justices. He wished he could do as well.

From the lectern that stood squarely in front of Chief Justice Pendleton, Sickles began his presentation, slowly, in a low voice, without notes. He was glad of the microphone on the lectern, but hoped it would not pick up the knocking of his knees. As in a dream, he heard his own voice echoing back from the maroon drapes behind the great bench. "My client stands convicted of murder, on evidence improperly admitted, in that it was obtained in violation of his constitutional rights."

"You refer to the rifle, with Tyson's palm-print?" demanded Justice Godwin.

Sickles groaned inwardly. Not ten seconds at the lectern, and the questions had begun. "Yes, your honor."

"You admit the ballistics tests?"

"Yes, your honor."

"And that this evidence was obtained by search warrant giving the warehouse address and where the rifle would be found in it?"

"Yes, your honor, but—"

"But what, Mr. Sickles? Proceed." Godwin's mustache twitched grimly as he leaned back.

"The warrant was not issued upon probable cause."

"The information was not sworn to?"

"Oh, it was sworn to. But the officer who gave the sworn information admits he obtained it from one Dr. Drago, who admitted that he obtained it by his own personal clairvoyance."

"You don't believe there's such a thing?" demanded Justice Burke.

Oliver Godwin said calmly, "Don't answer that, sonny." He turned a bland face to his outraged colleague. "Relax, Mr. Burke. What counsel thinks personally is irrelevant."

Sickles sighed. If he were back in Brooklyn, he would be comfortably leaning back in his old wooden swivel chair, dictating during coffee break. He said, "I'd like to answer that this way, your honor. If there is such a thing, then it's the same as wiretapping. Maybe worse. And any evidence obtained by its use cannot justify a warrant. The circumstances of the issuance can be examined in court.

This court has so ruled. And if the warrant issues wrongfully, the evidence obtained with the warrant is inadmissible, the same as if it had been obtained by wiretapping. Clairtapping . . . wiretapping . . . the legal consequences should be the same."

"There's no other evidence of Tyson's guilt?" asked Helen Nord.

"Not much, your honor. Just that of Dopher, the elevator operator. He testified he saw Tyson leaving the empty office, carrying an object in front of him. That alone is not enough to convict Tyson. His life or death depends on the admissibility of the rifle."

"Dr. Drago testified that clairvoyance is a fact?" asked Pendleton.

"He did, but he didn't offer proof beyond the bare statement, which was merely his own opinion."

"How about the camera in the safe, and Drago's predictions?" asked Edmonds.

"The contents of the safe are not actually in evidence, your honor. And as for his predictions . . . their value depends on the decision of this court. They have no present probative value."

"He predicted we'd grant the certiorari?" pressed Edmonds.

"He did, but—"

"And that we'd hold the warrant invalid, and reverse?"

"That is my expectation and hope, your honor."

"So that, if he turns out to be right, doesn't that prove clairvoyance, and would it not therefore follow that the warrant was in fact valid?"

"That involves a hopeless paradox, your honor. Anyhow, every case that is decided here is won by somebody, without benefit of clairvoyance."

Edmonds smiled. He had been thinking the same thing himself, but he wanted Sickles to make the point in open court.

"He! he!" Godwin slapped the bench with his open palm. "Well said, young man."

Sickles bowed to the aged justice—and wondered how many votes he had just lost.

"Mr. Sickles," said Helen Nord, "do you know what is in the safe—on the camera film, I mean?"

"No, your honor. I'm interested, of course. It may be nothing at all. But whatever it is, it can have no relevance in these proceedings."

"Suppose, Mr. Sickles," said the Chief Justice, "that it shows the face of the assassin?"

Sickles looked up at the great man in astonishment, then shrugged. "And who *is* the assassin, your honor? How would face and deed be connected? But I respectfully submit that the camera and its contents, whether present or prospective, are moot. Exhibit Q simply is not in evidence."

"Yes, that's true."

"Can electromagnetic radiation penetrate that safe?" asked Helen Nord.

"Quite impossible, your honor. The walls are one-inch steel and form a perfect Faraday box."

"So that, if psi does exist, and is a form of electromagnetic radiation, it would not be possible to penetrate the steel shell and affect the photographic emulsion in any way?"

"That's right, your honor."

"Then," asked Pendleton, "if we open the safe, and find the film activated, wouldn't this prove that psi is not a violation of Section six-oh-five of the Federal Communications Act, and hence that you have no benefit under *Nardone* v. *United States?*"

"That would seem to follow, your honor," said Sickles unhappily. He realized that he was being given the "treatment." The court frequently, at argument, forced both sides to admit they were in the wrong; then neither could complain if he lost. But he was not ready to admit defeat. "If the court please, I'd like to elaborate a little further on the constitutional question. I respectfully remind this court that under the British common law, before this country had a constitution, it was lawful to extract testimony on the rack. Farfetched, your honors? Similar things have happened here, and not too long ago. Your honors will recall the case of *Rochin* v. *California,* in which the police used a stomach pump to recover the 'evidence,' two capsules of narcotics, from Rochin's stomach. After lengthy appeals, it was finally held that Rochin's constitutional rights had been violated, and the exhibits were ruled inadmissible. Now, if a man's stomach is sacred, how much more so his mind!"

"But surely Tyson does not contend that his body is inviolate from the police for all purposes?" demanded Justice Blandford. "Surely they can still fingerprint him, measure him, take his picture, record his voiceprint, and test his blood and breath for alcohol, and do it all without his consent?"

"Well, yes, your honor."

"Then how does clairvoyance differ?"

"It's the degree of privacy. The attributes that your honor has just mentioned, fingerprinting and so on, well, these are pretty well exposed to the public anyhow. But a man's thoughts are not. If Americans lose their right to have private thoughts, freedom is gone."

Edmonds found himself nodding in agreement.

"But you contend there is no such thing as clairvoyance," said Justice Burke. "How then, this concern for privacy of thought?"

Sickles grinned crookedly. "Until this court rules that psi is nonexistent, I have to argue in the alternate: psi doesn't exist; but if it does, it was used in violation of Tyson's constitutional rights."

"Yes," agreed Burke. "Quite logical."

Sickles looked down at his wristwatch. He was done. There was no room in him to wonder whether he had saved a man's life. He felt only relief. He looked up at the Chief Justice. "I have nothing more, your honors."

"Thank you, Mr. Sickles. May we hear now from New York?"

Guy Winters took a deep breath and walked to the lectern, where he pulled off his watch and laid down a sheaf of notes. His eyes swept the faces at the bench without seeing them. He was tense, nervous. But he had rehearsed for hours, and knew exactly what he wanted to say—if they would let him.

"May it please the court, one issue alone is involved in this case—the question on which certiorari was granted, namely, whether the warrant was invalidly issued as based on clairvoyant information." He took another deep breath and wished he could do something about the perspiration soaking his armpits. "It is the position of New York that clairvoyance does exist, and that, although the state police did not explain that the information was obtained in this way, the magistrate, had he known, would necessarily have issued the warrant; and if this be so, the warrant was valid under the Fourth Amendment, the rifle was admissible under the Fifth, and Tyson's conviction must stand.

"The record below, through the testimony of Dr. Drago, is replete with a documentation of American psi, even to the very beginnings of history on this continent. With the court's indulgence, I'd like to digress for just a moment to present this historical background.

"As far as North America is concerned, historical psi began with the Aztec chief, Quetzalcoatl. When he was forced to abdicate the Aztec throne in ten nineteen, he predicted that in exactly five hundred years he would return in full war panoply and reclaim his dominions. That was why—in fifteen nineteen—the Aztec emperor Moctezuma was too paralyzed to act, when Hernando Cortes arrived at the gates of the Aztec capital.

"And psi is an integral part of the history of the United States. Many famous Americans were involved at one time or another with psi. In fact, we might reasonably infer that their psi abilities contributed to their fame. Their names include some of our best known writers, artists, politicians, poets, and religious leaders. One could turn to the *Index of American Biography* almost at random. Edgar Allan Poe said he did not know the meaning of *Ulalume,* the poem that describes a man wandering down a misty cypress-lined path, in the month of October, to the crypt where his wife lay buried. We can well understand his mental block. October, of course, was the month, a few years later, in which Poe followed *his* wife to the grave.

"And Sam Clemens—Mark Twain—dreamed he saw his brother Henry dead of a steamboat accident, lying in a metal casket, and that on his breast was a spray of white flowers centered with a single red rose. When he found him in Memphis, his brother was dying of injuries received in the explosion of the boilers of a river boat, the *Philadelphia.* On the fourth day, his brother died, and was placed in a metal casket. As Sam looked on, grieving, a lady walked up and placed flowers on the boy's chest. It was a spray of white blooms, and in the center was a single red rose. I might add that this final detailed touch, completing the dream, or vision, or hallucination, if you like, is quite common."

Pendleton broke in. "My question is perhaps not completely relevant, but I am curious. Is there any reason to believe that there is a psi on this court?"

Edmonds started, but continued to look at the assistant attorney general.

"I don't know for sure, your honor," said Winters. "But I think it likely, simply as a matter of statistical probability, that there are at least three psi's on this honorable court. And probably more." He stood there calmly as several of the justices leaned forward suddenly. There was a buzzing rustle in the crowded room behind him.

The Chief Justice rapped the gavel sharply. "Would you explain that, please?"

"Certainly, your honor. It's pretty difficult, of course, to take a census of psi's, although it's something the Bureau of the Census really ought to include in nineteen ninety. But fairly large samples have been made in the past. The English Society for Psychical Research canvassed seventeen thousand people in eighteen eighty, and ten percent reported that they had had psi experiences. The Boston Society for Psychical Research made a similar survey in nineteen twenty-five, and that time twenty percent reported psi experiences. In nineteen sixty-six, one hundred and fifteen students of Aberdeen University were similarly sampled. Thirty percent acknowledged a personal psi experience. The psi percentage of the population is certainly growing, but the rate is hard to determine. We may nevertheless estimate that at least thirty percent of this court is gifted in some phase of psi. And thirty percent of nine is about three. And, having regard to growth rate, and—forgive me, your honors—the fact that psi correlates strongly with intelligence, culture, and mental activity, one might reasonably expect to find four, possibly even five, psi's on the court."

"Incredible!" breathed the Chief Justice.

"Permit me to disagree, your honor. Many of us have some degree of psi, but are not consciously aware of it. Consider the studies of William E. Cox on train wrecks some years ago. He proved that the number of passengers on a train involved in a wreck was generally substantially less than the number for the same train the day before, or two, three, or four weeks before. He concluded that the missing passengers somehow had a 'hunch' about the impending wreck, and simply didn't make the trip. If they were Pullman passengers, they simply canceled the reservation."

Justice Blandford leaned forward. "That's curious indeed, Mr. Winters. It so happens I canceled a plane reservation to Miami tonight. Does that mean I'm clairvoyant?"

"I trust not, your honor. I mean, considering the circumstances, and the other lives involved. I merely make the point that psi is a generalized American experience, so common in fact that science must take notice, even though its possessors do not."

"I would go further than the Chief Justice," said Justice Burke. "This is not only incredible; it is absurd. Be that as it may, I think we are digressing."

"Yes, your honor. I was about to mention psi politicians. Lincoln is the prime example. He experienced autoscopy in eighteen sixty, shortly before he left Springfield, Illinois for Washington."

"Autoscopy?" said Helen Nord.

"It simply means seeing oneself. Lying on the horsehair sofa in his home in Springfield, he saw two images, one firm, one vague, in the mirror across the room, which was not positioned to reflect any image of him. He correctly understood that the strong image meant that he would serve out his first term, and that the weaker image meant he would die in his second term. And in the first days of April, eighteen sixty-five, he had his famous dream of his own mourner-lined catafalque lying in the East Room of the White House. 'The President has been killed by an assassin,' they told him in the dream. And he knew, at least subconsciously, when it would be. Every night previous, when he dismissed his guard, he had said 'Good-night, Crook.' But on *that* night, Good Friday, April fourteenth, as he left for Ford's Theatre, he said, *'Goodbye, Crook.'*

"And Chauncey Depew was another psi politician. We all know how Coleridge 'saw' the lines of *Kubla Khan* as he came out of an opium dream, and was busily writing them down when interrupted by a 'person from Porlock.' But how many of us know that Depew's speech nominating Colonel Theodore Roosevelt for governor of New York was similarly pre-recorded? He had a vision of the nominating convention, and of himself making the speech, while sitting on the front porch of his home on the Hudson. The vision faded, but the speech remained vivid in his mind, and he quickly wrote it down. And so Theodore Roosevelt was launched into national politics— by psi."

From time to time during this interplay Edmonds had

glanced down the bench where Oliver Godwin was busy taking notes. Godwin, he knew, had the remarkable faculty of abstracting and summing up a case during argument. He would turn his notebook over to Augusta Eubanks, who would flesh out the skeleton outline, cite the proper controlling decisions, and revise some of the old gentleman's language. (Augusta would write, "This is indeed a novel proposition, and one for which counsel urges no precedent in our judicial history," instead of Godwin's simpler "Sheep-dip.")

In a moment, Godwin would close his notebook and very likely doze off. Edmonds sighed.

"Let's get back to the camera," said Pendleton. "How can a camera inside a safe take a picture?"

"The technique is well established," said Winters. "Peter Hurkos in Holland and Ted Serios in this country were able to cause images to appear on film in a Polaroid camera. Fukurai and his associates in Japan did substantially the same thing, but caused Japanese ideograms to appear on the emulsion. Although the initial chemical mechanism within the emulsion is obscure, the subsequent steps of developing the latent silver image, fixing with hypo, and using the resultant negative to make positive prints or enlargements are the same as in conventional photography. One can only speculate as to how the sheer force of will, operating at a distance, could make certain molecules of silver bromide sensitive to the photographic developer, while leaving others unaffected."

Edmonds' temples were beginning to throb. He was glad when Burke interrupted.

"Tell me, counselor, why don't these clairvoyants play the ponies, or break the bank at Monte Carlo, or get rich in the stock market?"

"Apparently many do, your honor. But of course they would not publicize it."

Pendleton frowned. "My background in Wall Street is no secret. Are you suggesting that I am a psi?"

"I suggest nothing, your honor. But perhaps you will

agree, on the other hand, that your success is not inconsistent with the possibility."

"Hmph."

"If all these psi's have this power," demanded Burke, "why didn't they warn President Cromway in the first place?"

"Several claim they did. The data are still coming in. It's quite similar to the warnings attempted for Kennedy's benefit in nineteen sixty-two, by Jeane Dixon, John Pendragon, Helen Greenwood, and even Billy Graham. Jeane Dixon even named the day and the hour—and from fifteen hundred miles away."

"Even if all you say is true," said Edmonds bluntly, "you have offered nothing to prove that the particular clairvoyance in issue was used lawfully."

"I believe I can satisfy your honor on that point. If the court please, I would like at this time to place psi in its proper perspective in police technique. For it *is* a police technique, quite modern, but as useful in its way as the Bertillon measurement system, the Henry fingerprint system, the Keeler polygraph, radar for speeding, alcohol detection in the breath and bloodstream, spectroscopic analysis of dust, ballistics, blood analysis, differentation by blood groups, voiceprinting, and many others. Many police departments in Europe, and in Holland especially, use clairvoyants routinely. Professor W. H. C. Tenhaeff at one time maintained a whole team of 'paragnosts' for assistance to the Dutch police. And they are used in this country much more often than is generally realized. For example, Gerard Croiset, the Dutch clairvoyant, told the FBI in nineteen sixty-four where the bodies of three civil-rights workers would be found in Mississippi. And the equally famous Dutch clairvoyant, Peter Hurkos, assisted materially in the Boston Strangler case."

"But Hurkos failed on the Jackson case, in Virginia?" demanded Edmonds.

"The results were inconclusive, your honor. But these are not the only examples. Some years ago, a policeman in Grosse Pointe Woods, Michigan, was found to have the knack of locating the criminals before the crime had even been reported to the police."

"What *is* clairvoyance, Mr. Winters?" asked Pendleton.

The assistant attorney general shook his head. "I don't know, your honor. Even clairvoyants themselves don't know. I mean, they know when it happens to them, but they don't know *how* it happens. Clairvoyance, of course, is just one well-defined variety of psi experience. There are several others."

"Would you explain that?"

"Certainly. Clairvoyance is a unilateral extrasensory phenomenon. Only one person is involved—the percipient. He perceives a visual or aural experience taking place at a different time or place. Telepathy requires at least two people, a sender and a receiver. Telekinesis is the mental ability to control the motion of matter. Gamblers have it frequently with dice. Radiesthesia is a special kind of psi."

"Radi-*what?*" demanded Justice Moore.

"Radiesthesia, your honor. The lay word is dowsing— for the location of water with a forked hazel wand."

"Nonsense, Mr. Winters. Dowsing is dowsing. Nothing supernatural about it. Back in Louisiana my father was the village dowser. I've dabbled in it a little myself."

"I'm no expert, your honor. But I understand that at least five Nobel prize winners consider radi— dowsing, that is, a valid form of psi."

Edmonds stole a glance down at Godwin. The old man's head was propped in his cupped hand and his eyes were closed. Pendleton had better hurry up.

The Chief Justice interrupted. "We seem to have taken you somewhat over your allotted time with our questions, Mr. Winters. In fairness to opposing counsel, and since our two-thirty adjournment is nearly at hand, I will ask that you draw to a close."

"This concludes the case for New York, your honor."

"Thank you. We stand adjourned." He stood up.

The clerk began his intonation: "All rise . . ."

That judges of important causes should hold office for life is not a good thing, for the mind grows old as well as the body.

—Aristotle

In the robing hall Helen Nord took Godwin by the arm. "I'm having some friends over tonight. We want you to come. Ben can pick you up."

"Thank you, my dear. But I don't know. I'd just be in the way. It's disgraceful to be old. You know what they say. Tired old man. Helen, I know I should retire, and I'm going to. But I don't want Roly Burke to think he's forcing anything. Actually, my resignation is already written. I will send it to the President the day we decide *Tyson*."

"No!"

"Yes. Oh, I'm not truly senile. Not yet. With a little help from Gus I can still crank out a passable decision. But I'm tired, Helen. Tired." His mustache drooped. "That's the only reason. I've told Ben, and now you. Later, I'll tell Pendleton. Until then, this is all in confidence."

"Of course."

"And no fuss and feathers at the end. No stupid sentimental retirement banquet. No idiotic gold watch, no initialed attaché case, no desk set. Maybe just a photograph of something familiar with a farewell card that all of you can sign. I would treasure it."

"However you want it."

He stood silent a moment, thinking. "Your party. I miss Laura's parties. All the old friends are gone. Ah, the times we used to have in Georgetown. Till four, five in the morning. I wish Laura could have known you. She would have liked you." His face clouded.

"You can turn in any time. You know where the guest room is."

He brightened. "In that case, I think I'll come." He put his arm around her shoulders and tried for his best leer. "Just down the hall from your bedroom."

"And what's a mere eighty-five years between friends?"

"That's *my* line, you forward wench!"

These judges, you will infer, must have something of the creative artist in them; they must have antennae registering feeling and judgment beyond logical, let alone quantitative proof.

—Justice Felix Frankfurter

Helen Nord lived on a two-hundred-acre farm near Port Royal, Virginia, an hour's drive to the Court by superhighway. Washington had been born nearby. Grant and Lee had struggled here, and Private Corbett had shot John Wilkes Booth in a burning barn a few miles away. She had inherited the land from her Strachey ancestors, and John Nord had designed the big house himself. Her sons had been born and raised here, and now they were grown and gone. She was grateful now for other interests, other ties. A steady stream of her brother justices and their wives attended her dinners and weekend parties. Of course, she rarely had them all out together. The air was strained when Burke and Godwin were merely in the same room. Tonight was the "Godwin" group, namely those whom the old gentleman could insult without offense.

The ladies of the court had accepted her instantly as the lawful successor of Laura Godwin, and felt their own somewhat anonymous status enhanced by direct representation of their sex on the high bench. Millie Pendleton explained it to her. "Laura used to say Washington was full of famous men and the women they married when they were young. But at least we now have a friend in court."

Just now Helen was leading a group down the garden path behind the house.

Godwin left the path and walked over to the great oak tree. Its dead leaves from the previous year were still frozen to its branches. The others waited. He called back, "You're sure you don't mind?"

"I don't mind. But don't hurt yourself."

"Hah!" He kicked the tree trunk savagely, then danced for a moment. A forlorn dead leaf floated down and hung in his mustache. He flicked it off indignantly. As he rejoined the group, he explained matter-of-factly, "I was born in Manhattan, in a hospital next to the old Third Avenue El, in the days when they still used those wonderful steam locomotives. Laura loved the country, but I hate it, with its pure air and the crickets raising cain at night. So Helen lets me kick a tree when I come out here." (They had all seen this many times before.) "Now let's get on to this well."

Helen Nord laughed. "It's right over here, Judge." She led them to a pit some five feet in diameter, edged with a couple of layers of loose cinder blocks, then called back to Moore. "Nick, there's your well." She pointed to a length of pipe extending up from the pit. "We put the casing in today. The driller hit water at fifty feet—forty gallons a minute. He brought the county agent and the state geologist out. They just looked at it and shook their heads. The geologist had already proved from his maps it was impossible."

"But why all the excitement about a water-well?" demanded Godwin. "The way you're carrying on, anybody would think you had struck oil."

"When you're on a farm, twenty miles from a city main, water can be more important than oil. But the point I'm making is, Nick Moore showed me where to drill. That was after I had brought in three dry holes, one of them at a hundred twenty feet. Isn't that right, Nick?"

Moore grinned. "Right."

"What are you getting at?" asked Mrs. Pendleton.

"He did it by dowsing."

"No! Water-witching? But I thought that was an old wive's tale."

"It's real. Many people can do it. Actually, it's a recognized form of psi. At argument today we learned it has a fancy scientific name: radiesthesia."

"Fantastic!" breathed Millie Pendleton.

"We'd better be getting back."

"Bill," said Mrs. Blandford, "why do you keep looking up at the sky?"

"No reason at all, dear," said Blandford lamely. "Just thinking about the flight to Miami I canceled."

"I'm glad you did. You can go next week. This is much nicer."

"The farm is directly under the flight line from National Airport to Miami," said Helen Nord quietly. "We always see it out here. It seems to be late this evening."

After dinner she led them back into the parlor. Ben Edmonds followed with a tray of cigars and liqueurs.

When they were all settled, their hostess began, almost hesitantly: "I want to tell you a story, and then I am going to ask a question of each of you. This has a bearing on the Tyson case. To start, I think there is something about me all of you should know. Mr. Winters, at argument today, hinted very strongly that there were probably three or four psi's on the court. I don't know for sure, but I think I may be one of them. I do know that I have had at least one psi experience. I've even wondered whether I should disqualify myself on the Tyson case. At any rate, I'd like to tell you about it. It took place when my husband died in the first manned Mars flight. It was two-ten on a warm August morning when he lasered back to Orbit Central that the retro rockets wouldn't fire. They analyzed the trouble almost instantly. There was a relay malfunction. They lasered back and told him how to fix it. And he did fix it. And then the retros did fire. But it had taken three minutes for his message to travel thirty-five million miles to Earth, and another three minutes back to Mars. Six minutes was too long. He was barely eight hundred miles above the planet when the retros worked, and he was traveling over four thousand miles an hour. He hit ground at one thousand miles an hour. The ship—everything in it—simply vaporized. The point I wish to make is, when he pressed the retro button at two-ten, and nothing happened, I *knew*. And I knew at two-ten. Orbit Central didn't know until they actually received his call, at two-thirteen. I was with him all the way down. He talked to me." She looked over at Edmonds, almost curiously. "We held hands. And then I died with him. Except, of course, here I am. Some of the other astronaut wives have had similar experiences. Mine didn't surprise the medical people at NASA. In fact, they not only didn't tell me I was crazy—they put me to work in the Parapsychology Section. They were trying to develop psi as an alternate to laser communication, to avoid the time lag of six minutes for a round-trip message, or even to substitute completely in case of laser failure. Actually, there's nothing new about the principle. The Dutch psi Croiset had already demonstrated that engine defects can be diagnosed across the Atlantic Ocean by clairvoyance. Distance is no difficulty."

She paused and looked around at her guests. Mrs. Pendleton had drawn her chair closer and was sitting on the edge of the cushion. Moore's pipe had long since gone out. Ben Edmonds watched her with impassive eyes.

"It must have been a terrible experience," said Pendleton gravely. "But I'm glad you told us about it. It is indeed pertinent to the Tyson issue, especially on the question of psi transmission. But forgive me, Helen, I don't believe you were finished."

"I just wanted all of you to understand. For me, as an individual, psi exists. I agree with Mr. Winters that psi is a common human experience, that most people have had a psi experience of some type, and that the members of the Court eminently qualify. On the other hand, a certain stigma seems to attach to psi, and the higher our standing in our society, the more reluctant we are to admit our psi experiences or ability. So we will try this one by secret ballot. Ben, would you pass around pencils and paper? I would like each of you to write 'yes' if you have ever had a psi experience, or 'no' if you have not. Ben will collect the votes in this vase."

Godwin grumbled. "Woman, I'm old, but I'm not crazy. It's a silly game, and I won't play."

"No matter. Seven votes should tell us something." She picked the pieces of paper out of the vase. "Five yesses, two noes. You all know how I voted. So, not counting the judge, four of you have had a psi experience, and two have not. Messrs. Pendleton and Blandford are negative, I would assume. The majority vote seems to indicate that psi is a rather recurrent thread in the fabric of our daily lives. It's not something weird or strange, unless we make it so."

"Very dramatic, Helen," said Moore. "But if you believe in psi so strongly, doesn't it follow the search and seizure in *Tyson* was constitutional, and that he was lawfully convicted?"

"Of course not! I've already explained that. My intuition, my own psi, if you will, tells me Tyson is innocent. So I'm going to vote for reversal."

"You tell 'em, Helen," said Mrs. Pendleton firmly.

Their hostess leaned over and touched Edmonds on the sleeve. She pointed to Godwin, who was slumped in the deep maternal upholstery of the chair. His eyes were closed, and his outsize mustache ends vibrated with slow rhythm.

Edmonds got up softly, picked up the justice with hypnotic gentleness, as though the old man were a child, and with his burden held loosely against his chest, walked quietly toward the stairs.

The guests watched this in fascination. Mrs. Pendleton tried to catch the eye of Helen Nord, but Helen simply put her finger to her lips. Finally the muffled measured sound of steps died away above them.

Moore shook his head in wonder. "If anyone else tried that, the old gentleman would go through the ceiling."

"What a man," murmured Mrs. Pendleton. "What are you waiting for, Helen?"

"He's never asked me," said Helen Nord shortly. "Millie, will you help me with the coffee?"

The maid had already turned back the bed. Edmonds put a hand under Godwin's head and laid the old man down on the waiting sheets. Then he eased off the shoes, loosened the belt, and pulled up the coverlet. He then realized that Godwin was awake and watching him.

"Sit down, Ben. When are you going to pop the question to little Nell?"

"I don't know. Maybe never. She can't forget—him. And I have a personal problem. Anyhow, maybe we are both too old."

"Of course she still thinks of him. She ought to. But life goes on. Memories should be a garden, not a prison. Talk to the three boys. Get them on your side. Be firm with her. Oh, you are both so stupid. My last twenty years with Laura were the best of all. April Fool's Day coming up soon. She loved it. Laura . . . Laura . . ." He seemed to drift off.

Whenever Godwin spoke of his dead wife in this intimate, carefree way, Edmonds felt, on some deep subsensory level, an emptiness akin to despair in the old man. His chest tightened. Does Helen still feel this way about John Nord? What is this sweet hell called love? Can no end come?

He pulled the blanket up about the old man's shoulders and tiptoed toward the door.

"Where's my teddy bear?" mumbled Godwin.

"Go to the devil," growled Edmonds.

Even as he left the hallway and re-entered the living room, he knew something was wrong.

Everyone was facing away from him, toward the open door of the study across the room. In that doorway stood Helen Nord's maid, holding the phone, one hand over the mouthpiece.

"What is it, Mary?" said Mrs. Nord quietly.

"It's your messenger, mum, calling from National Airport. He said to tell you Flight Sixty-seven to Miami crashed on takeoff. He could just now get to a telephone."

"Thank you, Mary. Tell him he can go home now." Helen Nord turned somberly to Blandford, who was standing, staring rigidly at her.

Mrs. Blandford gasped and sat down. *"That* plane!"

"Yes. I think Bill had a hunch he shouldn't take it."

"But that . . . that means," stammered Blandford, "I . . . I'm a . . ."

Helen Nord simply nodded. "Yes, Bill, you are. Join the club."

Judges are apt to be naif, simple-minded men, and they need something of Mephistopheles.

—Justice Oliver Wendell Holmes

It was late Thursday night, and Shelley Pendleton was alone in his office, and pacing.

Already he knew how the *Tyson* vote would go at conference tomorrow. Five to reverse, four to affirm. He'd be with the majority. Another five–four; and on a case like this! The newspapers, the editorial writers—the whole country would say that even the Supreme Court didn't know whether Tyson was innocent or guilty. And it was actually going to be worse than that. Burke, for instance, would vote to reverse, because psi was illogical. Godwin didn't believe in it, either, but would affirm. And

Helen Nord, because she believed in her own psi (but not in Drago's!) would vote to reverse.

Women. *Sui generis*. On occasion incomprehensible. Yet indispensable. He could hardly complain: by ancient rumor, Laura Godwin had won his appointment by cheating in a poker game with the President's judiciary advisors.

There would be no sanity in the *Tyson* decision. And the public outcry would far dwarf the reaction to the Warren Report of the sixties. For the honor of the Court, he could not let it happen. And just how was he going to prevent it?

He resumed pacing and thinking. Had Tyson really pulled the trigger? Helen Nord seemed so certain he was innocent. Women and their intuition. But suppose she's right? (And I'll have to grant the validity of her psi experience with John Nord.) Can this Court intervene, *sua sponte,* to prove it? Certainly not. But can *I*? I have hunches, too. I've always had hunches. Made my money that way. Does this make me a psi? Maybe. I don't know. God! What a crew. Nord, Moore and his dowsing, Blandford and that plane to Miami . . . And what about Edmonds and those impossible photos? Is it actually conceivable that a human intellect can reach into the past and put what he sees on a camera film? Serios did it, and that Japanese fellow. It all begins to make sense. Edmonds is probably the worst of them. And if there will be no image on the film until Decision Day, how does it get there? What are the rules? Can one psi have a hunch about another psi? There's only one way to find out. And to find out, I will have to do a thing which, if done by one of my brother justices, would merit my strongest censure.

He stopped his slow striding and glared at the phone. He knew now that he would have no peace until he acted. In sudden resolution he seized the phone and dialed a number.

"Evans? Pendleton. I have a very delicate matter I

want you to handle, very confidential. You've heard of Philip Dopher? Yes, *that* one—elevator operator in *that* building. I want you to find him and give him a thousand dollars. Tell him it's expenses to hear the *Tyson* opinion firsthand. He'll have to be here every Monday until we hand it down. It'll take several weeks. My guess is about April First. Tell him he gets another thousand on Decision Day. But he's got to be in court then to get it. Make up something. Tell him it's sponsored by the Sons of Justice. Tell him anything. Just get him here. No, Evans, I can't talk about it. It's just a hunch. Oh, one more thing, bring him in the first day yourself, and show him where he has to sit—well up front, where Ben Edmonds can see him easily."

Tweedledee: If it were so, it would be; but as it isn't, it ain't. That's logic.

—Lewis Carroll, *Through the Looking Glass*

It was Friday Conference again.

"We have been discussing *Tyson* now for over two hours. Agreement seems impossible." The voice of the Chief Justice was measured, controlled. But Edmonds thought he detected a note of grim amusement. His other colleagues, in contrast, seemed morose, almost sullen, as though only now they realized certain impossible aspects of their task. Pendleton continued as though in brooding monologue. "We must make an end and vote, even though it but defines our differences. I will begin by summarizing my own position. If clairvoyance does not exist, then clearly the warrant was invalid, and we must reverse New York. But I cannot reach that conclusion. There are too many documented cases of clairvoyance. Yet it is admittedly erratic, cannot be called up at will, and generally requires verification by the normal senses. Its most fervid proponents do not claim that it has the certainty of ordinary seeing and hearing. Any magistrate called upon to issue a psi warrant would certainly be entitled, perhaps even *required,* to look into the antecedents and previous record of the psi-informant. Some psi's of international reputation and long histories of demonstrated police success might be sufficiently reliable to support a warrant if there were no other fault in the arrangement. But unfortunately for this argument, I think there *is* a fault, and a grave one. Granted this is not wiretapping. Neither the electric current nor electromagnetic radiation is demonstrably involved in psi transmission. A Faraday cage shuts out electromagnetic radiation but cannot shut out psi. Absent interception and publication of an electrically generated message, Section six-oh-five of the Federal Communications Act has not been violated. So our long line of wiretapping cases—*as such*—is not directly controlling. And yet an invasion of privacy has occurred in a depth that far surpasses wiretapping. The intrusiveness, and the breach of privacy goes far beyond the sounds and sights available to bugging and spy TV. Our very thoughts are laid bare. It's worse than truth serum: we needn't even be present to have it done to us. I think Tyson's constitutional rights were invaded. I think we should reverse. And now I'm done. Mr. Godwin?"

"I agree up to a point. The problem as I see it turns on whether this particular bit of clairvoyance involved reading Tyson's mind, that is, assuming there's such a thing as clairvoyance in the first place—which I very much doubt. I don't see how Tyson could have known exactly where the movers had put that particular box in the warehouse. Or even if he did know, we haven't been shown that it was Tyson's mind that was read. For all we know, the clairvoyant might have read the warehouseman's mind. Or nobody's mind. Tyson's privacy wasn't invaded unless his mind was read, and I just don't think it was read, whether or not psi is for real. But my main point is, we shouldn't interfere. These are very complex procedural matters better left to the state courts. Look at it this way. If a person is indicted for murder, the determination of his guilt or innocence should not be considered as a sporting event, to be governed by the Marquis of Queensberry Rules, but by a practical and actual determination of the guilt of the indictee, with the state, in order to prevail, being required to establish guilt beyond any reasonable doubt. In my view the State of New York has fully discharged its burden. Psi isn't even relevant. Roly?"

"Psi certainly *is* relevant, Mr. Godwin," said Burke calmly. "It's the sole question certified."

"I didn't vote to grant certiorari," said Godwin bluntly. "But now that we have the case, I can decide on any basis I like."

"Most illogical," snorted Burke. "But no matter." He turned to Helen Nord. "You say you believe in psi?"

"Yes."

"And also in logic?"

"Yes, at least as long as it makes sense."

The rotund justice looked over at her sharply. She returned his look with expectant interest. He knotted his jaw muscles and continued. "Logic by definition is that which makes sense: nothing more, nothing less. No miracles. No supernatural hocus-pocus. Everything that takes place, every event, every effect, is logically caused by something, something which preceded it in time, and which provided the physico-chemical causative chain that resulted in the effect. These premises are the foundations of our intellectual existence. Psi violates them. Therefore psi is false; it does not exist."

"I'm not very bright at logic," said Godwin, "but why can't you turn it around the other way? Psi exists: therefore the foundations of our intellectual existence are false."

"Just what I might have expected from you, Brother Godwin. You are using the conclusion to destroy the premise. The mental effort required for logical thinking is quite beyond a party of your years, I'm afraid."

Godwin sat up straight. His mustache began to twitch.

Helen Nord broke in hurriedly. "All that sounds very complicated."

"Perhaps so, perhaps so," conceded Burke, "at least to those unaccustomed to disciplined cogitative processes." He touched his fingertips together and considered the matter. "Perhaps we can benefit from an example, taken from a sub-species of logic known as operationalism. So. If a loaded gun is pointed at my heart, the trigger is pulled, and the bullet proceeds toward me in a straight line, I would certainly be killed, would I not?"

"Of course."

"My death is the effect of the bullet in motion?"

"Agreed."

"And the bullet in motion is the effect of the pressure of the hot gases within the barrel of the gun?"

"Yes."

"And the gases are the effect of the ignition of the gunpowder by the primer, in turn the effect of the firing pin striking the primer cap?"

"Certainly."

"And the movement of the firing pin is caused by the trigger pull, in turn the effect of the squeeze of the gunman's finger?"

"True."

"So we have a complete chain of cause and effect?"

"Yes."

"And it is logical to assume that every effect must have some identifiable cause? Nothing happens without a specific cause?"

"It may be logical. But there may be a reasonable doubt as to whether the rules of logic apply to psi. Psi seems to operate without any cause-effect linkage. For example, if psi takes over, your bullet might vanish in mid-air."

Burke sighed. "I give up. I absolutely give up."

Pendleton hid a grin.

Godwin leaned forward querulously. "Are we to understand, Roly, that in *this* case you are trying to get by on *logic?*"

The insinuation was insidious; it implied that Burke's analysis was superficial; and indeed, that the justice had not devoted the necessary time and study to grasp all the fine points of the case.

Burke's face turned slowly pink. He glared back at Godwin. "I would like you to understand exactly that. Law has no other basis."

But it was no good. The others were looking at him almost sympathetically. Who are they to judge me, he thought bitterly. Logic is . . . logic!

Pendleton cleared his throat. "We'll have to go on. Mr. Moore?"

"I agree with our brother Godwin. You call it clairvoyance. If that's what it is, nobody's mind was read. By definition, clairvoyance excludes telepathic cognition of the mental activities of another person. And if nobody's mind was read, there was no invasion of privacy protected by the Fourth. I would affirm."

"Mr. Blandford?"

"In my view the evidence shows clairvoyance exists, but it also shows it is erratic, often not available on call, generally not reproducible, so I feel that clairvoyance is too unscientific for use as 'probable cause.' Reverse."

"Mr. Lovsky?"

"I agree with Burke, *supra,* that clairvoyance is an impossibility. But I don't agree that it must follow that the warrant was improperly issued. The warrant was duly sworn. It pinpointed what was to be searched, and the rifle was in fact found, exactly as described on the information. Pendleton *contra,* I would affirm. *Cf.* Godwin, *id.*"

"Mr. Randolph?"

● CONCVR ●

"Mr. Edmonds?"

"Personally, I believe in psi. But I don't think it should be used as a police technique without the consent of the suspect, and any evidence thus discovered should be inadmissible. Reverse."

"Madam Nord?"

"I, too, believe in psi. And I think the warrant was valid and the rifle admissible. But I would reverse. Tyson didn't do it."

Pendleton took a deep breath. *"Why* do you think he didn't do it?"

She looked back defiantly. *"Because,* that's why."

Pendleton exhaled slowly, then smiled at her reassuringly. "Quite all right. So be it. Let me sum up. We have five to reverse, four to affirm. And in neither the majority nor the dissent do we have the slightest unanimity of rationale." He studied his notes. "Madam Nord, you're up next on the opinion list. Will you please draft the majority opinion? With the variation of views, and especially considering your own, your task will be cut out for you."

"I'll do my best," said Helen Nord. "In fact, in the interests of reconciliation of divergent views, I'll even go along with the rationale of the majority—that either psi doesn't exist, or if it does, the psi-based search warrant was defective."

"Yes?" said Pendleton, surprised.

"On one condition."

"Such as what?" demanded Burke suspiciously.

"That we open the safe on Decision Day."

"Preposterous!" cried Burke. "Exhibit Q was never properly admitted into evidence, and even if it had been, the question of its probative value would be within the exclusive jurisdiction of the trial court. The Supreme Court of the United States never decides facts except in rare cases of original jurisdiction!"

"Then I'll file a specially concurring opinion to reverse on the plain and simple ground I don't think Tyson is guilty!"

Godwin chuckled. "And she'd do it, too!"

"If I might make a suggestion," said Pendleton, with an enigmatic smile, "we could order the safe opened after handing down both the majority and dissent. It could of course have no bearing on our decision as then rendered, but both Tyson and New York could use it, if they choose, and if its contents truly merit it, as basis for re-hearing. Mrs. Nord? Gentlemen? Then it's agreed.

"Just one more point. Despite the gravity of the case, we have a duty to the defendant and to the country to act as promptly as possible. Hopefully, we can hand down the decision on April First."

When the penalty is death, we are tempted to strain the evidence and even the law in order to give a doubtfully condemned man another chance.

—Justice Robert H. Jackson

It was Monday, April 1, Decision Day, in the Marble Palace.

Practically every appellate court in the country—saving only the United States Supreme Court—distributes printed or typewritten copies of its decisions to its litigants as the sole means of stating the outcome of the case. But from time immemorial the Supreme Court—the only appellate court with its very own printing shop on the premises—had "handed down" its decisions orally. And "orally" means whatever the delivering justice chooses it to mean. It might mean reading an entire ninety-page opinion—a favorite tactic of Justice Lovsky; or it might mean a very brief oral summary of the salient law and facts, after the manner of Justice Randolph. Or, as in the case of Justice Burke, it would start out as a summary and develop, willy-nilly, into a profound exposition of logic-in-law, through the historical framework of the Justinian Code, the Magna Carta, Coke, Comyn's *Digest,* the Constitutional Convention, the probable (corroborative) views of John Marshall, and would inevitably conclude with appropriate selections from Burke's *Logic in Appellate Decisions*. The law students of George

Washington and Georgetown Universities might have to get the printed decision to discover who had won, but all agreed it was an enthralling experience.

After he was seated, Edmonds surreptitiously searched the first row of the pewlike red-cushioned seats and found there the face he had noted on previous Mondays, and the face he did not want to find: a bald man, burly, bearded, his eyes a study in controlled, violent cunning. Edmonds moaned inaudibly. Let this pass. But it would not pass. Everything was here, waiting. He looked over at the safe on the marshal's cart. It was still locked, still inviolate, but within minutes all that would be changed forever.

When he had taken office ten years ago he had sworn to uphold the Constitution and the laws of the United States. A month ago he had flung down Orwell's *1984* on the conference table. Beware! he had cried. And beware of whom? Of Benjamin Edmonds, Ph.D., J.C., Associate Justice of the United States Supreme Court, and psi extraordinary. For he thought it very likely that he was now going to violate his oath, and in so doing, the constitutional rights of another. And thereby he would strike down, besmirch, and discredit for decades the enhallowed institution he had sworn to preserve. For Helen Nord (and how did *she* know?) was right. Tyson had *not* pulled the trigger of that fateful rifle. He *knew*. (And for that matter, how did he know?) And so there remained a thing for him to do, a thing so simple, so devastating, that the Tyson case would be decided instantly and forever. It was not lawful; it had only justice to excuse it.

Edmonds noted that Pendleton seemed to be studying him from the corner of his eye. But then the Chief Justice turned and nodded gravely to Helen Nord, at the far left. She nodded back. She was on her own.

This, thought Edmonds, was the crowning paradox. Helen Nord, who knew that psi existed, had joined with four of her brothers in the majority opinion that would hold, in effect, that psi was unproven. And she would do

this because it would free a man whom she thought innocent.

The woman's voice was clear and strong. Briefly she
recited the undisputed facts, read the single question certified to the Court, then came directly to the point. "It is
the view of a majority of this Court that the search warrant was not issued upon probable cause, as is required
by the Fourth Amendment, in that the basis of the information was not explained to the magistrate who issued
the warrant. *Aguilar* v. *United States*. This finding requires the further finding that the evidence obtained by
the search is inadmissible under the Fifth Amendment.
And it must follow that Tyson's conviction must be reversed, and that he is entitled to a new trial, in which this
tainted evidence must be excluded."

There was more, but Edmonds now heard only
snatches. His eyes were looking into—and through—the
eyes of Philip Dopher. In a strange, nearly real sense,
both of them were for the next few minutes not even in
this great chamber, but in a deserted room in an office
building on Manhattan's East Side, where Dopher was
kneeling at an open window, caressing a rifle resting on
the window sill, and waiting.

Somehow, the voice of Helen Nord floated by, wisp-
like, fragmented. ". . . the consequences of the reason-
ing urged by New York . . . the thrust of the constitutional command . . . we do not recede from . . ."

And now he watched the kneeling figure grow tense
and still. The bearded cheek lay in lethal affection against
the wooden stock, the eye peering through the telescopic
cylinder, and the gloved finger beginning to squeeze its
unspeakable message to the trigger.

". . . if clairvoyance *does* exist—and this we do not
decide—this source of information should have been
brought to the magistrate's attention, so that he could
fully understand and evaluate what was being sworn to as
a fact . . . and assuming *arguendo* that clairvoyance exists, we rule, nevertheless, that it is not such a generally

accepted basis for experiential information that the magistrate could take judicial notice of it . . ."

One year and a couple of hundred miles away, a puff of smoke appeared at the muzzle of Dopher's rifle. Ben Edmonds closed his eyes and withdrew from the mind of the murderer.

"In summary, it is the decision of this Court that the warrant did not issue upon probable cause. The judgment of the Court of Appeals of New York is reversed and the cause remanded for further proceedings not inconsistent with this opinion."

She was done.

Everyone in the courtroom knew what had happened. It would be futile for New York to retry Tyson without the evidence of the rifle. He would have to be released, a branded assassin, the mark of Cain on his forehead, with every hand against him. How long had Tyson to live?

Dopher appeared to be reflecting silently. To Edmonds the man seemed only mildly disappointed. Dopher had no way of knowing what had just happened to him: that the image Dopher dreaded most, the horrid secret one, had been carefully lifted from his mind, and had been carried away and laid down in another place, and there made permanent, as a flowing modulated pattern of light-sensitized silver bromide molecules in a gelatin emulsion.

Edmonds knew that his face was covered with tiny drops of perspiration, and that he was cold.

As Helen Nord closed her case folder, the Chief Justice turned and nodded to Oliver Godwin.

The old man's voice rasped out. "I must respectfully dissent from the majority opinion, and my Brothers Moore, Lovsky, and Randolph have authorized me to state that they join in this dissent. We do not contend that the discovery of the rifle justifies the search, but we think this not the point. We think the search was made on a lawfully issued warrant, and that the rifle was properly admitted for that reason. In any event, the matter is procedural. We think, if perchance the constable blundered, this should not set the criminal free. Society has the right to be protected against the return of this man. A great deal has been said about psi and clairvoyance in the proceedings below, and here. Some of the authors of this dissent have asked me to confirm their satisfaction that the record amply supports the existence of psi. Personally, I am far from convinced. But no matter, for our dissent is not founded either on the belief or disbelief in psi. We might observe that the use of psi as a police technique necessarily requires corroboration. But the only useful corroboration necessarily involves the subject matter of the search. It seems to us of the minority, that when the clairvoyant (assuming he was such) has been duly corroborated, the warrant stands self-validated, and further inquiry is superfluous. In our minority view the warrant *was* issued upon probable cause. We would, therefore, affirm.

"And now, with the consent of our brothers representing the majority opinion, we turn to one final matter. In the record below there is explicit testimony to the effect that the contents of the safe—Exhibit Q—will prove that psi exists. Both majority and minority have of course reached our separate conclusions without benefit of the safe—which, indeed, is not even in evidence and can have no probative value in our decisions. We do now order that the safe be opened. Marshal?"

Walter Sickles leaped to his feet. "Objection, your honor! We have had no opportunity to examine the contents!"

"Overruled. Your opportunity will come." The old man added sternly, "And there is no such thing as an objection to this court."

Sickles sat down uncertainly.

"Will the marshal please proceed?" said Godwin testily.

"May I remind your honor," said the deputy marshal, "that I do not have the combination."

"Of course. Here it is." Pendleton swiveled his chair around and gave the waiting page an envelope.

In a moment the marshal had the safe open and was staring inside. "It's full—of something, your honor."

"Yes. I imagine that's the urethane foam. You'll have to tear it out with your fingers. But be careful when you get to the camera."

The deputy dug in gingerly. Finally he pulled out the camera, still encrusted with adherent bits of plastic foam.

There was a sudden excited buzz in the great chamber.

Pendleton banged twice with his gavel. "Silence! Or I will ask the sergeants to clear the room!" He added quietly to the marshal: "Remove the film. Do you know how?"

"Yes, your honor." He pulled the tab, counted off the seconds, then tore off the assembly and stripped the wet print. His eyes widened as he stared.

"If the court please!" Guy Winters was on his feet.

"The court recognizes New York."

"New York requests permission to see the print."

"Granted, Mr. Winters. And I assume Mr. Sickles would like to see it also?"

"Of course, your honor."

Together the two lawyers bent over the composite with the marshal, who held the black-and-white print by the tab as the three of them studied it.

Pendleton's voice was under control, but it had now risen by half an octave. He demanded: "What does the print show?"

Winters looked up at the Chief Justice in wonder. "It seems to be—*the* rifle. A puff of smoke . . . just been fired. It's *the* room . . . *the* window. And the man is still aiming . . ."

"Man?" demanded Pendleton.

"Yes, your honor. It looks like . . . Philip Dopher!"

"Dopher? The witness below?"

"Sure looks like him," affirmed Winters in irreverent wonder.

And now a commotion in front of the audience. A stocky bearded man exploded into the center aisle. His right hand held a pistol. The spectators shrank away from him.

He cried out, "Yes! I did it! Long live the revolution!"

The defiant, weaponed fist upraised, in weird confrontation of the ultimate lawless force versus the ultimate force of law.

Everyone in the audience was on his feet. A wide empty circle formed around the intruder.

Dopher boomed out again. "If I killed your President, you think I won't kill you? All of you, possessed by the devil! Only way you could know I did it. I have six bullets. I think maybe I start with your chief, Mr. Pendleton." He waved the pistol. "Nobody move! Maybe I miss, and hit the smart lady judge—you want that, eh?"

Edmonds felt his stomach caving in. The horror was complete. It was futile now, and much too late, to say, never, never again.

But now in the appalling silence, he felt a chill descending into the room. A cold wind struck his face, and he shivered. Behind him, the great maroon drapes were rustling.

He almost forgot Dopher. What? he wondered. Or—who?

"Laura . . . ?" Oliver Godwin, struggling out of his chair, mustaches trembling like questing antennae, had whispered the word. It was at once a statement and a question, fluttering, broken-winged, desolate. It made the hair stand stiff on Edmonds' neck.

Dopher's pistol arm swiveled to the new target. Paralyzed, Edmonds watched the fist squeezing, the dead aim. He heard, unbelieving, the deafening crack, then the reverberations.

Godwin did not fall. Edmonds knew he was untouched, and that a leaden pellet was somewhere sailing, lonely forever in stranger time and space. He turned back to the grotesque figure in the center aisle struggling between the two sergeants-at-arms.

Roland Burke now stumbled to his feet and leveled a shaking finger at Dopher. *"You!* Did *you* kill President Cromway? Answer me!"

"Don't answer that!" Thunder exploded from the throat of Oliver Godwin. He seemed to stand nine feet tall. "In this Court, the rights guaranteed by the Constitution will be respected. I admonish you, sir, to remain silent until you have the benefit of counsel. Be that as it may, Mr. Dopher, if such be your name, I now place you under arrest, on suspicion of murder of President Cromway, and for attempted murder here. We have no place of detention in this building, but in a moment I rather believe the District Police will arrive and transfer you to the District Jail, there to hold you for further proceedings in accordance with law. Mr. Sickles, will you accept Mr. Dopher as your client, until one of you shall request to the contrary?"

"Indeed yes, your honor. And I move that the Court impound and preserve this safe, camera, film, and all associated materials."

"Unless my brothers have any objection—" he did not even look at his colleagues. "So ordered."

As Dopher was led out into the main hall, Godwin turned to the Chief Justice. He was at this moment the reincarnation, the fusion, and the voice of all the great justices who in decades past had guided the flow of American legal thought. He was the great Marshall; he was Taney; he was Hughes. He was the immortal Holmes. "I apologize to my Brother Burke for interrupting him, and to the other members of this court, and most especially to my Brother Pendleton for any undue presumption of authority." But now he stood silent a moment, looking about the great room, wistful, searching. His body bent over a little, and he put a hand on the bench to steady himself. When he spoke again, the few reporters left in the front row had to strain to hear him.

"God's blessing on this place . . . on these, my brothers . . ." He looked up at Pendleton. "With the leave of the Court, I beg leave to retire."

Pendleton nodded to the clerk. "Adjourn the court."

The reporters, attuned to a generation of Washington arrivals and departures, caught it instantly. "It's *real*. He doesn't just mean retire, he means—*retire*. Godwin's finally retiring!" They were on their way to phones even as the crier was intoning, "All rise . . ."

I think it not improbable that man, like the grub that prepares a chamber for the winged thing it never has seen but is to be—that man may have cosmic destinies that he does not understand.

—Justice Oliver Wendell Holmes

"Thank all of you for coming," said Chief Justice Pendleton to the assembled justices. "After the events of this past noon, I thought it best for one last, highly informal conference, to tie up loose ends on *Tyson*. You've seen the afternoon papers?" He passed the copies around. "There seem to be all kinds of speculation. The *Evening Star* thinks Dopher's companions took the picture and got it into the safe somehow, and so betrayed him. The *Daily News* sees it as a plot to assassinate the Supreme Court. They demand a Congressional investigation with full TV and press coverage. Only the *Post* seems to have noticed that we released Tyson and simultaneously preserved Dopher's constitutional rights. They don't applaud either. But at least we need not be concerned further with Dopher. He's been extradited and is on his way to New York."

"And he'll bring the identical question right back here, evidence obtained by clairvoyance," said Moore.

"Not necessarily," said Pendleton cheerfully. "I think each and every member of this court is automatically disqualified to participate in any future cause of *Dopher* v.

New York. We were all witnesses. If we ever get a petition for certiorari, we would have to deny."

"So New York will have to handle it all by itself," said Helen Nord thoughtfully. "This time, with a confession in open court, in front of several hundred witnesses, how can Winters lose?"

"Especially if he won't have to worry about an appeal to this court," murmured Blandford.

"Why *are* we here, Mr. Pendleton?" asked Roland Burke.

"Well, I thought we'd have sort of a post-mortem discussion. And when we finish that, I'd like your signatures on a memento for Oliver Godwin. His resignation was effective at the close of court this afternoon."

"High time," breathed Burke.

Pendleton looked at him sharply, then cleared his throat. "A great deal has happened in this case that some of us do not understand. A picture has appeared as if by magic. Two pictures, as a matter of fact."

Burke sat up suddenly. *"Two* pictures?"

Pendleton peered at him noncommittally. "Yes, two. I'll come to that later on. I don't know what it all means, not really. Either we are faced with the most colossal fraud of our careers, a fraud that involves a number of people of good repute, or else . . . we have just experienced a three-ring circus of psi. A pistol was fired point-blank at Godwin. But the bullet, if there was a bullet, vanished in midair. Yes, there seems to be a great deal going on around me that I don't know about, and probably wouldn't understand if I did. I want to leave it alone. I will not inquire further. None of this need interfere with, nor is it truly relevant to, the continued performance of this Court. And therefore, in closing, let me assure you that I reprimand no one. Quite the contrary. I think we all owe a great debt to someone, or perhaps to several. Finally, I am very glad we are all alive."

Mr. Justice Burke was perplexed. "You mean that's the end of it? That we went through all that, and we're still not going to decide anything? What kind of logic is *that*? Shouldn't we withdraw our opinion, pull the whole case back for rehearing, and decide something?"

"And just what would we decide?" said Pendleton. "Should we take judicial notice that psi exists?"

"Of course not. You're twisting it all around. All I mean is, we can't dodge it forever. This is only the first case. Next term we'll have half a dozen."

"Exactly what do you think we ought to do, Brother?" asked Blandford.

"I don't know. I do know you're all against me." He stood up. "I would like to be excused from this conference."

"Just one more thing, Mr. Burke." Almost diffidently Pendleton turned around and picked up a portrait folder from the cart behind his chair. He passed it down to the justice. "This is the little farewell memento I mentioned earlier for Oliver Godwin. We wanted to give him a banquet and a suitable gift, but he flatly refuses. It's a photograph, with a signature card on the inside fold. We all plan to sign. Since you are now the Senior Associate Justice, we thought you might like to be the first."

"Of course. Very thoughtful." He opened the boards . . . and stared. "What on earth! Hands? A photograph of somebody holding hands?" He got out his fountain pen and unscrewed the cap, then looked over at Pendleton. "It's an old man's hand—in a black silk sleeve. It's Godwin, in robes, isn't it?"

"Yes."

Burke peered again at the portrait. "The other hand. It's a young woman's. The bracelet looks—familiar. Odd. Who is she?" He looked around the table uneasily. "Where did you get this?"

"It was on the negative from the *Tyson* camera. You may recall, I mentioned two pictures. The FBI developed the whole strip. This was on it, too. Ben Edmonds made the blowup."

"Who *is* she?" whispered Burke. He looked at Helen

Nord's wrist. "It wasn't you. *You* don't wear a bracelet like *that* . . . of laurel . . . leaves?" As he considered this, doubt began to undermine doubt, and finally left him at the edge of some awesome mental precipice, unbalanced, and clawing to return to his warm, predictable, three-dimensional continuum. "No!" he gasped. "It can't be. And even if it is, I don't have to believe it!"

Chief Justice Pendleton looked at the gray face. He said soothingly, "Of course you don't, Mr. Burke. In this country, and on this Court, nobody has to believe anything."

And now it seemed to Roland Burke that this cheerful band had been illuminated by a flash of lighting, that he was now seeing their faces for the first time—and they were strangers, knowing, powerful, and he was helpless, and innocent among them. There was something terrifying about it. Nothing could ever be the same again.

Ben Edmonds knew what must be passing through Burke's mind: psi existed. It was a living thing, without boundary of time, space, life, or death. It was not subject to the laws of logic, or to any law made by man. It was without probable cause.

Burke's pen clattered to the floor. From the great black table he picked up the current volume of *United States Reports,* clutched it to his breast as though it were a talisman to ward off a horrifying unknown, and walked slowly from the room.

Edmonds leaned over and took the photograph from Pendleton. "Helen and I will sign first," he said simply. "It would please them."

Harlan Ellison is one of the few writers who have sniffed the breath of corruption that puffs out of the dark places in our own world. Here is a story whose quiet horror comes not from Arkham or Otranto, but from the smell of weed in an opened doorway, candy wrappers and kitty litter in a fireplace, the flutter of wings in a hall.

SHATTERED LIKE A GLASS GOBLIN

By Harlan Ellison

So it was there, eight months later, that Rudy found her; in that huge and ugly house off Western Avenue in Los Angeles; living with them, all of them, not just Jonah, but all of them.

It was November in Los Angeles, near sundown, and unaccountably chill even for the fall in that place always near the sun. He came down the sidewalk and stopped in front of the place. It was gothic hideous, with the grass half-cut and the rusted lawnmower sitting in the middle of an unfinished swath. Grass cut as if in a placating gesture to the outraged tenants of the two lanai apartment houses that loomed over the squat structure on either side. (Yet how strange . . . the apartment buildings were taller, the old house hunched down between them, but *it* seemed to dominate *them*. How odd.)

Cardboard covered the upstairs windows.

101

A baby carriage was overturned on the front walk.

The front door was ornately carved.

Darkness seemed to breathe heavily.

Rudy shifted the duffel bag slightly on his shoulder. He was afraid of the house. He was breathing more heavily as he stood there, and a panic he could never have described tightened his fat muscles on either side of his shoulderblades. He looked up into the corners of the darkening sky, seeking a way out, but he could only go forward. Kristina was in there.

Another girl answered the door.

She looked at him without speaking, her long blonde hair half-obscuring her face; peering out from inside the veil of Clairol and dirt.

When he asked a second time for Kris, she wet her lips in the corners, and a tic made her cheek jump. Rudy set down the duffel bag with a whump. "Kris, please," he said urgently.

The blonde girl turned away and walked into the dim hallways of the terrible old house. Rudy stood in the open doorway, and suddenly, as if the blonde girl had been a barrier to it, and her departure had released it, he was assaulted like a smack in the face, by a wall of pungent scent. It was marijuana.

He reflexively inhaled, and his head reeled. He took a step back, into the last inches of sunlight coming over the lanai apartment building, and then it was gone, and he was still buzzing, and moved forward, dragging the duffel bag behind him.

He did not remember closing the front door, but when he looked, some time later, it was closed behind him.

He found Kris on the third floor, lying against the wall of a dark closet, her left hand stroking a faded pink rag rabbit, her right hand at her mouth, the little finger crooked, the thumb-ring roach holder half-obscured as she sucked up the last wonders of the joint. The closet held an infinitude of odors—dirty sweat socks as pungent as stew, fleece jackets on which the rain had dried to mildew, a mop gracious with its scent of old dust hardened to dirt, the overriding weed smell of what she had been at no one knew how long—and it held her. As pretty as pretty could be.

"Kris?"

Slowly her head came up, and she saw him. Much later, she tracked and focused and she began to cry. "Go away."

In the limpid silences of the whispering house, back and above him in the darkness, Rudy heard the sudden sound of leather wings beating furiously for a second, then nothing.

Rudy crouched down beside her, his heart grown twice its size in his chest. He wanted so desperately to reach her, to talk to her. "Kris . . . please . . ." She turned her head away, and with the hand that had been stroking the rabbit she slapped at him awkwardly, missing him.

For an instant, Rudy could have sworn he heard the sound of someone counting heavy gold pieces, somewhere off to his right, down a passageway of the third floor. But when he half-turned, and looked out through the closet door, and tried to focus his hearing on it, there was no sound.

Kris was trying to crawl back further into the closet. She was trying to smile.

He turned back, on hands and knees moved into the closet after her.

"The rabbit," she said, languorously. "You're crushing the rabbit." He looked down, his right knee was lying on the soft matted-fur head of the pink rabbit. He pulled it out from under his knee and threw it into a corner of the closet. She looked at him with disgust. "You haven't changed, Rudy. Go away."

"I'm outta the army, Kris," Rudy said gently. "They let me out on a medical. I want you to come back, Kris, please."

She would not listen, but pulled herself away from him, deep into the closet, and closed her eyes. He moved his lips several times, as though trying to recall words he had already spoken, but there was no sound, and he lit a cigarette, and sat in the open doorway of the closet, smoking and waiting for her to come back to him. He had waited eight months for her to come back to him, since he had been inducted and she had written him telling him, *Rudy, I'm going to live with Jonah at the house.*

There was the sound of something very tiny, lurking in the infinitely black shadow where the top step of the stairs from the second floor met the landing. It giggled in a glass harpsichord trilling. Rudy knew it was giggling at him, but he could make out no movement from that corner.

Kris opened her eyes and stared at him with distaste. "Why did you come here?"

"Because we're gonna be married."

"Get out of here."

"I love you, Kris. Please."

She kicked out at him. It didn't hurt, but it was meant to. He backed out of the closet slowly.

Jonah was down in the living room. The blonde girl who had answered the door was trying to get his pants off him. He kept shaking his head no, and trying to fend her off with a weak-wristed hand. The record player under the brick-and-board bookshelves was playing Simon & Garfunkel, "The Big Bright Green Pleasure Machine."

"Melting," Jonah said gently. "Melting," and he pointed toward the big, foggy mirror over the fireplace mantel. The fireplace was crammed with unburned wax milk cartons, candy bar wrappers, newspapers from the underground press, and kitty litter. The mirror was dim and chill. "Melting!" Jonah yelled suddenly, covering his eyes.

"Oh shit!" the blonde girl said, and threw him down, giving up at last. She came toward Rudy.

"What's wrong with him?" Rudy asked.

"He's freaking out again. Christ, what a drag he can be."

"Yeah, but what's *happening* to him?"

She shrugged. "He sees his face melting, that's what he says."

"Is he on marijuana?"

The blond girl looked at him with sudden distrust. "Hey, who are you?"

"I'm a friend of Kris's."

The blonde girl assayed him for a moment more, then by the way her shoulders dropped and her posture relaxed, she accepted him. "I thought you might've just walked in, you know, maybe the Laws. You know?"

There was a Middle Earth poster on the wall behind her, with its brightness faded in a long straight swath where the sun caught it every morning. He looked around uneasily. He didn't know what to do.

"I was supposed to marry Kris. Eight months ago," he said.

"You want to fuck?" asked the blonde girl. "When Jonah trips he turns off. I been drinking Coca-Cola all morning and all day, and I'm really horny."

Another record dropped onto the turntable and Little Stevie Wonder blew hard into his harmonica and started singing, "I Was Born To Love Her."

"I was engaged to Kris," Rudy said, feeling sad. "We were going to be married when I got out of basic. But she decided to come over here with Jonah, and I didn't want to push her. So I waited eight months, but I'm out of the army now."

"Well, do you or don't you?"

Under the dining-room table. She put a satin pillow under her. It said: *Souvenir of Niagara Falls, New York.*

When he went back into the living room, Jonah was sitting up on the sofa, reading Hesse's *Magister Ludi.*

"Jonah?" Rudy said. Jonah looked up. It took him a while to recognize Rudy.

When he did, he patted the sofa beside him, and Rudy came and sat down.

"Hey, Rudy, where y'been?"

"I've been in the army."

"Wow."

"Yeah, it was awful."

"You out now? I mean for good?"

Rudy nodded. "Uh-huh. Medical."

"Hey, that's good."

They sat quietly for a while. Jonah started to nod, and then said to himself, "You're not very tired."

Rudy said, "Jonah, hey listen, what's the story with Kris? You know, we was supposed to get married about eight months ago."

"She's around someplace," Jonah answered.

Out of the kitchen, through the dining room where the blonde girl lay sleeping under the table, came the sound of something wild, tearing at meat. It went on for a long time, but Rudy was looking out the front window, the big bay window. There was a man in a dark gray suit standing talking to two policemen on the sidewalk at the edge of the front walk leading up to the front door.

"Jonah, can Kris come away now?"

Jonah looked angry. "Hey, listen, man, nobody's *keeping* her here. She's been grooving with all of us and she likes it. Go ask her. Christ, don't bug *me!*"

The two cops were walking up to the front door.

Rudy got up and went to answer the doorbell.

They smiled at him when they saw his uniform.

"May I help you?" Rudy asked them.

The first cop said, "Do you live here?"

"Yes," said Rudy. "My name is Rudolph Boekel. May I help you?"

"We'd like to come inside and talk to you."

"Do you have a search warrant?"

"We don't want to search, we only want to talk to you. Are you in the army?"

"Just discharged. I came home to see my family."

"Can we come in?"

"No, sir."

The second cop looked troubled. "Is this the place they call 'The Hill'?"

"Who?" Rudy asked, looking perplexed.

"Well, the neighbors said this was 'The Hill' and there were some pretty wild parties going on here."

"Do you hear any partying?"

The cops looked at each other. Rudy added, "It's always very quiet here. My mother is dying of cancer of the stomach."

They let Rudy move in, because he was able to talk to people who came to the door from the outside. Aside from Rudy, who went out to get food, and the weekly trips to the Unemployment Line, no one left The Hill. It was usually very quiet.

Except sometimes there was the sound of growling in the back hall leading up to what had been a maid's room; and the splashing from the basement, the sound of wet things on bricks.

It was a self-contained little universe, bordered on the north by acid and mescaline, on the south by pot and peyote, on the east by speed and redballs, on the west by downers and amphetamines. There were eleven people living in The Hill. Eleven, and Rudy.

He walked through the halls, and sometimes found Kris, who would not talk to him, save once, when she asked him if he'd ever been heavy behind anything except love. He didn't know what to answer her, so he only said, "Please." and she called him a square and walked off toward the stairway leading to the dormered attic.

Rudy had heard squeaking from the attic. It had sounded to him like the shrieking of mice being torn to pieces. There were cats in the house.

He did not know why he was there, except that he didn't understand why she wanted to stay. His head always buzzed and he sometimes felt that if he just said the right thing, the right way, Kris would come away with him. He began to dislike the light. It hurt his eyes.

No one talked to anyone else very much. There was al-

ways a struggle to keep high, to keep the *group high* as
elevated as possible. In that way they cared for each
other.

And Rudy became their one link with the outside. He
had written to someone—his parents, a friend, a bank,
someone—and now there was money coming in. Not
much, but enough to keep the food stocked, and the rent
paid. But he insisted Kris be nice to him.

They all made her be nice to him, and she slept with
him in the little room on the second floor where Rudy
had put his newspapers and his duffel bag. He lay there
most of the day, when he was not out on errands for The
Hill, and he read the smaller items about train wrecks
and molestations in the suburbs. And Kris came to him
and they made love.

One night she convinced him he should "make it,
heavy behind acid" and he let the two sugar cubes dis-
solve on his tongue, and she was stretched out like taffy
for six miles. He was a fine copper wire charged with
electricity, and he pierced her flesh. She wriggled with the
current that flowed through him, and became softer yet.
He sank down through the softness, and carefully observed the intricate wood-grain effect her teardrops made
as they rose in the mist around him. He was downdrifting
slowly, turning and turning, held by a whisper of blue
that came out of his body like a spiderweb. The sound of
her breathing in the moist crystal pillared cavity that went
down and down was the sound of the very walls themselves, and when he touched them with his warm metal
fingertips she drew in breath heavily, forcing the air up
around him as he sank down, twisting slowly in a veil of
musky looseness.

There was an insistent pulsing somewhere below him,
and he was afraid of it as he descended, the high-pitched
whining of something threatening to shatter. He felt
panic. Panic gripped him, flailed at him, his throat constricted, he tried to grasp the veil and it tore away in his

hands; then he was falling, faster now, much faster, and afraid afraid!

Violet explosions all around him and the shrieking of something that wanted him, that was seeking him, pulsing deeply in the throat of an animal he could not name, and he heard her shouting, heard her wail and pitch beneath him and a terrible crushing feeling in him . . .

And then there was silence.

That lasted for a moment.

And then there was soft music that demanded nothing but inattention. So they lay there, fitted together, in the heat of the tiny room, and they slept for hours.

After that, Rudy seldom went out into the light. He did the shopping at night, wearing shades. He emptied the garbage at night, and he swept down the front walk, and did the front lawn with scissors because the lawnmower would have annoyed the residents of the lanai apartments, who no longer complained, because there was seldom a sound from The Hill.

He began to realize he had not seen some of the eleven young people who lived in The Hill for a long time. But the sounds from above and below and around him in the house grew more frequent.

Rudy's clothes were too large for him now. He wore only underpants. His hands and feet hurt. The knuckles of his fingers were larger, from cracking them, and they were always an angry crimson.

His head always buzzed. The thin perpetual odor of weed was saturated in the wood walls and the rafters. He read newspapers all the time, old newspapers whose items were imbedded in his memory. He remembered a job he had once held as a garage mechanic, but that seemed a very long time ago. When they cut off the electricity in The Hill, it didn't bother Rudy, because he preferred the dark. But he went to tell the eleven.

He could not find them.

They were all gone. Even Kris, who should have been there somewhere.

He heard the moist sounds from the basement and went down with fur and silence into the darkness. The basement had been flooded. One of the eleven named Teddy was there. He was attached to the slime-coated upper wall of the basement, hanging close to the stone, pulsing softly and giving off a thin green light. He dropped a rubbery arm into the water, and let it hang there moving idly with the tideless tide. Then something came near it, and he made a sharp movement, and brought the thing up still writhing in his rubbery grip, and inched it up the wall to a dark, moist spot on his upper surface, near the veins that covered its length, and pushed the thing at the dark-blood spot, where it shrieked with a terrible sound, and went in and there was a sucking noise, then a swallowing sound.

Rudy went back upstairs. On the first floor he found the one who was the blonde girl, whose name was Adrianne. She lay out thin and white as a tablecloth on the dining-room table as three of the others put their teeth into her, and through their hollow sharp teeth they drank up the yellow fluid from the bloated pus-pockets that had been her breasts and buttocks. Their faces were very white and their eyes were like soot-smudges.

Climbing to the second floor, Rudy was almost knocked down by the passage of something that had been Victor, flying on heavily ribbed leather wings. It was carrying a cat in its jaws.

He found Kris in the attic, in a corner breaking the skull and sucking out the moist brains of a thing that giggled like a harpsichord.

"Kris, we have to go away," he told her. She reached out and touched him, snapping her long, pointed, dirty fingernails against him. He rang like crystal.

In the rafters of the attic Jonah crouched, gargoyled and sleeping. There was a green stain on his jaws, and something stringy in his claws.

"Kris, please," he said urgently.

His head buzzed.

His ears itched.

Kris sucked out the last of the mellow good things in the skull of the silent little creature, and scraped idly at the flaccid body with hairy hands. She settled back on her haunches, and her long, hairy muzzle came up.

Rudy scuttled away.

He ran loping, his knuckles brushing the attic floor as he scampered for safety. Behind him, Kris was growling. He got down to the second floor and then to the first, and tried to climb up on the Morris chair to the mantel, so he could see himself in the mirror, in the light from the moon through the flyblown window. But Naomi was on the window, lapping up the flies with her tongue.

He climbed with desperation, wanting to see himself. And when he stood before the mirror, he saw that he was transparent, that there was nothing inside him, that his ears had grown pointed and had hair on their tips; his eyes were as huge as a tarsier's, and the reflection of the light hurt him.

Then he heard the growling behind and below him.

The little glass goblin turned, and the werewolf rose up on its hind legs and touched him till he rang like fine crystal.

And the werewolf said with very little concern, "Have you ever grooved heavy behind anything except love?"

"Please!" the little glass goblin begged, just as the great hairy paw slapped him into a million coruscating rainbow fragments all expanding consciously into the tight little enclosed universe that was The Hill, all buzzing highly contracted and tingling off into a darkness that began to seep out through the silent wooden walls . . .

"By February the lump was the size of a bushel basket and had separated itself from him except for a gristly shining skin-covered tube, that pulsed with his heart like an obscene umbilicus. . . ."

THIS CORRUPTIBLE

By Jacob Transue

And so, after thirty-five years, they would be face to face again.

Andrew eased his car up under a big white pine and cut the motor. The place didn't look like much. One old pickup truck parked between the two quonsets, a barn tucked against the forest, an unmowed meadow full of daisies and black-eyed susans on the south.

Andrew got out of the car and stood in the shade of the pine. His sense of uneasiness increased sharply. Of course, he was alone out here. He wasn't used to being alone anymore. He was used to traveling with a swarm of secretaries, servants and assorted sycophants. He felt naked.

It ought to be refreshing. No planes, no cars, no engines of any kind. Nothing but the sputtering of summer insects. A wilderness. Anything could happen out here and no one would ever know.

Nonsense. Paul was a scientist. Men like him were too selfish, too single-minded to risk the interruption of their work for anything so sterile as vengeance. Paul always had been secretive. It was characteristic of him to insist Andrew come alone.

Andrew crossed the brown pine-needled ground toward the huts.

"Hello!" he called.

A leggy brown-haired girl wearing trousers peeped through the door and vanished as silently as a deer.

"Paul?"

And there, suddenly, was Paul behind the screening. "Hello, Andrew."

The nylon netting was a dazzle of white between their faces, too blinding to penetrate. Then the door opened and Andrew stepped through, his hand extended in greeting. But Paul had already turned away to lead him inside.

It was cool and gloomy and dimly sparkling with long rows of chemical glass, glass cabinets, two tall glass closets so steamed with interior humidity their contents could not be seen. A long work counter ran the entire length of the building, with sinks and shelves, burners, centrifuges and other equipment he did not recognize. Off in one corner, squeezed between two huge filing cases, was an old gray metal desk.

"Sit down," said Paul, seating himself behind the desk. "I'm sorry we're rather primitive here. Take that crate."

Andrew sat down uncomfortably. It had been years since his flesh had had to accommodate itself to such makeshifts.

"Well," said Paul, "it's been a long time."

Able to see him clearly at last, Andrew clenched his jaws in surprise. It must be true, then, the incredible rumor his investigators had brought him. Paul had not changed at all. His thin dark hair, perpetually on the brink of baldness, was the same. The round child's face had no dewlaps, no wrinkles. The beanpole body was still taut and narrow. Andrew's hand crept surreptitiously under his coat. His tailor had again altered his measurements two months previously in London.

"Yes, a long time," said Andrew. "What are you doing away out here?"

"Cheap land. Cheap labor. I have one girl here in the lab and a man up at the barn for the heavy work. Local people. I never had much money to operate with, you know."

Was it a cut at him? Andrew felt for his cigar case, extended it and, when Paul shook his head, fumbled one out for himself.

Paul watched him light it. "I see your hands mended quite nicely. I didn't think you'd ever be able to use them again."

Andrew held them out for him to see. The palms and fingers, clear to the tips, were scar tissue, hard and white. The other memento of their last day of partnership. Scars on his hands and a fortune in his pocket.

"A whole beaker of acid," said Paul. "It's amazing you have hands at all."

"I was preoccupied that day."

"It was even convenient for you, wasn't it. It gave your departure such logical urgency."

"It ruined me for working," said Andrew. He flexed his hands, stiffly, clumsily.

"Fortunately, you don't need them for work," said Paul and smiled thinly. "Tell me, how did you manage to find me?"

"It took me three years."

"You must want something very badly."

"You know what I want," said Andrew.

Paul was silent, gazing at his desk-top. Andrew watched him narrowly. What was going on in his mind? Was that satisfaction, to have Andrew come seeking him out at last? Or was it perhaps caution, after what had happened so long ago?

"Now look," said Andrew bluntly. "I'm not skillful at working people around. Power does that to you, I suppose. You get used to giving orders."

"You have a great deal of power, haven't you."

"Yes. Now, I regret that thirty-five years have gone by since we worked together. But I make no apologies. You and I were different kinds of men. You were after knowledge. You've got it. I was after power. I've got it. You know yourself that in order to get what you wanted, you had to eliminate a lot of things from your life. I imagine you've had to slice your ethics pretty thin sometimes. So have I."

"What have ethics to do with it?" asked Paul.

"You're right," said Andrew. A cloud of fragrant cigar smoke drifted between them. "Men like you and me operate on a different code. We have no families, no private lives. We each had one goal and everything else was sacrificed."

"You mean that when you sacrificed me, it was according to your code."

"In a manner of speaking. But you had what you wanted when you discovered that formula. It was of no further use to you. On the other hand, it was of great use to me. I've built an empire with it. At the time I had no money to either buy or lease that formula from you. Now, however, it's a different story. Perhaps I can make it up to you."

Paul's spectacles flashed as he turned his head away. "That is not what you have come here for."

Andrew lipped his cigar in silence for a moment. "All right," he said at last. "My investigators picked up rumors of your work. At first I doubted the whole thing. Then I put my secretary on it and his report seemed to confirm the rumors. Now that I see you myself, I have to believe them."

"What do you want?"

"Look at me. And look at you. We're both sixty-eight years old."

"Well, the exercise of power is rather hard on the organism, I should think. I lead a quiet life."

What did he want? To see the rich man crawl? Andrew studied him in silence for a moment. "My investigators tell me you have found a way to lengthen the life-span indefinitely. To reverse the aging process."

"Science is always the subject of wild rumors. You know that."

"They have seen your eight-year-old monarch butterfly and your ten-year-old shrew."

That got to him. The pause lengthened as Paul fingered his lower lip. At last he said, "Which of my assistants was indiscreet?"

Andrew gave a grunt of amusement. "Money talks. I heard it from my checkbook."

Paul stood up and went to the window. Outside, the meadow shimmered in the sun, the insects chittered and buzzed.

Andrew leaned forward on the crate. "I'm prepared to give you half of everything I possess."

Paul smiled. "You said yourself that money was not my goal."

"No, but knowledge is power, they say. Maybe we're not so different after all."

Paul turned toward him. It was impossible to see his face against the light pouring in through the window. "We're entirely different," he said. "I would never have allowed that formula to get out of my hands. I knew from the beginning it would be put to a lethal use—"

"But this isn't lethal!"

"Oh, think, man! The planet is already staggering under its superfluous populations. Nobody deserves to live indefinitely. Why, death by superannuation is the only thing that frees us from pampered dictators in all walks of life—of whom you are one, more than likely. What makes you think that you should live forever? Do you contribute something so precious to the world?"

"Do you?"

"Certainly not."

"Then what's the use? Why did you involve yourself in this?"

"Curiosity." He could hear the smile in Paul's voice.

"Then it's futile!"

Paul's narrow shoulders lifted in a shrug. "In the last analysis, it's all futile. All ultimates are ultimate nothing, from the human point of view. We pass our tiny span with tiny games—bridge or biology, it makes little difference."

"Nevertheless," said Andrew, "I don't believe you'd look the way you do in the natural course of time."

"As I said, I lead a quiet regular life. I'll probably outlive you by a good many years."

Andrew lapsed into silence again and a strange little sensation came over him. He had felt it before. Ephemeral as a spiderweb, it closed over him and left its small stickiness, its impalpable repulsiveness. It was the sense of approaching death. He felt like a child, ready to cry out in wild anger and rebellion. It was not fair! Here he was with unlimited opportunities. It took years to reach such a position and what good was it if time was about to run out? It was so preposterous, so badly arranged, so paradoxical. Why should life be so idiotically perverse? And there stood that prim ass with the secret in his skull, presuming to withhold it.

"You've become quite a moralist, haven't you," he said ironically. "Fit to judge the whole world!"

"I'm not judging you, Andrew."

"If you have the means to keep me alive and you don't use it, that constitutes a judgment."

"Why should I give it to you and not someone else?"

"Because I know you."

"I know lots of people."

"Because I know you can."

"Now you're tempting me, Andrew." Paul sat down again at his desk, pressing his hands flat on the top of it. "My two vulnerable points. Curiosity and a logical aversion for you."

Craftily, Andrew kept quiet. There always came a time when you had to be quiet and let a man talk himself into doing what you wanted.

"I've succeeded with animals, but a human being— with the unpredictable human mind. I ought to be willing to sacrifice you, since you've already found me expendable. Here you are urging me, offering yourself. I can't imagine why I hesitate."

"Liar," said Andrew calmly, watching his obviously youthful face.

For a moment they were both quiet, eyeing each other with mutual skepticism.

"You have no idea what it entails, Andrew," said Paul at last. "You see, your investigators didn't get it quite right. I don't lengthen the life of your organism. I have a procedure by which you produce yourself a new one."

Andrew puffed at his cigar. "What's the difference?"

"The psychological hazard. It's terrifying."

"You can do it, then!"

"It's also very painful."

"Worse than dying?"

"It would take a year."

"Give me six weeks to get my business in order."

"You're determined, then?"

Andrew carefully scraped the ash off his cigar into the saucer on the desk. Now why was the man so carefully decontaminating himself of all trace of responsibility? Was there more he had not disclosed? Or was it a last attempt to frighten him off? Oh, I know you, Paul. You'd complete an experiment if it cost your own life, much less saving mine. "Yes."

When Andrew returned to the laboratory, the hardwoods were turning color and the katydids had replaced the locusts. He brought with him a physician's report, which Paul had insisted upon, attesting to the soundness of his heart, lungs, liver and kidneys.

Changes had occurred at the laboratory during the interval. A new cinderblock wing jutted from the end of the quonset. It housed a small operating room and the room which Andrew would occupy for a year.

"I have some tests of my own to make, first," Paul told him, and for two weeks Andrew submitted to brief agonizing encounters with tubes, needles and the rest of the distasteful panoply of research. The experience of suffering was new to him. Not even the accident to his hands had hurt very much—too much nerve tissue had been destroyed. Now, for the first time in his healthy life, he suffered the intrusion of reality upon his intellectual horizon, a reality that probed deeper and deeper into the fortress of his mind, laying waste whole concepts by the quick dazzle of pain, the hollow echoes of relief. He was astounded and exasperated at the ease with which his body could dominate his attention. His buffeted ego retched, too, as he lay vomiting after one particularly trying exploration. He might have quit the whole attempt then and there had it not been for the old cold habits of his years in commercial chemistry. One did not easily relinquish the fruit of a three year search. Any new enterprise was like a boil, growing more tense and painful until it finally erupted in success.

The experiment itself commenced with a small operation. The large artery in Andrew's groin had to be moved to the outer side of his thigh. This was for mechanical ease, Paul explained.

"I'm not much of a surgeon, but no reputable doctor would perform such an operation so you have no choice. Are you still interested?"

"Yes."

"Once we go this far, there will be no turning back."

Andrew nodded brusquely, took the sedatives Paul gave him and climbed into bed. Paul snapped out the light, the door closed, all was quiet.

So, here he was suddenly. In this small room, this great

bed, facing the large window that looked out on the meadow and part of the woods. The rising moon, three-quarters full, shed its placid light on the world, the curtains moved beside the partly opened window and it was as though nothing but this room had ever existed. I will not go out of this room on these legs, he thought, and abruptly the gamut opened before him.

Thoughts of life and death lined either side, thoughts a healthy man should never think. How fragile life was! One blow and it was gone. There lay the bones and tissues, but the life was gone, emptied out so easily. How vulnerable it was, how final its departure! How short its tenure seemed, at best. If something were to go wrong, it would be as though he had never lived at all. Consciousness was no more than an abstraction, a geometrical point in the void, preceded by mindless infinity, succeeded by mindless infinity. How mad, the commotion this abstraction could produce. Between the two infinities, what difference did a few years make? And yet how precious they seemed. It was worthless. A man would never buy anything so problematical. Yet he had.

This is not the way to think. You can die thinking such thoughts. You have to fight. Now, fight, he told himself. Cling. Think of being alive!

Oh, but pain. It was a problem. Those additional tests Paul had made. Painful. Pain required a certain mental attitude. You had to alienate yourself, draw apart from your body, set it out there where you could look at it and see it was just a kind of automobile. Made the pain bearable. The pain was bad when you confused it with yourself, whatever yourself was. What is the self? This mysterious seer, hearer, thinker, this insubstantial entity that desires to continue, that hates these wincing tissues on which it depends. Repulsive, failing, dying stuff. Suddenly, he felt as though he were perched precariously in a small boat tossed on a wild sea of organic matter that would drown him if he let it.

But I will not be drowned, he told himself. I'll cling to this boat and tomorrow in the daylight it will be better.

When he awoke, leaves were swirling past the window. It was a windy October day and he felt hungry. He pressed the button and Paul came in carrying a small tray with sterile implements on it.

"Well," said Andrew heartily. "I feel ready for anything. Give me some breakfast and let's get on with it."

"The operation is over," said Paul.

Andrew gaped at him, and in the silence Paul set down the tray on the table by the bed. Scissors, cotton, alcohol, a small vial with a plain darning needle stuck through the cork. Andrew turned away and instead looked at his hands. They were the same as always. But what matter if they were stiff and numb? They worked, didn't they? He clenched them slowly. Good hands.

"Already past the point of no return, eh?"

"That's right," said Paul.

And then the reaction. This is not me. I'm in it, but it isn't me. And the mad scramble back into the boat.

Paul lifted the bandage where the relocated artery pulsed. He swabbed a tiny patch of skin and picked up the vial.

"You see," he said, extracting the cork with the needle, "in this process we take advantage of the fact that every cell of the body has in it the complete genetic equipment. We merely encourage one to divulge what it knows." And he pricked the skin deeply.

"Is that all?"

"That's the beginning."

It itched, but Andrew, clinging to the cockleshell of his identity, refused to scratch it. The body was itching, not he.

"I'll bring in your breakfast now," said Paul, replacing things on the tray. "You're going to have to eat quantities. Six meals a day. And unfortunately, special and not very tasty preparations. But it'll be better in a couple of weeks. You won't have to force yourself anymore. The new body is parasitic."

Andrew said nothing. Instead, he watched with great attention as Paul recorked the vial. Small hard sounds of glass on metal, the movements of hands, footfalls as Paul went out.

Then what does one do with the mind?

One had to use these senses. They were all one had. But curse these sneaking side-glances at the machinery!

Leaves fell, dipping and kiting. Puffs of cloud drew their shadows over the blue hills. A flight of crows clamored noisily from tree to tree. One wondered what all the conversation was for. Why didn't they just leave? It was as though they were saying, Where's that report from the Florida labs? Dammit, Pete, I told you to take care of that. Their costs are running too high! Who's that? Representative from Rupert Chemical. Get him out of here, damn spy!

He spent an hour watching a downy woodpecker go up and down the pitchpine just outside his window, picking and picking, softly and imperturbably, while the jays swooped, perched, bowed and brashly quoted prices. That woodpecker was like Paul. Research. The jays, salesmen, in and out all the time, bright-eyed and predatory. The starlings, speculators, always traveling in flocks.

And at last, breakfast came in on a wheeled tray pushed by Erna, the mountain girl, who looked at him white-eyed and served him at arm's length.

Three days later there was a pimple on his leg. He got out of the boat long enough to touch it gingerly with an exploratory forefinger.

"What's that?"

"That is how it begins," said Paul.

Andrew turned to the window irritably. November was forecast by gray gusts of rain. "I wish it were spring."

A month later, when the first snow lay feathered like a herring-cloud among the brown weeds of the meadow, the pimple had become a huge lump, the size of a grapefruit, and the pain had begun in earnest. It was a queer kind of pain, as though everything in him were being sucked through a pinhole.

"Is everything all right?"

"Yes," Paul would say, each time he asked the fretful question.

But his suspicions grew. Then the practical self would take command again. You had to stick to the conviction that everything was fine! Maybe it wasn't, but if not, it still was not practical to dwell on it. Stick with the paying premise.

"I've got to have something to do!"

"If you don't mind Erna, I'll send her in to play cards with you or something."

"Anything!"

So Erna, the freckled, long-legged girl, sidled in with a pack of cards, and they played endless, wordless games of Russian bank, in between endless, tasteless meals. And, during the hour each morning. afternoon and evening, when Erna was up at the barn helping Paul with the experimental animals, Andrew played obsessive solitaire.

By February the lump was the size of a bushel basket and had separated itself from him except for a gristly shining skin-covered tube, that pulsed with his heart like an obscene umbilicus.

"That's what it is," said Paul.

"Cover it up!" Andrew ordered. "I don't want to see it!"

Paul and Erna rigged a curtain between Andrew's side and the lump's side of the bed.

Yet, when the March winds started roaring over the quonset, he could no longer bear being in ignorance. He swept aside the curtain to see, and Paul came running at his sudden cry.

"My God, is that it? What's gone wrong?"

It lay like a huge grub beside him, the head all frontal lobes, so large they wrinkled forward between the blind tumescent bulbs that should have been eyes. Its small caterpillarlike arms were curved in over the wrinkled chest.

"Nothing is wrong. It's just shaped like a fetus at this stage."

"It's hideous!"

Paul jerked the curtain across the bed again and laid a barbiturate on the table. "Take that and stop thinking."

Andrew gulped it down and replaced the water glass with a trembling hand. "That isn't me," he said hoarsely. "That could never be me."

"Try to stop thinking."

"What have you done to me?"

"What you insisted I do."

"I want to stop. Cut it off. Kill it. Get rid of it!"

"If I did, you would die."

"I don't believe you."

"You would die. Your body processes are altered now." He went out and returned with a mirror which he handed Andrew in silence. Glaring at him, Andrew took it, then he glanced in it, handed it back. He didn't want to see. He had shriveled like a burnt leaf. His skin was leathery and stretched tight over the high bones of his cheeks and forehead and chin, sucked in in prunelike wrinkles around his mouth and eyes. He was aware suddenly of how very weak he had become. He closed his eyes tightly, withdrawing to the tiny boat, clinging to it, rocking and rocking in the now loathsome sea, hearing the suck and surge of his old body's fluids, the receding tide of his blood.

He had made a mistake. He should not have left his business behind. That was the function of his mind, to keep him from being overwhelmed by this decaying carcass.

He demanded a *Times,* and Erna made a special trip in the pickup to get it. Thereafter, every day she went in to the distant county seat and brought one back to him. He began to write to his secretary, and large envelopes arrived in the mail once a day. It preoccupied him, and he congratulated himself on getting back to his proper activities again. But by June he was too weak to continue.

That day, when he admitted he could not write any longer, or even leaf stiffly through the contents of the latest brown envelope, Paul pushed back the curtain again. At first, Andrew refused to look.

"It has changed," Paul assured him. "Take a look."

At last Andrew turned his head on the pillow.

Beside him, head in the opposite direction, lay a young man.

"That isn't me."

"It's you, all right."

"It doesn't look like me. I never looked like that." He struggled to sit up, but was too feeble. Paul came around and helped him.

"The differences are only wear and tear," said Paul. "This is a fully mature body, but it's unmarked by experience. The feet, for example. No calluses, no deformities. They've never worn shoes. And the face. Even the face of a four-year-old child is altered to a certain extent by thought."

Andrew gazed at it, rapt. It was eerie, lovely, locked in prenatal composure. "All the orifices are still shut," he whispered.

"They'll open shortly now," said Paul.

Andrew hunched forward as far as he could. "Let me see the hands."

Paul lifted one hand and held it up for Andrew to see the palm, smooth, flexible, traced like a baby's with innumerable tiny lines. Andrew studied it avidly.

"I wonder how it will be to touch things again and be able to feel them," he said, letting Paul help him lie down again.

They kept the curtain back after that so that Andrew, propped up on pillows, could watch the last changes taking place, the slow unsealing of the eyelids, the lips.

"Why doesn't he wake up?" Andrew asked.

"This is not your son," said Paul. "This is you, remember?"

"How do I get in there?"

"Wait and see."

Andrew was becoming too weak to worry. He avoided looking at his hands, which were so dessicated that the details of the bone structure could be seen through the darkening skin. Erna had to feed him, spoonful by spoonful, a long tedious process that seemed to do him no good at all anymore. Between meals he would sink into a torpor from which he roused sluggishly to be aware that for half-conscious hours he had been carrying on a long dialogue with himself, feebly insisting, heavily denying.

Live! Live!

Oh, it's too weary, it's too far away. I'm too tired.

That's the trap of the flesh, the weakness of the mind. Don't believe it. Don't listen to it. Live!

And he would pick up the enormous load of his identity and struggle back to seeing once more.

And drift away again, down and down, deeper and deeper . . .

It was warm again and he could smell the meadow, a fragrance compounded of warm grasses and a hint of wild strawberry, immensely sweet. He lay breathing it in, feeling for the first time in months a sense of ease, the quitting of innumerable pains and aches. I'm dead, he thought. And the faraway voice of Paul saying over and over again, "Andrew!" seemed the last echo out of time. So it does go on, he thought. This little I in the dinghy. Well, I'm glad to be out of it. How good to have no sensation but this pleasant scent . . .

And then he opened—his eyes? But there was Paul, bent over the blackened shell, touching it gently, speaking to it. Loathsome thing. How could he bear to bend so close to it?

And then he blinked. Blinked what? Slowly down, glance over these limbs?

He could not speak.

There, Paul, you bloody genius, it hasn't worked. Something has gone wrong and I can't even tell you that I anticipated it and did not arrange to endow you with half my worldly goods.

Ah, there at last. Paul was looking toward him. If he couldn't speak, he could smile. He knew he must be smiling, because Paul straightened slowly and came toward him, his academic frown shattered into wonder, his hand extended tentatively.

"Are you there?" Paul's voice gently inquiring, curious, concerned.

Andrew smiled again.

"Can you speak?"

Can this head be moved? It's extremely heavy, ah, but it can be shaken back and forth on the pillow, with effort, yet the effort is not painful, merely difficult.

"Don't be anxious," said Paul. "These delicate neural complexities of speech will need some training. Everything is there. You just need a little time. Erna!"

The girl came running. glanced at him wildly, turned away, turned back. He could have laughed, if he had been able, watching the comic graceful pirouette of alarm and curiosity and amazement.

"We must get some fluids going," said Paul to her. "That thing—" a thumb over his shoulder toward the other form in the bed "—is not quite defunct. We can keep it operating a little longer and give him a margin."

She vanished out the door, returned quickly with the bottled fluid and the rack. They suspended it over the other one, jabbed the needle into the papery vein.

"Get this one something to sip at. We've got to get it functioning!"

Erna ran out again while Paul wrapped a blood-pressure band and listened to his heart. meanwhile glancing at him with eyes that seemed filled with new unsuspected perplexities, eyes newly gentle, newly troubled and searching. Had something gone wrong?

Paul folded his stethoscope, patted his hand and waited until Erna returned with a tall glass of fruit juice. "Hold it for him," he said to her, and she sat down beside the bed and put the straw in his mouth. Andrew drank greedily, and instantly was filled with such an intensity of pleasure that tears sprang to his eyes. All that was new and waiting and ripe functioned smoothly, joyously, and was in turn rejoiced by the cool liquid flowing into the receptive stomach. Andrew tongued aside the straw for a moment to smile reassuringly at Paul. It works, he wanted to say. You see, it does work. Don't worry. All will be well. Poor old Paul.

Old Paul?

Andrew squinted at him, trying to manage the unsteady focusing of these sharp new eyes with their exquisitely flexible lenses. Ah, there it was! The tiny webbing of lines around Paul's eyes. And the papery look of the skin under his chin. Old Paul. My God. Andrew turned his head and gazed at Erna, really seeing her for the first time. Here was genuine youth. This luminous skin, the high round contours of cheeks outlined in light, contours to be understood not by their bones or their lines, but by the simple fruit-like bloom of skin.

Andrew lifted one hand uncertainly. It wavered but it rose, and he studied the skin of his forearm. There it was. The moist pellucid bloom of youth.

So Paul had not lied. He had never passed through the process. He really was the fortunate possessor of a type of organism that aged very inconspicuously.

"We'll teach you to talk," Paul was saying. "That can be Erna's job."

And so he learned to speak again from Erna, who had once so diffidently played cards with him in his old person. He watched her lips form the syllables, and from the syllables his attention was drawn to the lips that formed them. How was it possible he had associated with her for a year and never seen her at all, save as someone to be sent or summoned? Why, she was lovely, brimming with whimsical grace, warm and attentive.

Beware, whispered old experience, drawing him back into the boat. The sea is the sea. Today the sun shines on it, but remember the darkness.

Oh, but life is so sweet again! All these senses—surely they should be tried for their own sakes. This body has so many potentials besides just carrying around an ego and a calculator.

Hormones, came the ironic reply. The subtle secretions of a new set of endocrines. Did I endure that year for a pretty hillbilly?

How marvelous she is! These textures, these fragrances, this animation!

Even Paul seemed to consider her a more appropriate companion for him (youth to youth, perhaps), for days went by when Andrew did not see him at all except for the daily blood-count. He did not care. He was too charmed with the small pleasures of each succeeding day, the exercises he could do in bed, shaving, eating (real food again, meat and fruit and vegetables), looking at Erna.

"Oh, but I want to get my feet on the ground," he said moving his legs restlessly. "I want to walk out in the meadow."

Erna had been sitting in the open window, obviously longing to go outside almost as much as she wanted to stay with him. Now she turned with a grin. "Let's ask Paul," she said, slipping from the window.

The next morning Paul gave him a pill and prepared him for the final operation. He awoke at noon to find himself free at last, with a small bandage on his navel, and the still sinister form of his past gone forever.

During the following week he learned to walk again, first simply getting in and out of bed, or standing up, then wobbling around the room holding fast to things. His strength increased rapidly and in five days he was able to walk up and down the corridor. A week later he was ready to try the meadow and, leaning on Erna's round arm, he went slowly out through the daisies and beebalm and wild chicory.

"Not too far the first time," said Erna.

"Just to the pines," he begged, so they went down and into the shade of the pines where she helped him to sit down to rest on the brown needles. He was no sooner securely on the ground than he tightened his arm around her shoulders and dragged her down to him and kissed her on the mouth. After one start of surprise, she threw her arms around him and very happily kissed him back.

He laughed. "I knew it would be good to kiss you!"

"How could you know!"

"Because I've watched your mouth for weeks. It's so sweet and fresh." He let her sit up beside him. "And so am I! No old dental plumbing! No tobacco stains! No jaded tissues!" And he touched her cheek with his fingertips, relishing the texture of silky skin.

He remembered the first sight he'd had of her. Wild and shy as a deer. And like a deer, confidence made her playful. What did it matter if she was a mountain girl? What did education matter? She spoke well enough. Paul's influence, perhaps. But she was young and pretty and healthy and bright. What more could a man want? Besides, she was guileless. Nothing haughty there, nothing combative. With a girl like this you could be two against the world instead of each other. Marriage was one thing he'd never tried.

"Erna," he said, "I realize I'm too old for you. I'm sixty-eight, after all. But I want to marry you anyway."

Her bright eyes looked into his, a little abashed. Then she grinned. She had such a fetching open-hearted smile. "You've got it backwards! I'm ancient compared to you. You'll only be two months tomorrow!"

They laughed and hugged each other and then she leaned contentedly on his chest and tucked her head underneath his chin. "I'd love to marry you, Andrew. Only do you suppose we could live here in the woods?"

"I'll buy you two thousand acres of your very own and you can fence out the hunters and tame all the varmints."

"I'd like that!" She lifted her head and looked into his face. "How did you know?"

Andrew, holding her in his arms, smiled dreamily out at the meadow. "I seem to know a lot of things all of a sudden. Maybe I never had time before."

And without a backward glance, there under the pine trees, he left the dinghy and slipped into the welcoming sea.

That evening after dinner, Paul came in, listened to his heart and said he was doing very well.

"Sit down," said Andrew.

Erna was sitting on the edge of the bed beside him. Paul sat down in the chair. "It's time," he said cryptically.

"Well," said Andrew, "I feel it's time, anyway." He glanced gratefully at Erna. "I doublecrossed you, Paul."

"That was too long ago to think about," said Paul.

"No. I mean, I did it again. I said I'd give you half of everything I had. Why didn't you ask about it? Why didn't you insist on seeing it legalized before you went through with this?"

Paul looked at him in silence.

"Well, it doesn't matter, anyway," Andrew went on. "I've been thinking about a great many things. I regret so much. Half of what I have is more than you'd ever need. But I want to reestablish what we had, what I wrecked thirty-five years ago. I know I can trust you, but I want you to know you can trust me, now. I thought we could work out some way for you to be joint owner with me of everything. It belongs to you probably more than it does to me, anyway."

"It won't work," said Paul.

"Yes, it will," said Andrew. "I've been going over it in my mind and I've a good idea how to go about it. I'm going to bring my lawyers up here and we'll put the whole thing on paper once and for all. I know you aren't interested in money, but don't tell me you'd turn down unlimited funds for your laboratory."

Paul smiled his habitual thin smile. "It would be very nice, but it won't work." He glanced at Andrew wearily, with a touch of his old irony. "You see, Andrew, your personality has changed. Oh, I'm almost certain you're the same entity, but there are dozens of significant little differences that make you a human being instead of a monster."

"I suppose I should be grateful . . ."

"But there are ramifications," Paul continued. "I mean, you haven't asked how you can prove your identity. Can you make your lawyers believe you're a sixty-eight-year-old man? Will they believe you?"

Andrew blinked at him. "We'll do it by mail," he said.

Paul took his notepad and pencil from his breast pocket. He laid them carefully on the table beside Andrew. "Sign your name."

Still gazing at him in bewilderment, Andrew picked up the pad, curled his fingers around the pencil. Then he bent his head and concentrated on the absurdly difficult task of writing his name. A childish scrawl met his eyes. He looked up at Paul, startled. "But I'll learn to write again! A little practice . . ."

"Certainly." Paul nodded. "But the difference between your present personality and your—'late'—personality, would make any graphologist testify against your claim." He paused, then added softly. "And then, doubtless many of your associates are quick men to grasp an opportunity. Can you trust them not to find it to their interest to deny your identity?"

Slowly, Andrew leaned back on his pillow. It was true enough. The high ridges of industrial finance had their quota of predators. Even as he digested his predicament, he felt the slow stirring of his own old instinct, rousing to prowl again. And with it came the old cunning: you bare your fangs when you have power, but while you're jock-eying for it, you go quietly, head down. "Well," he said.

He glanced at Erna who was watching him with wide-eyed concern. So sweet, so desirable. But that would have to wait awhile. "What'll I do?" He lifted his hands and looked at them. "No fingerprints that are any use. But they're good again, Paul. Can you give me a job here for a while?"

Paul smiled suddenly, with relief, it seemed. "That's an idea. Then it really would be like old times." He rose. "Well, we have to get up to the barn. I'm delighted with the way you've come along, Andrew. And very happy with the way you've taken this turn of events."

"You did what you said you would," said Andrew. "I'm the luckiest man in history. And if I hadn't tried to cheat you, I wouldn't have cheated myself, would I?"

Paul sighed. "I admit it. It was my breaking point. The idea of letting you cut yourself off without a penny was irresistible. But now I'm genuinely sorry, Andrew."

"Forget it."

Erna slipped off the bed and followed Paul out, touching Andrew's hand as she passed. He listened to their footsteps going down the corridor, then the soft closing of the door as they left the building to go up to the barn. After that, he lay still, thinking and thinking, while contempt and rage slowly accumulated force. At last he snaked quietly out of bed and stood barefoot on the floor, his entire being poised, cold, feral.

Work for you again! Work for you! Why, you stupid vindictive old ass! To annihilate the fruits of a lifetime for a moment's spite! You dried-up academician! You might be satisfied to spend sixty years with your eyes plastered to a microscope but I have other fish to fry. And this time I won't waste fifteen years getting started.

He knew they would be at the barn for an hour at least. He slipped down the corridor, past the operating room, into the laboratory. It was dark, save for one small light above Paul's desk. In a moment his eyes adjusted as he went softly and slowly down the long aisle, examining Paul's equipment as he went, touching things here and there, recognizing, remembering as the knowledge seeped back with his other reviving powers. Halfway down the long continuous bench, he stopped. There, in a glass cabinet, in front of several rows of similar little vials, was the one with the darning needle stuck through the cork. He looked at it impassively.

"Will he be all right?"

Erna's voice. He froze.

"Are you in love with him?"

At the sound of Paul's voice, Andrew realized he was listening to an open intercom between the laboratory and the barn. He looked about for it, then spotted it a little to his left where he had passed it in the dark.

"Guess I am."

Now he could hear, faintly in the background, the nicker of a horse and the intermittent whining of a dog. He relaxed and turned back to the cabinet, his eyes fixing on the vial.

A chuckle from Paul. *"He's going to make it."*

"How can you be sure?"

It was worth millions, that vial. Untold millions. Every fortune in the world would come tumbling into his lap. The idle rich, politicians, athletes, movie stars . . .

"The rats, Erna."

Stealthily, Andrew slid open the door of the cabinet. His hands closed over the vial. Then he paused, assessing the other little bottles ranked on the shelves. Did they all contain the same fluid?

"Which ones? The first two died."

"Ah, but they served their purpose! If they hadn't remembered the maze after processing, we never would have suspected we had preserved the same entity."

Andrew turned the vial in his fingers. Well, then. Perhaps I shall work for you awhile, after all. Long enough to observe, to learn. I can go whenever I'm ready.

"But the next four rats forgot the maze and had to learn it all over again. It's been so in every case, Erna. The ones that remember the maze are the ones whose

blood production fails after a few weeks. It's as if the entity had to make a massive realignment to survive. I'm happy to say Andrew's a changed man."

Andrew, hearing Paul's dry reassuring chuckle, felt the vial grow heavy in his hand.

Carol Emshwiller studied art at the University of Michigan, met Ed Emshwiller and married him, went to France on a Fulbright, and did not even think of writing until she was almost thirty. Her stories have an enigmatic simplicity. Like walnut shells with landscapes inside, they achieve a curious, and habit-forming, inversion of perspective. Her stories have appeared recently in Cavalier, City Sampler, Transatlantic Review, *and in Harlan Ellison's* Dangerous Visions.

ANIMAL

By Carol Emshwiller

The first day of the animal the sun came up yellow over fog. A woman from the Century Arms Apartments walked her three dogs early but hurried back within ten minutes. Her breath was visible. Later on a man, carrying a cane and wearing a tan overcoat, paused at the corner of the small park where the woman had walked the dogs and buttoned up his collar. The sun of the first day of the animal had, by now, turned orange and the man's breath was not visible. The animal, as might be expected on his first morning, slept late. At eleven he was given a bowl of shredded wheat, a glass of milk and two slices of buttered toast but he refused to eat any of it. This was expected, too. He did, however, drink 16 ounces of water from a pail left in the corner for him and this was considered a very good sign.

He was found, of course, in the deepest part of the forest.

The second day of the animal all the windows frosted over. People woke up early and even the night watchmen went home whistling. Something in the air. The barometer was rising. The man of the tan overcoat took ten deep breaths, blowing out alternately from the right and left nostril. The woman who loves dogs enjoyed the cold on this, the second morning. She has never been married and she has a history of dating unsuitable men in spite of the dignity and self-assurance of her manner.

The animal still does not eat. He has watched out the window for a long time. What is he dreaming? his keepers wonder. That confinement is a question of degree? measured less by bars than by the perspectives behind them? so the question may not be, after all: Are the doors locked? but where would they lead to once they are opened, if such a time might come? And are the answers, whatever they may be, all the freedoms he can hope for?

It was said, on the second day, that he did not look too unhappy. At lunchtime a keeper of a particular sensitivity brought him both a grilled cheese sandwich and a hamburger so that it might be seen what his preferences were, but still he ate nothing.

Some intelligence seems to shine in his eyes. The keepers all feel he may be conscious of some meaning in their words, no doubt interpreting them in his own way. The keepers say he may dimly understand the significance of his position in their midst. Perhaps he wishes for more elements from which to draw conclusions. One keeper feels that if he had a drum and a flute he might make some kind of music and these are supplied but he only taps his fingers on his chin.

There's much to do: wash him, cut his nails, clip his mane (all those curls and underneath his head is found to be the same size as everyone's). Also his skin, under the dirt, seems like theirs except for a ruddiness probably due to constant exposure.

There are no marks of the capture on the animal except where the ropes had rubbed into his wrists and ankles. It was said he had suffered no more than a nose-bleed at the time and yet he had killed two of the hunters with his bare hands.

They had dropped him as they entered the city early that morning. He was tied, hands and feet, to a pole and supported by four of them and they had come into the city singing rounds and swinging him jauntily. This was after the last bus had gone back to the center and after the last bus driver had gone to bed and not a taxi in sight. They had stumbled as they came down the embankment and he hit the sidewalk with the back of his head and grunted. His nose began to bleed again; however, many of the hunters had had worse than that from him so not one of them thought to apologize.

On the third day the animal ate . . . scrambled eggs and bacon, toast, orange juice, and it was considered that the most important hurdles were over and, since the weather continued fair, it was felt by most of them that no one would object if the animal was allowed some fresh air in some small, nearby park, provided some pants could be put on him and kept on. Still, it was argued by a minority that this was not necessary for an animal. Others said that it wasn't at all a philosophical question as to when and when not animals might need to wear trousers or even what might constitute animalness, but more a question of simple physiology and that anyone with eyes could answer it and, what's more, would answer it undoubtedly in favor of pants.

Since the keepers all dress alike in gray coveralls, it was decided that one of these would be the simplest to keep on him and, with a small suitcase combination lock at the top of the zipper, there could be no danger that the animal might remove it himself at some inappropriate time.

The woman walks her dogs four times a day. She is tall and always wears black or white with a red hat. Father figures tempt her, hunters and keepers, men she can count on to give her advice and encouragement though one wouldn't suspect this from her expressed attitudes.

The animal is graying at the temples. His eyebrows have grown bushy. There are hairs in his ears. Perhaps his hard life in the deepest part of the forest has aged him. Actually the man in the tan coat appears to be the same age and might make a proper husband for the woman who walks dogs even though he hasn't yet been married and, at his time of life, one would suspect strange vices. Yet he could afford a wife and he has kept himself remarkably fit. He doesn't smoke. Unfortunately he never passes the Century Arms at quite the right times for any chance meetings to occur and neither do the animal and the woman meet, on this, the third day, but if he has an odor, subtle and savage, that is certainly what makes her take off her white scarf and open the top button of her coat. What if she is conscious of some secret origins? (perhaps all the townspeople are) then she may feel some organic kinship at this smell and from it she might draw conclusions about her past and maybe even about her future. Now the dogs slink with their tails between their legs. They are black retrievers though she can have no use for their inborn talents at the Century Arms. The only water they ever see is in their bowls or rain but the weather continues fair. It grows warmer. It is thought that the animal might be permanently installed in the small park where he would see the sun and yet be out of the public's way to some extent. It is thought an imitation cave with a heater and a cot might do well enough and a private bathroom with shower stall. Some keepers wonder if even a heavy wire mesh will be strong enough to hold him. It must cross the top of the cage for he is nimble enough to climb almost anything with a toehold. There happens to be a suitable spot there already which once housed squirrels, foxes, a raccoon and an owl. It only needs enlarging and refurnishing.

Chance encounters sometimes lead to warm friendships and at their first meeting she offers the animal a cigarette which he accepts graciously with a little nod of thanks. Unfortunately, under these circumstances, she would have to play rather the dominating role in the relationship and yet appearances are so important that his expression alone may lead her to believe in his abilities as advisor and encourager. The mesh makes things simpler in many ways. She might bring him little presents of coffee in containers to go, or ice cream or something she has baked herself and she will never need to wonder why he hasn't brought anything to her. She can put herself in a mother role and act out a part she would prefer he played, perhaps thinking he will learn from her, yearning to tuck blankets round his chin, to rub his back, always speaking softly.

Others come and watch him as they watch the goldfish in the pond or how far the crocus has come up. Someone has somehow taken pictures of him naked and sold them surreptitiously. The man in the tan overcoat bought a set of five but he doesn't meet the woman that day in front of the animal's cage as the creature chins himself on a branch of his ginkgo tree. If he were here, she might pay some attention to the man in the tan coat, more than she ordinarily would. Everything has become physical and even under their overcoats they would have felt themselves to be there in the flesh.

Neither of them have yet received the invitations to the party that will celebrate the installation of the animal in the park. There has been a delay in hopes that warmer weather will come in the next week or two. The hunters and keepers will be there as well as most of the people in the nearby apartments such as the Century Arms. It is felt that perhaps the animal will pick up some valuable hints on the nature of civilized behavior from this event, though, of course, he can't be blamed for the two killings that occurred at his capture. Some of the townspeople have wondered what would have happened at that time had he been captured by other townspeople than hunters, had, for instance, the behaviorists come upon him first. Some of the keepers, themselves, and many have become quite fond of him, argue that there would have been no deaths, yet others say he has turned on them in anger more than once, though they managed to get out of his way in time, but they can't say for sure if these were only threatening gestures.

Yet suddenly, before the invitations can be sent, the animal escapes. No one can understand quite how. At night there's the policeman to check now and then. The lights are kept burning all around the park and yet he's gone. There are reports of four rapes that night, and goodness knows, the townspeople say, how many unreported. One can't be sure who committed them. (There has already been much thought about his possible animal wife or wives, his animal children, perhaps whole colonies of animals living in shelters under the roots of fallen trees, nested in coarse skins and covered with lice. Perhaps they run in packs.) In any case, it may be that the women of the townspeople seem extraordinarily desirable to him or perhaps it's just his superb physical shape or his animal nature, but then maybe he isn't responsible for the rapes at all.

Once the woman had come in late afternoon and whispered "Apartment 5A" as though by some miracle he could come to her open window five floors up. Many of the townspeople have exaggerated ideas of the animal's abilities, but still, he has escaped miraculously, no one can tell how. Perhaps as he shaved himself in the mornings, his thoughts had turned to the functioning of doors and locks and maybe the woman had left him a bobby pin or dropped one by the wire mesh where he could reach it. Perhaps the key to her apartment, by some strange coincidence, also fit the door of his cage.

And certainly, these moonlight nights, the woman would have liked to reinvent love on a higher plane, liked to consider it from many angles and choose those most likely to satisfy in the longest run of all. And suppose there are to be thoughts also on the new man or a new mankind? a new movement of which the animal might be the leader and she might play the part of sister to the animal, a position without emotional dangers, in which she can permit herself a certain degree of closeness while waiting for some ritual sacrifices to take place. And she wants love-tests also for herself to pass, and a period of fasting, a building up of muscles and mental capacities, some way to prepare herself while she waits for his token, a severed finger, ear or toe? Who knows what rites he practices?

He was found ten days later eating a hamburger and French fries in a diner in a distant city, wearing an astrakhan hat, sunglasses, and smoking Marlboros. He did not resist recapture and was taken by taxi to the airport with no incidents. Positive identification wasn't difficult even though he had changed his name and adopted many new mannerisms.

A double lock is put upon his door and a guard to warn the townspeople not to come too near. It is felt new hobbies will have to be found to occupy his time. Someone has contributed an old upright piano, others have brought last month's magazines, paint sets, colored pencils, a banjo. There is a general understanding among the townspeople that there comes a time in everyone's life when new decisions must be made, new directions taken, new resolutions formulated. The townspeople recognize this phase as it becomes manifest in the actions and attitudes of the animal. After all he is, they estimate, at about that age when such a change is due, and he must understand, in some vague way of his own, that in spite of his marvelous physical condition he has passed the peak of his powers. And so they are watching the new self-awareness bloom in him along with new generosities

and new dissatisfactions. Surely he is asking not only
what is the purpose of life, but more specifically, what
will he make the purpose of his own life. Now he takes
up new pleasures and discards old ones. He revolves
slowly to music by the townspeople's best loved, long-
dead composers. He dances with his eyes shut. He taps
on the mesh. He seems to understand or at least to react
to counterpoint and fugue. He receives a daily newspaper
and a good deal of mail addressed to occupant. He
writes: Once I crouched, fleabitten, eating raw roots.
Once I never heard of shirttails, socks and tie tacks. I
slept on ferns.

By now it is the fifty-first day of the animal.

He is writing poems on shredded wheat cardboards
and old envelopes, but this time of year the younger
townspeople roller-skate in the park. The sound of their
wheels on the sidewalks bothers the animal as he sits
thinking what to write down next or when he is studying
a book on style. He has a list of nouns expressing movement and a note to remind himself to put a short sentence
next to a long one. Lately he has studied the role of mystery in fiction of every form, but now, probably because
of some special feeling for the lady with the dogs and
knowing her address from before, he writes: Dear
Madam; I must apologize for the night of April second,
1969 . . . She won't be sure what he is apologizing for
even though it was not a fulfilled night for her as it may
have been for the animal.

He has already attended two cocktail parties in his
honor and one literary tea and he has returned to his
cage without complaint. The extra guard may soon be removed. Someone has given him a tan corduroy jacket
with leather patches on the elbows. Many townspeople
have found him extraordinarily attractive, especially in a
cocktail party setting. The combination of a rugged, even
dangerous looking face, white teeth, a well cut jacket, a
delicate touch upon a Martini glass and a bit of primeval
shyness forms an irresistible combination and none of the

male townspeople have blamed the female townspeople for their susceptibility. One woman has sent him three bottles of champagne, another a suede vest and an imported shoehorn. One has knit him a sweater which he will certainly put to good use since the heating in his cave is not particularly good and the imitation stone door has never closed well. He would have liked an electric blanket, which might not have been much more expensive than the champagne, but he certainly must know that he cannot choose in his position.

One woman has asked if he might be let out in her custody. She has, no doubt, realized the distractions of the park with its roller-skating and its gaping visitors, with even the guard wanting to join into some sort of communication with the animal. She has felt this isn't in the best interests of his art.

She would like to install him in a section of her summer house where he might have a suite of rooms over the garage. She hopes he will be of use as a fourth for bridge and secretly she imagines that the animal will not be aware of her age as she is interested in a certain aspect of his animal nature. The morals of a case like this may be questioned, but the answer is certainly not clear-cut.

This would be just for the Easter vacation and perhaps for next summer. Of course she realizes that the townspeople need this attraction for their park and that the animal belongs to all the people and not just to her but she feels he needs a change if only for the sake of his art. Where will his new ideas come from? she asks, and wouldn't a wild creature do better in the suburbs than in the center of town? at least for a while? People must have sympathy and understanding for all their animals and if she can't have this one she might consider taking a gibbon instead, or a young fox.

She has already gone to the jeweler's to have a silver chain made with which to lead him to breakfast, lunch and dinner.

But he has written: Dear Madam; I would like to accept your kind offer of the use of your house in the country, but I'm afraid I have other plans over Easter. However I may be available for the summer, especially after August first. Perhaps you will consider some alternative since, as you are well aware, all of us wild creatures would enjoy a week outside the town. I would suggest you contact the keepers as to which animals will be the most suitable. Very truly yours, the Animal.

The young male townspeople imitate the animal. They stand at the street corners with their heads at a noble angle, their cigarettes between thumb and forefinger. They all have political opinions now and they fondle stray cats.

The woman still walks her dogs four times a day as usual. She has bought three red leashes for them.

There is much conjecture as to whether the animal is actually capable of experiencing real love in spite of the complications of his political beliefs and the nuances of his art. One never knows how imitative such things may be. But it does look as though the animal considers the three dogs exceptionally graceful. It looks as though he is interested in becoming friendly with dogs, but he has recently given up smoking and there is no longer any excuse for her offering him cigarettes. Perhaps cough drops if he coughs a bit and she notices, but she doesn't.

There are changes afoot. Professors have come to study his reflexes and they have found that they are in no way different from those of the townspeople. This hasn't surprised anyone since they have all, long ago, recognized their animal origins. Yet there is a general sense of foreboding. There has been a reorganization in the department of parks. Younger townspeople are coming in to replace older men. There will certainly be new theories on the influences of such a creature as the animal living in plain view of everyone. Many studies are already underway as to whether there has been more or less crime since his capture. Attitudes of the teenage townspeople are being questioned by teams of graduate students and the animal's writings are being studied by experts in animal behavior. The animal himself has expressed the view that he would like to be considered as an individual as well as an animal. Soon there will be a symposium. Everyone has a theory or two. The lady with the three dogs will be there as representative of the citizen's council of residents of the park area. It is said that the animal himself will preside as chairman, though he will have no real say in the proceedings. No doubt it will be broadcast.

The animal has not yet expressed any opinion of his own. Most likely he is waiting for the results of the various studies to be published. The townspeople are eagerly waiting for him to speak out for they are sure, as with all his other writings, that what he says will not be ordinary.

The woman with the dogs feels her responsibilities deeply and is even more inclined to wear black than ever, but she still allows herself red leashes. She doesn't think it proper for her to discuss anything with the animal at the present time.

On sunny Sundays the park is full of dogs including the three with the red leashes. Townspeople who own dogs can always find something to talk about with each other. It's too bad the animal doesn't own a dog. There is so much he could join into. Later the townspeople will remember this and think, if only we had given him a dog since he had to live in the park anyway. But of course it's too late now.

He has evidently come to a decision and walked away into the deepest part of the forest without writing a single word on the question of his good or bad influences. He has left all the townspeople with an empty feeling inside. Their park seems deserted.

The woman walks with her head up. There are rumors about her but nothing anyone can prove. Her dogs act as though they own the park. Not a single tree is sacred to them. Many townspeople wonder were they really that way before? What if she has shown the animal some secret results from some secret studies? Had she some in-

formation not yet released to the general public? Or is it
that she has finally grown bold enough to realize her love
and confess it? and was he, after all, capable of some sort
of loving response of the same nature as the townspeople's reponses? But how will they ever know now all that
their animal might have been capable of? And they will
always be wondering why he went just at this particular
time before the symposium had even begun. They will
think how great was his need to return to the land of his
origin. They will say he pined for his animal family, his
possible animal wives and children, or they will say that
he searches for his youth in the places where he once was
young or that it is for the townspeople's sake, because of
his influence, perhaps sinister and yet so subtle only he
was aware of it, that he has hidden himself there, alone
and lonely, writing out his poems on birchbark and whistling themes from the music of their long-dead composers, able to avoid capture this time because of his greater
knowledge of the townspeople's methods.

Oh come back to us, they sometimes call out silently
towards the forest, come and write us your animal opinions. Sit in our park. Adorn our cocktail parties. Crime
wave or no, you were really good for us in the long run,
and even if that may not be true, why you belonged to us
and no other town had one like you.

But there's nothing for them to do but to await the
sons and daughters of the animal, those conceived on the
nights of freedom, if it really was the animal who was responsible for (and capable of) that rash of rapes. Will the
children of the animal, they wonder, follow him back to
the deepest part of the forest by instinct, off in search of
their father as soon as they are old enough? And what of
the youngest, the one that some of the townspeople believe must have been conceived the night he left? will he
or she stay as a gift to the townspeople from the animal,
decorating first their schools, their birthday parties, base-
ball games, even roller-skating in the very park where her
father spent so much of his time, later the college, the

dances, contributing to the courses in logic and philology, majoring in history or French and then marrying one of the townspeople and conceiving sons and daughters of her own?

Surely, the townspeople think, surely the blood of the animal is with us still and will, in some future time, be a part of us all.

There is an ethnic flavor to the following story; I am unable to define it with exactness, but would almost be willing to venture the opinion that it is Irish. It is certainly mad; it has in addition that determined and violent gaiety that somehow makes me think of large, jug-eared men with scars on their knuckles.

The author, R. A. Lafferty, might well adopt the proud phrase used by John Collier to describe his Fancies and Goodnights; *his stories are "tales unlike other tales."*

ONE AT A TIME

By R. A. Lafferty

Barnaby phoned up John Sourwine. If you frequent places like Barnaby's Barn (there is one in every port city of the world, and John is a familiar in all of them) you may already know John Sourwine; and you will know him as Sour John.

"There's an odd one down here," Barnaby told him.

"How odd?" asked Sour John. He collected odd ones.

"Clear coon-dog crazy, John. He looks like they just dug him up, but he's lively enough."

Barnaby runs a fine little place that offers eating and drinking and conversation, all of them rare and hearty. And John Sourwine is always interested in new things, or

149

old things returned. So John went down to Barnaby's Barn to see the Odd One.

There was no need to ask which one he was, though there were always strangers and traveling men and seamen unknown to John in the Barn. The Odd One stood out. He was a big, spare, rough fellow, and he said that his name was McSkee. He was eating and drinking with a chortling pleasure, and they all watched him in amazement.

"It's his fourth plate of spaghetti," Smokehouse confided to Sour John, "and that is the last of two dozen eggs. He's had twelve hamburgers, six coney islands, six crab-burgers, five foot-long hot dogs, eighteen bottles of beer, and twenty cups of coffee."

"Blind blinking binnacles! He must be getting close to some of the records of Big Bucket Bulg," Sour John exclaimed with sudden interest.

"John, he's broken most of those records already," Smokehouse told him, and Barnaby nodded assent. "If he can hold the pace for another forty-five minutes, he'll beat them all."

Well, the Odd One was still a spare fellow, with a great gangling frame designed to carry fifty or sixty pounds more than the lean fellow now owned. But he began to fill out even as John watched him; and it was not only that he bulked larger almost by the minute, it was also as though a light was being turned on inside him. He glowed. Then he shone. Then he began to sparkle.

"You like to eat, do you, oldtimer?" Sour John asked the Odd One, the amazing McSkee.

"I like it well enough!" McSkee boomed with a happy grin. "But, more than that, it's just that I'm a bedamned showoff! I like everything in excess. I love to be in the roaring middle of it all!"

"One would think that you hadn't eaten in a hundred years," Sour John probed.

"You're quick!" the illuminated McSkee laughed. "A

lot of them never do catch onto me, and I tell them nothing unless they guess a little first. Aye, you've got the hairy ears, though, and the adder's eyes of a true gentleman. I love a really ugly man. We will talk while I eat."

"What do you do when you've finished eating?" asked John, pleased at the compliments, as the waiters began to pile the steaks high in front of McSkee.

"Oh, I go from eating to drinking," McSkee munched out. "There's no sharp dividing line between the pleasures. I go from drinking to the girls; from the girls to fighting and roistering. And finally I sing."

"A bestial procedure," said John with admiration. "And when your pentastomic orgy is finished?"

"Oh, then I sleep," McSkee chuckled. "Watch how I do it some time. I should give lessons. Few men understand how it should be done."

"Well, how long do you sleep?" Sour John asked, "and is there something spectacular about your sleeping that I don't understand?"

"Of course it's spectacular. And I sleep till I waken. At this also I set records."

And McSkee was wolfing the tall pile of steaks till Sour John had a mystic vision of a steer devoured entire except for head and hide and hooves, the slaughterer's take.

Later, they talked somewhat more leisurely as McSkee worked his way through the last half-dozen steaks—for now the edge was off his great appetite.

"In all this ostentatious bestiality, was there not one gluttony more outstanding than the others?" Sour John drew him out, "one time when you outdid even yourself?"

"Aye, there was that," said McSkee. "There was the time when they were going to hang me with the new rope."

"And how did you eat your way out of that one?" Sour John asked.

"At that time and in that country—it was not this one —the custom was new of giving the condemned man what he wanted to eat," the incandescent McSkee limned it out in his voice with the lilt of a barrel organ. "I took advantage of the new usage and stripped the countryside. It was a good supper they gave me, John, and I was to be hanged at sunup. But I had them there, for I was still eating at dawn. They could not interrupt my last meal to hang me—not when they had promised me a full meal. I stood them off that day and the night and the following day. That is longer than I usually eat, John, and I did outdo myself. That countryside had been known for its poultry and its suckling pigs and its fruits. It is known for them no longer. It never recovered."

"Did you?"

"Oh certainly, John. But by third dawn I was filled. The edge was off my appetite, and I do not indulge thereafter."

"Naturally not. But what happened then? They did not hang you, or you would not be here to tell about it."

"That doesn't follow, John. I had been hanged before."

"Oh?"

"Sure. But not this time. I tricked them. When I had my fill, I went to sleep. And then deeper and deeper into sleep until I died. They do not hang a man already dead. They kept me for a day to be sure. John, I get a pretty high shine on me in a day! I'm a smelly fellow at best. Then they buried me, but they did not hang me. Why do you look at me so oddly, John?"

"It is nothing," said Sour John, "a mere random objection which I will not even dignify with words."

McSkee was drinking now, first wine to give a bottom to his stomach, then brandy for its rumpled dignity, then rum for its plain friendliness.

"Can you believe that all breakthroughs are achieved by common men like myself?" this McSkee asked suddenly.

"I can't believe that you're a common man," Sour John told him.

"I'm the commonest man you ever saw," McSkee insisted. "I am made from the clay and the salt of the Earth, and the humus from decayed behemoths. They may have used a little extra slime in making me, but I contain none of the rare earths. It had to be a man like myself who would work out the system. The savants aren't capable of it; they have no juice in them. And by their having no juice in them, they missed the first hint."

"What is that, McSkee?"

"It's so simple, John! That a man should live his life one day at a time."

"Well?" Sour John asked with towering intonation.

"See how harmlessly it slides down, John. It sounds almost like an almanac maxim."

"And it isn't?"

"No, no, the thunder of a hundred worlds rumbles between them. It's the door to a whole new universe. But there's another saying: 'Man, thy days are numbered.' This is the one inexorable saying. It is the limit that will not be bent or broken, and it puts the damper on us hearty ones. It poses a problem to one like myself, too carnal to merit eternal beatitude on another plane, too full of juice to welcome final extinction, and anxious for personal reasons to postpone the hardships of damnation as long as possible.

"Now, John, there were (and are) smarter men than myself in the world. That I solved the problem (to an extent) and they did not, means only that the problem was more pressing on me. It had to be a coarse man to find the answer, and I never met a man with such a passion for the coarse things of life as myself."

"Neither did I," Sour John told him. "And how did you solve the problem?"

"By a fine little trick, John. You'll see it worked if you follow me around through the night."

McSkee had left off eating. But he continued to drink

while he indulged in girls, and in fighting and roistering, and in singing. His girly exploits are not given here; but there is a fruity listing of them on the police blotter of that night. Go see Mossback McCarty some night when he is on desk duty and he will get it out and let you read it. It is something of a classic around the station house. When a man gets involved with Soft-Talk Susie Kutz and Mercedes Morrero and Dotty Peisson and Little Dotty Nesbitt and Hildegarde Katt and Catherine Cadensus and Ouida and Avril Aaron and Little Midnight Mullins all in one night, you are talking about a man who generates legends.

McSkee *did* stir things up around town, and John Sourwine stayed with him. John fit in with McSkee well. There are many who would not.

There are persons of finely-tuned souls who cringe when a companion becomes unusually boisterous. There are those who wince when a hearty mate sings loudly and obscenely. There are even those who attempt to disassociate when the grumblings of the solid citizenry rise to a sullen roar; and who look for cover when the first little fights begin. Fortunately, Sour John was not such a person. He had a finely-tuned soul, but it had a wide range.

McSkee had the loudest and most dissonant voice in town, but would an honest friend desert him for that?

The two of them cut a big swath; and a handful of rough men, rubbing big knuckles into big palms and biding their time, had begun to follow them from place to place: men like Buffalo-Chips Dugan and Shrimp-Boat Gordon, Sulphur-Bottom Sullivan, Smokehouse, Kidney-Stones Stenton, Honey-Bucket Kincaid. The fact that these men followed McSkee angrily but did not yet dare to close with him speaks highly of the man. He was pretty woolly.

But there were times when McSkee would leave off his raucous disharmony and joyful battling, and chuckle somewhat more quietly. As—for a while—in the Little Oyster Bar (it's upstairs from the Big Oyster).

"The first time I put the trick to a test," McSkee confided to John, "was from need and not from choice. I have incurred a lot of ill will in my day, and sometimes it boils over. There was one time when a whole shipful of men had had enough of me. This time (it was far away and long ago in the ancient days of small sail) I was shackled about the ankles and weighted and dropped overboard. Then I employed the trick."

"What did you do?" Sour John asked him.

"John, you ask the damnest questions. I drowned, of course. What else could any man do? But I drowned calmly and with none of that futile threshing about. That's the trick, you see."

"No. I don't see."

"Time would be on my side, John. Who wants to spend eternity in the deep? Salt water is most corrosive; and my shackles, though I could not break them, were not massive. After a long lifetime, the iron would be so eaten through that it would part with any sudden strain. In less than one hundred years, the shackles gave way, and my body (preserved in a briny fashion but not in the best of condition) drifted up to the surface of the sea."

"Too late to do you any good," Sour John said. "Rather a droll end to the story, or was it the end?"

"Yes, that is the end of that story, John. And another time, when I was a footsoldier in the service of Pixodarus the Carian (with his Celtic Mercenaries, of course)—"

"Just a minute, McSkee," Sour John cut in. "There's something a little loose about all your talk, and it needs landmarks. How long have you lived anyhow? *How old are you?*"

"About forty years old by my count, John. Why?"

"I thought your stories were getting a little too tall, McSkee. But if you're no more than forty years old, then your stories do not make sense."

"Never said they did, John. You put unnatural conditions on a tale."

McSkee and Sour John were up in night court, bloodied and beatific. It was only for a series of little things that they had been arrested, but it was really to save them from lynching. They had a palaver with all those fine officers and men, and they had much going for them. Sour John was known to them as an old acquaintance and sometime offender. It was known that John's word was good; even when he lied he did it with an air of honesty. After a little time was allowed to pass, and the potential lynchers had dispersed, Sour John was allowed to bail them both out on their strong promise of good behavior.

They swore and forswore that they would behave like proper men. They took ringing oaths to go to their beds at once and quietly. They went on record that they would carouse no more that night; that they would assault no honest woman; that they would obey the quirks of the laws however unreasonable. And that they would not sing.

So the police let them go.

When the two of them were out and across the street, McSkee found a bottle handy to his hand on the sidewalk, and let fly with it. You'd have done it yourself if you'd been taken by a like impulse. McSkee threw it in a beautiful looping arc, and it went through the front window of the station house. You have to admire a throw like that.

We record it here that they are *not* patsy cops in that town. They are respectable adversaries, and it is always a pleasure to tangle with them.

Off again! And pursued by the Minions with shout and siren! It was close there! Half a dozen times it was close! But Sour John was a fox who knew all the dens, and he and McSkee went to earth for the while.

"The trick is in coming to a total stop," said McSkee

when they were safe and had their breath again. They were at ease in a club less public than Barnaby's Barn and even smaller than the Little Oyster. "I tell you a little about it, Sour John, for I see that you are a man of worth. Listen and learn. Everyone can die, but not everyone can die just when he wants to. First you stop breathing. There will be a point where your lungs are bursting and you just have to take another breath. Do not do it; or you will have the whole business to go through again. Then you slow your heart and compose your mind. Let the heat go out of your body and finish it."

"And then what?" Sour John asked.

"Why, then you die, John. But I tell you it isn't easy. It takes a devilish lot of practice."

"Why so much practice for a thing you do only once? You mean to die literally?"

"John, I talk plain. I say die, I mean die."

"There are two possibilities," said Sour John. "One is that I am slow of understanding. The other is that you are not making sense. On other evidence, I know the first possibility to be impossible."

"Tell you what, Sour John," said McSkee, "time's running short. Give me twenty dollars and I'll overlook your illogic. I never did like to die broke, and I feel my time is upon me. Thank you, John! I had a full day, both before and after I met you, and a full night that is nearly over. I had a pleasant meal, and enough booze to make me happy. I had fun with the girls, especially Soft-Talk Susie, and Dotty, and Little Midnight. I sang several of my favorite songs (which are not everybody's favorites). I indulged in a couple of good solid fights, and I've still got bells ringing in my head from them. Hey, John, why didn't you tell me that Honey-Bucket was lefthanded? You knew it, and you let him sneak the first punch on me.

"It's been fun, John. I'm a boy that gets a lot out of this game. I'm a real juicy one, and I try to jam everything into a day and a night. You can get a lot into a period if you heap it up. Now, let's gather up what's left in the bottles, and go down to the beach to see what we can provoke. The night needs a cap on it before I go to my long slumber."

"McSkee, you've hinted several times that you had a secret for getting the most out of life," said Sour John, "but you haven't told me what it is."

"Man, I haven't hinted; I've spoken plainly," McSkee swore.

"Then what in hog heaven is the secret?" John howled.

"Live your life one day at a time, John. That's all."

Then McSkee was singing an old hobo song, too old a song for a forty-year-old man, not a specialist, to have known.

"When did you learn that?" John asked him.

"Learned it yesterday. But I learned a bunch of new ones today."

"I noticed, a few hours back, that there was something curiously dated about your speech," John said. "But it doesn't seem to be the case now."

"John, I get contemporary real fast. I've a good ear, and I talk a lot and listen a lot, and I'm the perfect mimic. I can get up on a lingo in a day. They don't change as fast as you'd imagine."

They went down to the beach to put the cap on the night. If you're going to die, it's nice to die within the sound of the surf, McSkee had said. They went down beyond the end of the sea wall and into the stretches where the beach was dark. Aye, McSkee had guessed it rightly, there was excitement waiting for them, or actually it had been following them. It was the opportunity for a last glorious fight.

A tight dark group of men had been following them—fellows who had somehow been insulted during the day and night of carousing. The intrepid pair turned and faced the men from a distance. McSkee finished the last bottle and threw it into the midst of the group. The men were bad-natured; they flamed up instantly, and the man who was struck by the flying bottle swore.

So they joined battle.

For a while it seemed that the forces of righteousness would prevail. McSkee was a glorious fighter, and Sour John was competent. They spread those angry men out on the sand like a bunch of beached flounder fish. It was one of those great battles—always to be remembered.

But there were too many of those men, as McSkee had known there would be; he had made an outlandish number of enemies in a day and a night.

The wild fight climaxed, crested, and shattered, like a high wave thunderously breaking under. And McSkee, having touched top glory and pleasure, suddenly ceased to battle.

He gave one wild whoop of joy that echoed the length of the island. Then he drew a grand breath and held it. He closed his eyes and stood like a grinning rigid statue.

The angry men toppled him and swarmed him; they stomped him into the sand and kicked the very life out of the McSkee.

Sour John had battled as long as there was a battle. He understood now that McSkee had withdrawn for reasons that were not clear. He did likewise. He broke and ran, not from cowardice, but from private inclination.

An hour later, just at the first touch of dawn, Sour John returned. He found that McSkee was dead—with no breath, no pulse, no heat. And there was something else. McSkee had said, in one of his rambling tales, that he got a pretty high shine on him. John knew what he meant now. That man got ripe real fast. By the test of the nose, McSkee was dead.

With a child's shovel that he found there, Sour John dug a hole in the side of one of the sand cliffs. He buried his friend McSkee there. He knew that McSkee still had the twenty-dollar bill in his pants. He left it with him. It isn't so bad to be one or the other, but to be both dead and broke at the same time is an ignominy almost past enduring.

Then Sour John walked into town to get some breakfast, and quickly forgot about the whole thing.

He followed his avocation of knocking around the world and meeting interesting people. The chances are that he met you, if there's anything interesting about you at all; he doesn't miss any of them.

Twelve years went by, and some weeks. Sour John was back in one of the interesting port cities, but with a difference. There had come the day as it comes to many (and pray it may not come to you!) when Sour John was not flush. He was as broke as a man can be, with nothing in his pockets or in his stomach, and with very little on his back. He was on the beach in every sense.

Then he bethought himself of the previous times he had been in this city. There had been benders here; there had been antics and enjoyments. They came back to him in a rush—a dozen happy times, and then one in particular.

"He was an Odd One, a real juicy cove," Sour John grinned as he remembered. "He knew a trick, how to die just when he wanted to. He said that it took a lot of practice, but I don't see the point in practicing a thing that you do but once."

Then Sour John remembered a twenty-dollar bill that he had buried with that juicy cove. The memory of the incandescent McSkee came back to Sour John as he walked down the empty beach.

"He said that you could jam a lot of living into a day and a night," John said. "You can. I do. He said something else that I forget."

Sour John found the old sand cliff. In half an hour he had dug out the body of McSkee. It still had a high old shine on it, but it was better preserved than the clothes.

The twenty-dollar bill was still there, disreputable but spendable.

"I'll take it now, when I have the need," Sour John said softly. "And later, when I am flush again, I will bring it back here."

"Yes. You do that," said McSkee.

There are men in the world who would be startled if a thing like that happened to them. Some of them would have gasped and staggered back. The meaner ones would have cried out. John Sourwine, of course, was not a man like that. But he was human, and he did a human thing:

He blinked.

"I had no idea that you were in such a state," he said to McSkee. "So that's the way you do it?"

"That's the way, John. One day at a time! And I space them far enough apart that they don't pall on me."

"Are you ready to get up again, McSkee?"

"I sure am not, John. I had just barely died. It'll be another fifty years before I have a really good appetite worked up."

"Don't you think it's cheating?"

"Nobody's told me that it's disallowed. And only the days that I live count. I stretch them out a long while this way, and every one of them is memorable. I tell you that I have no dull days in my life."

"I'm still not sure how you do it, McSkee. Is it suspended animation?"

"No, no! More men have run afoul on that phrase than on any other. You think of it like that and you've already missed it. You die, John, or else you're just kidding yourself. Watch me this time and you'll see. Then bury me again and leave me in peace. Nobody likes to be resurrected before he's had time to get comfortable in his grave."

So McSkee put himself carefully to death once more, and Sour John buried him again in the side of the sand cliff.

McSkee—which in hedge Irish is Son of Slumber—the
master of suspended animation (no, no, if you think of it
that way you've already missed it, it's death, it's death),
who lived his life one day at a time, and those days separated by decades.

The title of this story might seem to suggest Long-fellow's Elizabeth: *So on the ocean of life we pass and speak one another, / Only a look and a voice; then darkness again and a silence. And indeed this is part of its meaning; the other part, which is less pleasant, I leave you to discover.*

PASSENGERS

By Robert Silverberg

There are only fragments of me left now. Chunks of memory have broken free and drifted away like calved glaciers. It is always like that when a Passenger leaves us. We can never be sure of all the things our borrowed bodies did. We have only the lingering traces, the imprints.

Like sand clinging to an ocean-tossed bottle. Like the throbbings of amputated legs.

I rise. I collect myself. My hair is rumpled; I comb it. My face is creased from too little sleep. There is sourness in my mouth. Has my Passenger been eating dung with my mouth? They do that. They do anything.

It is morning.

A gray, uncertain morning. I stare at it awhile, and then, shuddering, I opaque the window and confront instead the gray, uncertain surface of the inner panel. My room looks untidy. Did I have a woman here? There are

163

ashes in the trays. Searching for butts, I find several with lipstick stains. Yes, a woman was here.

I touch the bedsheets. Still warm with shared warmth. Both pillows tousled. She has gone, though, and the Passenger is gone, and I am alone.

How long did it last, this time?

I pick up the phone and ring Central. "What is the date?"

The computer's bland feminine voice replies, "Friday, December fourth, nineteen eighty-seven."

"The time?"

"Nine fifty-one, Eastern Standard Time."

"The weather forecast?"

"Predicted temperature range for today thirty to thirty-eight. Current temperature, thirty-one. Wind from the north, sixteen miles an hour. Chances of precipitation slight."

"What do you recommend for a hangover?"

"Food or medication?"

"Anything you like," I say.

The computer mulls that one over for a while. Then it decides on both, and activates my kitchen. The spigot yields cold tomato juice. Eggs begin to fry. From the medicine slot comes a purplish liquid. The Central Computer is always so thoughtful. Do the Passengers ever ride it, I wonder? What thrills could that hold for them? Surely it must be more exciting to borrow the million minds of Central than to live a while in the faulty, short-circuited soul of a corroding human being!

December 4, Central said. Friday. So the Passenger had me for three nights.

I drink the purplish stuff and probe my memories in a gingerly way, as one might probe a festering sore.

I remember Tuesday morning. A bad time at work. None of the charts will come out right. The section manager irritable; he has been taken by Passengers three times in five weeks, and his section is in disarray as a result, and his Christmas bonus is jeopardized. Even though it is customary not to penalize a person for lapses due to Passengers, according to the system, the section manager seems to feel he will be treated unfairly. So he treats us unfairly. We have a hard time. Revise the charts, fiddle with the program, check the fundamentals ten times over. Out they come: the detailed forecasts for price variations of public utility securities, February–April 1988. That afternoon we are to meet and discuss the charts and what they tell us.

I do not remember Tuesday afternoon.

That must have been when the Passenger took me. Perhaps at work; perhaps in the mahogany-paneled boardroom itself, during the conference. Pink concerned faces all about me; I cough, I lurch, I stumble from my seat. They shake their heads sadly. No one reaches for me. No one stops me. It is too dangerous to interfere with one who has a Passenger. The chances are great that a second Passenger lurks nearby in the discorporate state, looking for a mount. So I am avoided. I leave the building.

After that, what?

Sitting in my room on bleak Friday morning, I eat my scrambled eggs and try to reconstruct the three lost nights.

Of course it is impossible. The conscious mind functions during the period of captivity, but upon withdrawal of the Passenger nearly every recollection goes too. There is only a slight residue, a gritty film of faint and ghostly memories. The mount is never precisely the same person afterwards; though he cannot recall the details of his experience, he is subtly changed by it.

I try to recall.

A girl? Yes: lipstick on the butts. Sex, then, here in my room. Young? Old? Blonde? Dark? Everything is hazy. How did my borrowed body behave? Was I a good lover? I try to be, when I am myself. I keep in shape. At 38, I can handle three sets of tennis on a summer afternoon without collapsing. I can make a woman glow as a woman is meant to glow. Not boasting: just categorizing. We have our skills. These are mine.

But Passengers, I am told, take wry amusement in controverting our skills. So would it have given my rider a kind of delight to find me a woman and force me to fail repeatedly with her?

I dislike that thought.

The fog is going from my mind now. The medicine prescribed by Central works rapidly. I eat, I shave, I stand under the vibrator until my skin is clean. I do my exercises. Did the Passenger exercise my body Wednesday and Thursday mornings? Probably not. I must make up for that. I am close to middle age, now; tonus lost is not easily regained.

I touch my toes twenty times, knees stiff.

I kick my legs in the air.

I lie flat and lift myself on pumping elbows.

The body responds, maltreated though it has been. It is the first bright moment of my awakening: to feel the inner tingling, to know that I still have vigor.

Fresh air is what I want next. Quickly I slip into my clothes and leave. There is no need for me to report to work today. They are aware that since Tuesday afternoon I have had a Passenger; they need not be aware that before dawn on Friday the Passenger departed. I will have a free day. I will walk the city's streets, stretching my limbs, repaying my body for the abuse it has suffered.

I enter the elevator. I drop fifty stories to the ground. I step out into the December dreariness.

The towers of New York rise about me.

In the street the cars stream forward. Drivers sit edgily at their wheels. One never knows when the driver of a nearby car will be borrowed, and there is always a moment of lapsed coordination as the Passenger takes over. Many lives are lost that way on our streets and highways; but never the life of a Passenger.

I begin to walk without purpose. I cross Fourteenth Street, heading north, listening to the soft violent purr of the electric engines. I see a boy jigging in the street and know he is being ridden. At Fifth and Twenty-second a prosperous-looking paunchy man approaches, his necktie askew, this morning's *Wall Street Journal* jutting from an overcoat pocket. He giggles. He thrusts out his tongue. Ridden. Ridden. I avoid him. Moving briskly, I come to the underpass that carries traffic below Thirty-fourth Street toward Queens, and pause for a moment to watch two adolescent girls quarreling at the rim of the pedestrian walk. One is a Negro. Her eyes are rolling in terror. The other pushes her closer to the railing. Ridden. But the Passenger does not have murder on its mind, merely pleasure. The Negro girl is released and falls in a huddled heap, trembling. Then she rises and runs. The other girl draws a long strand of gleaming hair into her mouth, chews on it, seems to awaken. She looks dazed.

I avert my eyes. One does not watch while a fellow sufferer is awakening. There is a morality of the ridden; we have so many new tribal mores in these dark days.

I hurry on.

Where am I going so hurriedly? Already I have walked more than a mile. I seem to be moving toward some goal, as though my Passenger still hunches in my skull, urging me about. But I know that is not so. For the moment, at least, I am free.

Can I be sure of that?

Cogito ergo sum no longer applies. We go on thinking even while we are ridden, and we live in quiet desperation, unable to halt our courses no matter how ghastly, no matter how self-destructive. I am certain that I can distinguish between the condition of bearing a Passenger and the condition of being free. But perhaps not. Perhaps I bear a particularly devilish Passenger which has not quitted me at all, but which merely has receded to the cerebellum, leaving me the illusion of freedom while all the time surreptitiously driving me onward to some purpose of its own.

Did we ever have more than that: the illusion of freedom?

But this is disturbing, the thought that I may be ridden without realizing it. I burst out in heavy perspiration, not merely from the exertion of walking. Stop. Stop here. Why must you walk? You are at Forty-second Street. There is the library. Nothing forces you onward. Stop a while, I tell myself. Rest on the library steps.

I sit on the cold stone and tell myself that I have made this decision for myself.

Have I? It is the old problem, free will versus determinism, translated into the foulest of forms. Determinism is no longer a philosopher's abstraction; it is cold alien tendrils sliding between the cranial sutures. The Passengers arrived three years ago. I have been ridden five times since then. Our world is quite different now. But we have adjusted even to this. We have adjusted. We have our mores. Life goes on. Our governments rule, our legislatures meet, our stock exchanges transact business as usual, and we have methods for compensating for the random havoc. It is the only way. What else can we do? Shrivel in defeat? We have an enemy we cannot fight; at best we can resist through endurance. So we endure.

The stone steps are cold against my body. In December few people sit here.

I tell myself that I made this long walk of my own free will, that I halted of my own free will, that no Passenger rides my brain now. Perhaps. Perhaps. I cannot let myself believe that I am not free.

Can it be, I wonder, that the Passenger left some lingering command in me? Walk to this place, halt at this place? That is possible too.

I look about me at the others on the library steps.

An old man, eyes vacant, sitting on newspaper. A boy of thirteen or so with flaring nostrils. A plump woman. Are all of them ridden? Passengers seem to cluster about me today. The more I study the ridden ones, the more convinced I become that I am, for the moment, free. The last time, I had three months of freedom between rides. Some people, they say, are scarcely ever free. Their bodies are in great demand, and they know only scattered bursts of freedom, a day here, a week there, an hour. We have never been able to determine how many Passengers infest our world. Millions, maybe. Or maybe five. Who can tell?

A wisp of snow curls down out of the gray sky. Central had said the chance of precipitation was slight. Are they riding Central this morning too?

I see the girl.

She sits diagonally across from me, five steps up and a hundred feet away, her black skirt pulled up on her knees to reveal handsome legs. She is young. Her hair is deep, rich auburn. Her eyes are pale; at this distance, I cannot make out the precise color. She is dressed simply. She is younger than thirty. She wears a dark green coat and her lipstick has a purplish tinge. Her lips are full, her nose slender, high-bridged, her eyebrows carefully plucked.

I know her.

I have spent the past three nights with her in my room. She is the one. Ridden, she came to me, and ridden, I slept with her. I am certain of this. The veil of memory opens; I see her slim body naked on my bed.

How can it be that I remember this?

It is too strong to be an illusion. Clearly this is something that I have been *permitted* to remember for reasons I cannot comprehend. And I remember more. I remember her soft gasping sounds of pleasure. I know that my own body did not betray me those three nights, nor did I fail her need.

And there is more. A memory of sinuous music; a scent of youth in her hair; the rustle of winter trees. Somehow she brings back to me a time of innocence, a time when I am young and girls are mysterious, a time of parties and dances and warmth and secrets.

I am drawn to her now.

There is an etiquette about such things, too. It is in

poor taste to approach someone you have met while being ridden. Such an encounter gives you no privilege; a stranger remains a stranger, no matter what you and she may have done and said during your involuntary time together.

Yet I am drawn to her.

Why this violation of taboo? Why this raw breach of etiquette? I have never done this before. I have been scrupulous.

But I get to my feet and walk along the step on which I have been sitting, until I am below her, and I look up, and automatically she folds her ankles together and angles her knees as if in awareness that her position is not a modest one. I know from that gesture that she is not ridden now. My eyes meet hers. Her eyes are hazy green. She is beautiful, and I rack my memory for more details of our passion.

I climb step by step until I stand before her.

"Hello," I say.

She gives me a neutral look. She does not seem to recognize me. Her eyes are veiled, as one's eyes often are, just after the Passenger has gone. She purses her lips and appraises me in a distant way.

"Hello," she replies coolly. "I don't think I know you."

"No. You don't. But I have the feeling you don't want to be alone just now. And I know I don't." I try to persuade her with my eyes that my motives are decent. "There's snow in the air," I say. "We can find a warmer place. I'd like to talk to you."

"About what?"

"Let's go elsewhere, and I'll tell you. I'm Charles Roth."

"Helen Martin."

She gets to her feet. She still has not cast aside her cool neutrality; she is suspicious, ill at ease. But at least she is willing to go with me. A good sign.

"Is it too early in the day for a drink?" I ask.

"I'm not sure. I hardly know what time it is."

"Before noon."

"Let's have a drink anyway," she says, and we both smile.

We go to a cocktail lounge across the street. Sitting face to face in the darkness, we sip drinks, daiquiri for her, bloody mary for me. She relaxes a little. I ask myself what it is I want from her. The pleasure of her company, yes. Her company in bed? But I have already had that pleasure, three nights of it, though she does not know that. I want something more. Something more. What?

Her eyes are bloodshot. She has had little sleep these past three nights.

I say, "Was it very unpleasant for you?"

"What?"

"The Passenger."

A whiplash of reaction crosses her face. "How did you know I've had a Passenger?"

"I know."

"We aren't supposed to talk about it."

"I'm broadminded," I tell her. "My Passenger left me some time during the night. I was ridden since Tuesday afternoon."

"Mine left me about two hours ago, I think." Her cheeks color. She is doing something daring, talking like this. "I was ridden since Monday night. This was my fifth time."

"Mine also."

We toy with our drinks. Rapport is growing, almost without the need of words. Our recent experiences with Passengers give us something in common, although Helen does not realize how intimately we shared those experiences.

We talk. She is a designer of display windows. She has a small apartment several blocks from here. She lives alone. She asks me what I do. "Securities analyst," I tell her. She smiles. Her teeth are flawless. We have a second round of drinks. I am positive, now, that this is the girl who was in my room while I was ridden.

A seed of hope grows in me. It was a happy chance that brought us together again, so soon after we parted as dreamers. A happy chance, too, that some vestige of the dream lingered in my mind.

We have shared something, who knows what, and it must have been good to leave such a vivid imprint on me, and now I want to come to her conscious, aware, my own master, and renew that relationship, making it a real one this time. It is not proper, for I am trespassing on a privilege that is not mine except by virtue of our Passengers' brief presence in us. Yet I need her. I want her.

She seems to need me, too, without realizing who I am. But fear holds her back.

I am frightened of frightening her, and I do not try to press my advantage too quickly. Perhaps she would take me to her apartment with her now, perhaps not, but I do not ask. We finish our drinks. We arrange to meet by the library steps again tomorrow. My hand momentarily brushes hers. Then she is gone.

I fill three ashtrays that night. Over and over I debate the wisdom of what I am doing. But why not leave her alone? I have no right to follow her. In the place our world has become, we are wisest to remain apart.

And yet—there is that stab of half-memory when I think of her. The blurred lights of lost chances behind the stairs, of girlish laughter in second-floor corridors, of stolen kisses, of tea and cake. I remember the girl with the orchid in her hair, and the one in the spangled dress, and the one with the child's face and the woman's eyes, all so long ago, all lost, all gone, and I tell myself that this one I will not lose, I will not permit her to be taken from me.

Morning comes, a quiet Saturday. I return to the library, hardly expecting to find her there, but she is there, on the steps, and the sight of her is like a reprieve. She looks wary, troubled; obviously she has done much thinking, little sleeping. Together we walk along Fifth Avenue. She is quite close to me, but she does not take my arm. Her steps are brisk, short, nervous.

I want to suggest that we go to her apartment instead of to the cocktail lounge. In these days we must move swiftly while we are free. But I know it would be a mistake to think of this as a matter of tactics. Coarse haste would be fatal, bringing me perhaps an ordinary victory, a numbing defeat within it. In any event her mood hardly seems promising. I look at her, thinking of string music and new snowfalls, and she looks toward the gray sky.

She says, "I can feel them watching me all the time. Like vultures swooping overhead, waiting, waiting. Ready to pounce."

"But there's a way of beating them. We can grab little scraps of life when they're not looking."

"They're *always* looking."

"No," I tell her. "There can't be enough of them for that. Sometimes they're looking the other way. And while they are, two people can come together and try to share warmth."

"But what's the use?"

"You're too pessimistic, Helen. They ignore us for months at a time. We have a chance. We have a chance."

But I cannot break through her shell of fear. She is paralyzed by the nearness of the Passengers, unwilling to begin anything for fear it will be snatched away by our tormentors. We reach the building where she lives, and I hope she will relent and invite me in. For an instant she wavers, but only for an instant: she takes my hand in both of hers, and smiles, and the smile fades, and she is gone, leaving me only with the words, "Let's meet at the library again tomorrow. Noon."

I make the long chilling walk home alone.

Some of her pessimism seeps into me that night. It seems futile for us to try to salvage anything. More than that: wicked for me to seek her out, shameful to offer a hesitant love when I am not free. In this world, I tell myself, we should keep well clear of others, so that we do not harm anyone when we are seized and ridden.

I do not go to meet her in the morning.

It is best this way, I insist. I have no business trifling with her. I imagine her at the library, wondering why I am late, growing tense, impatient, then annoyed. She will be angry with me for breaking our date, but her anger will ebb, and she will forget me quickly enough.

Monday comes. I return to work.

Naturally, no one discusses my absence. It is as though I have never been away. The market is strong that morning. The work is challenging; it is mid-morning before I think of Helen at all. But once I think of her, I can think of nothing else. My cowardice in standing her up. The childishness of Saturday night's dark thoughts. Why accept fate so passively? Why give in? I want to fight, now, to carve out a pocket of security despite the odds. I feel a deep conviction that it can be done. The Passengers may never bother the two of us again, after all. And that flickering smile of hers outside her building Saturday, that momentary glow—it should have told me that behind her wall of fear she felt the same hopes. She was waiting for me to lead the way. And I stayed home instead.

At lunchtime I go to the library, convinced it is futile.

But she is there. She paces along the steps; the wind slices at her slender figure. I go to her.

She is silent a moment. "Hello," she says finally.

"I'm sorry about yesterday."

"I waited a long time for you."

I shrug. "I made up my mind that it was no use to come. But then I changed my mind again."

She tries to look angry. But I know she is pleased to see me again—else why did she come here today? She cannot hide her inner pleasure. Nor can I. I point across the street to the cocktail lounge.

"A daiquiri?" I say. "As a peace offering?"

"All right."

Today the lounge is crowded, but we find a booth somehow. There is a brightness in her eyes that I have not seen before. I sense that a barrier is crumbling within her.

"You're less afraid of me, Helen," I say.

"I've never been afraid of you. I'm afraid of what could happen if we take the risks."

"Don't be. Don't be."

"I'm trying not to be afraid. But sometimes it seems so hopeless. Since *they* came here—"

"We can still try to live our own lives."

"Maybe."

"We have to. Let's make a pact, Helen. No more gloom. No more worrying about the terrible things that might just maybe happen. All right?"

A pause. Then a cool hand against mine.

"All right."

We finish our drinks, and I present my Credit Central to pay for them, and we go outside. I want her to tell me to forget about this afternoon's work and come home with her. It is inevitable, now, that she will ask me, and better sooner than later.

We walk a block. She does not offer the invitation. I sense the struggle inside her, and I wait, letting that struggle reach its own resolution without interference from me. We walk a second block. Her arm is through mine, but she talks only of her work, of the weather, and it is a remote, arm's-length conversation. At the next corner she swings around, away from her apartment, back toward the cocktail lounge. I try to be patient with her.

I have no need to rush things now, I tell myself. Her body is not a secret to me. We have begun our relationship topsy-turvy, with the physical part first; now it will take time to work backward to the more difficult part that some people call love.

But of course she is not aware that we have known each other that way. The wind blows swirling snowflakes in our faces, and somehow the cold sting awakens honesty in me. I know what I must say. I must relinquish my unfair advantage.

I tell her, "While I was ridden last week, Helen, I had a girl in my room."

"Why talk of such things now?"

"I have to, Helen. You were the girl."

She halts. She turns to me. People hurry past us in the street. Her face is very pale, with dark red spots growing in her cheeks.

"That's not funny, Charles."

"It wasn't meant to be. You were with me from Tuesday night to early Friday morning."

"How can you possibly know that?"

"I do. I do. The memory is clear. Somehow it remains, Helen. I see your whole body."

"Stop it, Charles."

"We were very good together," I say. "We must have pleased our Passengers because we were so good. To see you again—it was like waking from a dream, and finding that the dream was real, the girl right there—"

"No!"

"Let's go to your apartment and begin again."

She says, "You're being deliberately filthy, and I don't know why, but there wasn't any reason for you to spoil things. Maybe I was with you and maybe I wasn't, but you wouldn't know it, and if you did know it you should keep your mouth shut about it, and—"

"You have a birthmark the size of a dime," I say, "about three inches below your left breast."

She sobs and hurls herself at me, there in the street. Her long silvery nails rake my cheeks. She pummels me. I seize her. Her knees assail me. No one pays attention; those who pass by assume we are ridden, and turn their heads. She is all fury, but I have my arms around hers like metal bands, so that she can only stamp and snort, and her body is close against mine. She is rigid, anguished.

In a low, urgent voice I say, "We'll defeat them, Helen. We'll finish what they started. Don't fight me. There's no reason to fight me. I know, it's a fluke that I remember you, but let me go with you and I'll prove that we belong together."

"Let—go—"

"Please. Please. Why should we be enemies? I don't mean you any harm. I love you, Helen. Do you remember, when we were kids, we could play at being in love? I did; you must have done it too. Sixteen, seventeen years old. The whispers, the conspiracies—all a big game, and we knew it. But the game's over. We can't afford to tease and run. We have so little time, when we're free—we have to trust, to open ourselves—"

"It's wrong."

"No. Just because it's the stupid custom for two people brought together by Passengers to avoid one another, that doesn't mean we have to follow it. Helen—Helen—"

Something in my tone registers with her. She ceases to struggle. Her rigid body softens. She looks up at me, her tearstreaked face thawing, her eyes blurred.

"Trust me," I say. "Trust me, Helen!"

She hesitates. Then she smiles.

In that moment I feel the chill at the back of my skull, the sensation as of a steel needle driven deep through bone. I stiffen. My arms drop away from her. For an instant, I lose touch, and when the mists clear all is different.

"Charles?" she says. *"Charles?"*

Her knuckles are against her teeth. I turn, ignoring her, and go back into the cocktail lounge. A young man sits in one of the front booths. His dark hair gleams with pomade; his cheeks are smooth. His eyes meet mine.

I sit down. He orders drinks. We do not talk.

My hand falls on his wrist, and remains there. The bartender, serving the drinks, scowls but says nothing. We sip our cocktails and put the drained glasses down.

"Let's go," the young man says.

I follow him out.

The planet called Tu is a world of oceans and scattered archipelagoes. Tu has a sister planet, Seraph, hanging eternally fixed in her sky—a more tantalizing goal for space flight than our Moon. But Tu's thousand-year-old civilization has almost no metals. With a wood-glass-and-plastics technology, the island people have hydrofoils, telescopes, even photography, but no heavier-than-air craft, let alone spacecraft: they can only look up and wonder.

Stories like this, as C. S. Lewis pointed out, are written for the delight of imagining a whole new world, with its continents, islands, plants, animals, people. Here, then, is the story of the Chainpearl Archipelagate, of Krirsarque and Bayfast; of the Tarulle Barge; of Tatja Grimm and Svir Hedrigs—and of their bold attempt to steal from Tar Benesh, the Regent of Crownesse, the only complete collection of a seven-hundred-year-old magazine called Fantasie, *whose motto is, "Things are not what they seem."*

GRIMM'S STORY

By Vernor Vinge

The tavern was old, luxurious—even respectable. Its sloping dance floor and high ceiling created the illusion that the hall was an open amphitheater. Crystal spheres cast an even, unwavering twilight over tables and patrons. Svir Hedrigs squinted gloomily at the newly polished table surface. Barely visible under the varnish were three centuries of minor vandalism. Krirsarque had been a university city for almost ten generations, and during that time, unnumbered students had carved their names in the durable furniture of the Bayside Arbor.

It was still early and not a third of the tables were occupied. The jongleurs were up on their platform, playing songs and doing acrobatics. So far their amusements had not drawn a single couple onto the dance floor. Hedrigs grunted his disgust, and extended long knobby legs under the table. He absently caressed the furry body of the creature sitting on the table. The animal turned its outsize head toward him and regarded the man with limpid black eyes. A deep purring sound came from its wide, pointed ears. Then it turned away and scanned the hall, its tall ears flicking this way and that. Far across the hall, a waiter looked severely in their direction, began walking toward them. When he got to within three tables of Hedrigs, he stopped, puzzled, with the air of someone who has forgotten his purpose. The waiter shook his head confusedly and headed back to the bar.

"Good boy," murmured Hedrigs. Tonight he didn't want to argue with anyone about his pet's presence in the tavern. Svir had come out for one last fling before sailing tomorrow. Fling—ha! He knew he would just sit lumpishly till closing time. For the thousandth time he cursed his bad luck. Who'd have thought that his thesis topic would require him to sail all the way to Crownesse? Because of the season, that was more than ten days' sailing time, unless one could afford hydrofoil passage—which he certainly could not.

The hall was filling now, but as he surveyed it, Hedrigs concluded with sick self-pity that this night he didn't have the courage to tour the tables, importuning unattached girls. He slouched back and made a determined effort to finish his drink in one draft.

"May I join you?" The soft voice came from behind and above. Hedrigs choked violently on his *skaal,* spewing the liquid in all directions. His fit of choking gave him a chance to see that the speaker was as pretty as her voice.

"Please do!" He gasped painfully, trying to regain some shred of poise. "Miss, uh——?"

"Tatja Grimm." The miracle lowered herself gracefully into the chair next to his, and set her drink on the table next to Ancho's right forepaw. Svir felt himself staring. He daydreamed of encounters like this constantly, but now that he was confronted by reality he didn't know what to do or say. Tatja Grimm was certainly not pretty: she was beautiful, beautiful in an especially wonderful way. From a distance she would have appeared to be a slender girl with a superb figure and reddish-brown hair. But Tatja Grimm was more than six feet tall—nearly as tall as Hedrigs himself. Her hands were slim and delicate—and larger than the hands of most men. But the most wonderful thing of all was the look of genuine interest and intelligence in her gray-green eyes. She was interested in him.

"And your name?" Tatja smiled dazzlingly.

The wheels went round and Svir remembered his name: "Svir Hedrigs."

Tatja rubbed Svir's pet about the neck. "And that," said Svir, happy at finding something to say, "is Ancho."

"A dorfox? They're awfully rare, aren't they?"

"Uh-huh. Only a few can survive ocean voyages."

Tatja played with Ancho for a few seconds. The dorfox responded with satisfied humming. The human female was accepted.

Hedrigs' hopes were shattered almost as quickly as they had crystallized. Three men came over and sat down, without a word to Svir.

"Miss Grimm, did you——?" one began. Then he noticed the dorfox. The newcomers sat silently and watched her and the animal. Svir didn't know what was going on, but now he didn't care. There was obviously more competition here than he could handle.

Tatja Grimm looked up from the dorfox. "Men, this is Svir Hedrigs. Svir, meet Brailly Tounse, Rey Guille, and Kederichi Maccioso. They are respectively the First Proofreader, General Fiction Editor, and Ship's Captain for *Fantasie* magazine. I serve as the Science Editor."

Like hell, thought Svir. He knew he was being taken. Svir was a naturally gullible person. Once, in this very tavern, a couple of netscrapers had managed to convince him they were hot-air balloonists. Since then, he had been always on his guard. There were several good reasons why his new "friends" were frauds. In the first place, the Tarulle Publishing Barge wasn't due in the Krirsarque area for another three days. Svir had been very upset to learn that his ship would stay a day ahead of the Tarulle fleet as the publishing company sailed slowly east along the Chainpearl Archipelagate. He wouldn't receive the latest copies of *Fantasie*—all two years' worth—until he reached Bayfast in Crownesse. In the second place, the Tarulle Barge rarely landed at minor places like Krirsarque. The Barge dispatched its hydrofoil sailing boats for such contacts. These boats delivered the company's publications, and took aboard supplies and manuscripts. People like Rey Guille and Ked Maccioso were far too important and busy to leave the Barge. The frauds at his table had aimed far too high in their impersonation. Of all the literary corporations in the world—fiction or non-fiction, periodical or book—*Fantasie* was perhaps the most prestigious. Hedrigs had always admired Rey Guille and the managing editor, Spektr Ramsey. And never had he seen a Science Section in *Fantasie,* or heard of Tatja Grimm.

Well, determined Svir Hedrigs, *I can trade them lie for lie.* Aloud he said, "So happy to meet you. I find a lot of your stuff especially provocative since my specialty is astronomy."

"An astronomer?" They were obviously impressed.

Even the over-muscled bruiser identified as Ked Maccioso seemed interested.

"That's right," Svir affirmed. And, actually, he was an astronomer. But the others naturally assumed from his unmodified assertion, that he was one of those intrepid souls who manned the ninety-inch reflector in the Doomsday Mountains on The Continent. Life at the Doomsday Observatory was a constant struggle against asphyxiation, cold, mountain apes, and Hurdic tribesmen. "I came out here to deliver some speeches at Krirsarque University." This last was an inversion of the truth. Svir was a graduate student in astronomy at Krirsarque. For the last two years he had worked with the thirty-inch telescope at the university. The most recent publisher coming west from The Continent had brought news that the men at Doomsday had duplicated some of Hedrigs' work. Now Svir had to journey all the way to the coast of The Continent to meet with one of the Doomsday astronomers and thrash the problem out.

"What's your preference in astronomy?" asked Tatja. "Seraphy?"

"No," replied Svir. "Seraph's not visible from Doomsday. I'm in a new field—parallax astronomy. Using very delicate trig techniques, I've measured the distances to some of the nearer stars."

"Really! I bought an article on that very subject for the latest issue." She snapped her fingers. "Braffly Tounse" reached into a side pouch and handed Tatja a magazine. She gave it to Svir. "See."

Svir gasped. There was the familiar masthead of *Fantasie*. In small letters beneath it were the words: "Issue of the 162nd Meridian. Whole Number 10,039." Here was physical proof that the Tarulle fleet had already arrived. With the quivering ecstasy of a long-time addict, he drooled over the Togoto cover, and then the table of contents. Beneath the magazine's famous motto, "Things are not as they seem," were listed fifteen stories and novelettes by authors from all over the world. A new short by

Ivam Alecque, a serial by Tsumish Kats . . . Svir flipped through the pages and came across one that caught on his fingers. It wasn't made of the usual seaweed pulp, but of some heavier, lacquer-coated material. At the top of that page was written: "Meet the *Fantasie* staff." Below were six portraits done in tones of green. But they weren't acid-etch prints, or even hand paintings. These pictures were green-tinted windows revealing perfect likenesses of Tatja Grimm and the men seated at Svir's table.

Hedrigs wondered if he looked as embarrassed as he felt. These people were everything they claimed to be. And now Tatja Grimm was even more desirable—if that were possible—than she had been before.

Grimm placed her hand on his forearm as she saw what Svir was looking at. "How do you like those pictures? That's a development we picked up in the Osterlei Archipelagate. Those pictures are made by a machine that looks at its subject and instantly 'paints' the picture, just like in the Diogens stories." Tatja slipped her hand down onto his. For a moment Svir's vision blurred. A warm glow spread through his body. "My picture is at the bottom there because the Science Department was only introduced last year, when dear old Spektr gave in to the increased popularity of contrivance fiction.

"I can tell you are a fan. How long have you been reading *Fantasie*?"

"Ever since I was seven. Twenty years. The Tarulle Barge has come through the Archipelagate ten times in that period. I've looked forward to each arrival more and more eagerly. I've even collected some issues from the last century."

Tatja laughed, a friendly, intimate chuckle. The men at the table receded into the back of Svir's consciousness. "That's a worthwhile project. Do you know that in all the world, there is only one complete collection of *Fantasie*?"

"You mean the proof copies on the barge?"

"No. Not even the Tarulle Company has a complete set. Remember, there was a fire on Old Barge three hundred years ago, and all the copies to that date were lost. Up to twenty years ago, there were more than twenty-five complete collections, but a series of accidents has destroyed all but one." She put a faint accent on the word "accidents."

Hedrigs had never thought about it, but it certainly was possible that only one complete collection existed. As the Tarulle Company toured the world, they sold their magazines, and printed extra copies to drop off at later island chains. Delivery was quite unreliable compared to a subscription service, such as some island magazines used. Thus it was very difficult to get a continuous sequence of issues. And *Fantasie* was seven hundred years old. Even though most issues had been recopied and their stories anthologized, so that any major library contained thousands of stories from the magazine, there were still "lost" issues unavailable on the Chainpearls.

The person or government that possessed the complete set must be very wealthy and dedicated to culture. "Who has the collection?" asked Svir.

"The Regent of Crownesse, Tar Benesh," Tatja answered.

Svir frowned. Tar Benesh had never impressed him as a man of high taste. He almost missed what Tatja Grimm said next. She was looking directly at him, and her lips barely moved. She seemed to be preoccupied with something far away.

"It's too bad Benesh is going to destroy them."

"What! Why? Can't he be stopped?" His shocked questions tumbled over each other. Why would anyone want to destroy seven hundred years of *Fantasie?* The epic cycles, the ingenious short stories—all those glimpses into worlds-that-are-not—would be lost.

Tatja's hand tightened around his. Her face came near his and he heard her say, "Perhaps there is a way to stop him. With you and your dorfox perhaps—"

"*Please,* Miss Grimm, not here!" Ked Maccioso leaned forward tensely, at the same time glancing around the tavern. Svir's domain of attention expanded. He realized that now the Arbor was crowded, the dance floor overflowing, and the jongleurs in fine form on their resonation platform. Tatja's presence had made him completely unaware of the changes.

Grimm nodded to the heavy ship's captain. "I suppose you're right, Ked." She turned back to the astronomer. "When were you planning to return to The Continent, Svir?"

Return? Then Svir remembered the lie he had told them. But he couldn't reveal his fraud to her now. He wanted, needed, the interest Tatja was showing him.

"I sail tomorrow for Bayfast."

"Would you like to come on the Tarulle Barge? It's slower than hydrofoil, but we'll get you there just the same."

"I certainly would." The words came spontaneously, but he felt no desire to retract them. Imagine sailing off with a beautiful, famous girl—into adventure. His previous reality seemed pale indeed beside these prospects.

"Why don't you come out to Barge with us tonight? We'll show you around." She looked straight into his eyes. The men with her watched carefully, too. They couldn't talk here.

"Okay." Svir set Ancho on his shoulder. They all stood up and worked their way to the door. The music and party sounds faded as they descended the ancient stone stairs that led from Highrock to the wharves of the Krirsarque harbor.

Soon Maccioso was paddling them out to sea. Apparently the landing was a secret. It was well into the night sleep period and no other craft were moving. A breeze swept across the water, splashed luminescing algae into the boat.

Half an hour passed. No one spoke. Ancho shivered quietly, fearful of the water. They left the glowing waters of the harbor behind. It was quite cloudy, so even the light of Seraph was denied them. Gradually Svir con-

vinced himself that there was a greater darkness on the
water ahead of them. And then he was sure. The huge
pile of the Tarulle Publishing Barge rose tier upon tier
out of the ocean. Beside it floated the smaller forms of
scout hydrofoils. All were without lights.

They pulled over to the hulk, and a group of company
sailors pulled the little boat into a freight bay. A section
leader saluted Maccioso. She said, "XO's compliments,
sir, and no exterior activity noted."

Maccioso returned the salute. "Have him take us out
past the shelf."

Svir was escorted up a long corridor, into the heart of
the vessel. They entered a luxurious, brightly-lit room.
Just the maintenance of the algae pots must cost several
man-hours a day. The five seated themselves around a
table, on which was fastened a detailed map of Bayfast,
the capital of Crownesse.

"This must all seem a bit melodramatic, Svir," said
Tatja, "but Tar Benesh has an efficient spy system extending from Crownesse on The Continent all the way to
the Osterlei Archipelagate. The Regent is ambitious without limit. He—"

Ancho began nibbling at the map. As Svir pulled him
back, the animal keened an almost inaudible whistle. For
an instant everyone in the room felt stark terror. Then
Hedrigs patted the little animal, and the dorfox relaxed.
The feeling of panic disappeared. Ancho turned his large
eyes toward Hedrigs as if to ask forgiveness.

Tatja smiled shakily. "Tar Benesh is also an extremely
intelligent, capable individual. And he is—mad. Or perhaps he is just alien. Some rumors hint that he is actually
a Wildman from the center of The Continent.

"Since he came to power twenty years ago, he has been
a collector of *Fantasie*. And to enhance the value of his
wealth, we believe that he sabotaged other collections."

"We know for a *fact* that he has destroyed other collections," Rey Guille interrupted.

"Every five years, Benesh holds the Festival of the

Ostentatious Consumption. You may have heard of it—"

Svir gulped. "You're not trying to tell me that the *Fantasie* collection is going to be one of the sacrifices?"

Tatja nodded her head slowly, "Yes, that's it exactly. The Festival is scheduled to begin ten days from now. We plan to arrive in Bayfast on the night wake period of the Consumption." She gestured to the map of the Bayfast area, and the detailed floor plans of Tar Benesh's Keep. "I can't go over the details of the plans now, but we are going to try to save that collection. Our magazine has the unconditional backing of the entire Tarulle Company," she nodded at Maccioso, "in this venture. It's not going to be easy. But I think we could succeed if we had Ancho's help. And we need you too. You know Ancho best, and can persuade him to cooperate."

Svir glanced down at the little mammal, who sat licking his paws, unaware of the plans being made for him. "Yes," the astronomer answered, "dorfoxes are strange that way. They will answer to only one master at a time. And no one can predict exactly when they will change loyalties."

"Svir, this will be dangerous. But we need you. And some of the stories Benesh has, exist nowhere else. Will you come with us and help?" She was pleading.

Hedrigs suddenly realized what he was being asked to do. He could get killed—and all for some magazines. Before now he had been uneasy at the mere thought of traveling to Crownesse, and now he was going to risk his life in a plot against the government of that country. Some sensible element within him was screaming *No—no—no!* But he saw the pleading in Tatja's eyes. "Yes," he quavered, then continued more strongly, feigning confidence, "I'll be glad to do anything I can."

"Wonderful!" said Tatja. She stood up. "Now I'm sure you'll want to go ashore and get your stuff together. Ked will have a boat take you back." The group left the room and walked toward the outer hull. About halfway there, Tounse and Guille left them for the typeset area. The

walk gave Svir time for some heart-stopping second
thoughts. He had a vivid imagination and it was working
overtime now. Ancho responded uneasily to his fright,
moving nervously on his neck.

They reached the landing bay, and Maccioso went off
to get a crew. Tatja turned to Svir. She grasped his hand
gently and moved close. "Thank you, Svir. I want to save
that collection very much. But I think I want to see you
again even more. You'll be back tomorrow, won't you?"

She slipped her arms around him. He felt her body
against him, her lips against his. His fears and half-conscious plans to junk the whole project were erased. He
would be back.

It was well past midmorning. Hedrigs stood, with
Ancho on his shoulder, at the edge of the false deck
which reinforced the Barge's bowform. Tatja had said
she'd meet him here and take him on a tour.

The Tarulle Barge was especially impressive by day.
Over the centuries, it had grown helter-skelter. New
barge platforms had been added and built upon—then
built over again, until the mass resembled nothing so
much as a man-made mountain of terraces, cupolas, and
cranes. The top offices and printshops were of spun glass
—the most modern construction material. The bottom-
most members of the Barge were moldering timbers three
hundred years old. From the top of the mainmast to the
bottom of the lowest hold was almost three hundred feet.

Now the huge filmy sails were close-hauled as the
Barge tacked in the thirty-mile Monsoonal Drag that blew
steadily off The Continent.

Hedrigs grabbed the terrace rail to steady himself in
the wind. Just looking up at those masts was enough to
make him dizzy. He turned his attention to the ocean and
the whitecapped waves that stretched out to the horizon.
In winds like this, the sailing hydrofoils were at top
efficiency, getting up to almost fifty miles an hour. Two
Company scouts cut through the farther waters as they

sailed out to minor ports of the Chainpearl Archipelagate.

And the Tarulle fleet was not alone on the main. Svir could pick out three cargo barges at various distances. The Chainpearls lay along one of the busiest trade routes in the world.

For all their cultural importance, the publishing lines accounted for only a small fraction of total ocean tonnage. Most publishing enterprises were operated landside, and contracted with freighting companies to serve other islands. Relatively rare nowadays were the huge publishing barges, like Tarulle, which toured the entire world and printed a variety of books and magazines.

"Hey, Svir!" Tatja's voice came clearly over the wind. He turned to see her striding toward him. Her hair was caught in a soft reddish swirl tied with a clip to the front of her tunic. Even so the wind blew it back and forth to caress the side of her face. She seemed small and delicate even in her baggy work coveralls, but when she came near, her eyes were level with his. Her smile sent a long shiver down his spine.

"I'm sorry we couldn't get together earlier in the morning," she continued, "but things are really moving around here. This Chainpearl run is always the busiest of the circuit, and when we have Monsoon winds, every printer is running at the breaking-point."

"Uh, that's all right—I've had plenty to see," he replied. As a matter of fact, the wake period had been something of a bore so far. The crew was distinctly hostile toward nonessential personnel. Since lunch he had wandered about the decks. His ears still burned from insults received when he walked in a door marked TRIPULATION ONLY. The people weren't really stranger-haters, though. They just didn't want nonprofessionals messing up their work.

Svir and Tatja started toward a nearby stairway. Grimm looked at the dorfox. "Say, I'm glad you brought Ancho. He looks fine. Can I carry him? We'll have to be real careful: some of the areas I'll show you could affect him. But I want to see how hardy he is."

Svir handed the dorfox over. Ordinarily the little animal didn't enjoy being fondled by others, but he had taken a liking to Grimm. Ancho had recovered from his initial fear of sailing, though even now he clutched at Tatja's shoulders tightly. Dorfoxes came from a single island far around the world. They were long-lived and relatively infertile. Most dorfoxes became mortally seasick when taken aboard a ship. Ancho was an exception. Betrog Hedrigs, the great Continental explorer and Svir's grandfather, had brought the animal to Krirsarque forty years before. Ancho was probably the only dorfox in the Chainpearls. Pehaps it was just as well though, for if dorfoxes had been common, they would have turned society upside down. Their strange abilities would give criminals almost supernatural powers.

Svir and Tatja descended two flights to the vat holds. It was a different world, a claustrophobe's nightmare. The wind was no longer audible, but there was an ominous creaking from the hull of the barge platform. Dim orange light filtered from half-dead algae pots. Worst of all was the smell. Svir had been raised near the ocean, and so was virtually unaware of any special odor associated with the seas. But here, in these vats, the essence of those smells was being distilled.

Some of the workers actually smiled at them: Tatja's presence was safe conduct.

Tatja pointed to where the ocean water came in through the bowform. "The whole paper-making operation runs at just the speed that water can flow through these hulls. We're at the input now. If we walk to the stern, we'll see every stage of the processing."

The seawater flowed through the underpart of the Barge like a subterranean river. Narrow catwalks hung inches above the dark water. Every forty feet, they had to climb a short flight of steps and then down again, as they moved from the hull of one barge platform to the next.

They walked about two hundred feet through the gloom. Hedrigs admired the graceful way Tatja moved along the catwalk, and cursed his own fearful, halting pace. Below them the liquid had thickened and now flowed slowly past grinding wheels. Beyond this, it was divided into several streams, depending on which reagents were to be added to the conglomeration of sargasso, algae, and animalcules that composed the slimy mass. They followed the stream of sludge that was destined to become paper.

All the way, Tatja gave a running account of what was going on. She also kept a close eye on Ancho for any signs of nausea or disorientation. But the dorfox seemed quite calm. It was a different story for Svir. The stench was beginning to get to him. Finally he asked, "How can the hull take these chemicals? I should think it would rot in a matter of months."

"That's a good question," the Science Editor responded. "The processing seems to have just the opposite effect. The carbonates and silicates in this sludge replace the wood fiber on a microscopic level. Over the years the hull has actually become stronger. And what we discharge beneath the hull is so concentrated, it kills any parasites that might otherwise nest there. Oops!"

She slipped on the walk. Svir's arm reached out and grabbed her waist as Ancho caught at his collar. The three of them teetered precariously for a moment. Then Tatja laughed nervously. "Thanks."

Svir felt obscurely proud. He might move more slowly than she, but when it came to a test, his caution paid off. He didn't remove his arm from her waist.

At last they reached the stern. Here the remaining water was pressed from the bleached mass, and the paper was actually formed. The fine sheets hung for several days before they were wound on drums and taken up to Printing.

They walked up to the next deck, where tons of newly printed magazines were stored. Here too the light was dim, but there was only a faint musty smell. Thank God the final product didn't smell like seaweed, thought Svir.

Tatja hung close on his arm and became more talkative. The Tarulle Company put out five different magazines every sixteen days. *Fantasie* and a couple of girlie magazines accounted for four hundred thousand copies per issue, and provided the bulk of the Tarulle income. Since it was necessary to stock copies for as long as two years before they were sold, the Barge normally carried eight tons of magazines. Over the centuries it had been a race to keep up with world population increase. The Barge was now more than ten times as large as its first platform. All the latest machinery was employed. But even with increased landside printing and the prospect of writing machines to replace hand type-setting, they were still falling behind.

It suddenly came to Hedrigs that he was being chased. It was subtle, but this girl was falling all over herself to please. She gave forth with a continuous stream of highly animated speech, and at the same time took every opportunity to draw him out. Hedrigs felt himself warm even more to the miracle at his side.

They came to one of the loading ports. The sound of the wind came strong, and beyond that huge hole in the hull was a panorama of sky and sea. Less than twenty feet away floated one of the fifty-ton hydrofoils that did most of the delivery work for the Barge. Its sails were reefed and its boom masts were in the vertical position, permitting it to move close to the larger vessel. A fifteen-ton load of magazines was being hoisted onto the hydrofoil by one of the Barge's cranes.

They watched the scene for several minutes. Finally the operation was complete, and the boat pushed away from the Barge. Its booms were lowered and the sails—like sheets on a clothesline—were hung out. As it moved out of the Barge's wind shadow, it gathered speed, and the outermost studding sails tilted queerly into the wind. The whole affair lifted up on the slender stilts of its foils, and the boat moved away at nearly forty miles an hour. Then the Barge's crewmen closed the loading port and everything was dim again.

Tatja frowned. "You know, I've always wondered why they tilt the studding sails like that."

Hedrigs grinned broadly and gave her an explanation of Dertham's pressure theories, complete with an analogy to tacking. Grimm's eyes showed scarcely concealed admiration. "You know, Svir, that's the first clear explanation I've ever heard of that. You ought to try writing it up. I could use some decent articles."

Hedrigs' collar shrank about three sizes.

Then he noticed Ancho. "He's glazing over," he said, indicating the animal's eyes.

Tatja agreed, "So I see. We'd better cut things short. It's almost suppertime anyway. We'll just take a short look at the print deck, and leave the typeset and editorial offices for another time."

They went up another stair and entered a low room filled with whirling gears. Hedrigs wondered if all vessels were this crowded. It destroyed the romantic air he had always associated with sailing. He noticed that Tatja kept a close hold on the dorfox and petted him comfortingly. This was no place for Ancho to run about unprotected.

There were two machines in the room, but only one of them was in operation. At one end of the printer, a yard-wide roll of sea-paper unwound. The paper slid between two rotating drums. The upper one was inked and with every swift revolution it pressed at least twelve feet of print on the flowing paper. Beyond this first pair of drums, a second pair did the same for the underside of the sheet. The paper finally moved under a whirling glass flywheel that cut it into neat, yard-square sheets that landed in a small dolly, ready to be taken to the cutting and binding section. The machine was driven by a spinning shaft connected to the windmills on the main deck.

One of the print men looked up angrily and started toward them. Then he recognized Tatja Grimm, and his

manner changed. Up close, Hedrigs saw that the ink-
stained face belonged to Brailly Tounse. "Day, ma'am,"
Tounse shouted over the din. "Anything we can do for
you?"

"Well, if you have a couple minutes, could you describe your operation, Brailly?"

Tounse seemed momentarily surprised, but agreed. He
took them down the print line and traced the progress of
the paper through the machine. "Right now we're doing
almost five thousand impressions an hour—that's about
one hundred thousand pages after cutting. Sometimes we
go for months with hardly a breeze, but when we move
into the Drag we have to make up for it. I'm pushing
these machines at their physical limit right now. If you
could get us just twenty ounces of steel, Miss Grimm, we
could make some decent bearings, and run these things as
fast as the wind can blow—about twelve thousand
impressions an hour." He looked at Tatja expectantly.

Grimm smiled, and shouted back. "Brailly, I'll bet
there isn't fifty ounces of steel in the whole Barge."

Hedrigs was confused. Since when does a Chief Proofreader ask a Science Editor for mechanical help—and for
something as ridiculous as steel! Perhaps the fellow was
just teasing, though he certainly looked serious enough.

Tounse grimaced, wiped his greasy hand over his bald
head, leaving a broad black streak. The man was obviously exhausted. "Well," he said, "you might as well
stick around and see them install a new print board on
the other machine." He indicated the idle printer.

Several crewmen brought in four yard-square sheets of
rubbery printboard. The elastic base made it possible for
them to stretch the type across the drum and fasten down
the edges. The ironwood-sap type-pieces gleamed dully in
the light. In a few moments they would be black with ink.
When the first four sheets were properly tied down, the
workers moved down the line and tacked four more on
the underside printer. Then they handfed twenty feet of
roll paper through the machine.

Tounse nodded to the man at the clutch. The gearing engaged. Perhaps the fellow released the clutch too fast. Or perhaps the gearing was fatigued. Svir never knew the exact cause, but the machine was transformed into a juggernaut. Gears splintered and paper billowed wildly about him. The first print-drum precessed madly and then flew off its spindle, knocking all three of them against the first machine. The glass blade at the far end of the room shattered and slivers flew about the room. Even though declutched, the machinery took seconds to slow and stop.

Hedrigs picked himself up carefully. Tounse was all right, though he seemed on the verge of breaking down himself—printing machines just weren't supposed to behave like this! Svir dragged Tatja from beneath the drums. She sat up and looked at him, dazed.

"Svir, are you all—where's Ancho!"

The dorfox was gone. Tatja swore in a most unladylike manner. She picked herself up and declutched the first machine. "Tounse! Forget your damn machines. We've got to find that animal." Soon Tounse and his whole work gang were searching the print rooms for Ancho. Hedrigs wondered briefly if the dorfox could be deceiving them all with an I'm-not-here signal. Ancho hadn't pulled a trick like that in five years. If he had not been killed in the mangle, he was probably scared witless. His panic combined with his general fear of the sea, had probably driven him outside and to some higher deck.

Svir left the others and ran outside. He glanced quickly about and ran up to the next level. Soon he had reached the mast deck. He stopped, gasping for breath. The wind was much stronger here. From the sails and rigging above him came a continuous, singing hum. He was alone except for a single sailor in a short semi-skirt. She was climbing a rope ladder that stretched down from the mainmast. Svir wondered what she was doing—the rigging was adjustable from down in the navigation section. Besides, it was too windy to climb safely. Then he looked up past the girl. Almost forty feet above her, he saw Ancho's furry form. Hedrigs ran across the deck, toward the mainmast. The dorfox moved awkwardly up the rope. Dorfoxes are, at best, only fair climbers. He was trying to retreat from all the things that frightened him, and going up was the only direction left. Svir debated whether he should follow the sailor, then saw that it would just upset her precarious balance. The wind blew the ladder into a clean catenary form. As the sailor rose higher, she was forced to climb with her back to the ground and the rope above her. Ancho was radiating helpless distress—even down on the deck it made Hedrigs faint with fear. Its effect on the sailor must have been nearly intolerable. For a heart-stopping instant it looked as if she were going to fall. Her feet slipped from the rope and she hung by her hands from the ladder. Then she hooked her leg around the ladder and inched forward. She was no longer climbing. One hundred fifty feet above the deck, the ladder was blown nearly horizontal.

Finally she reached Ancho. She seemed to coax him. The dorfox clutched at her neck, or the top of her shirt. The two came slowly down the long, curving ladder.

The girl collapsed at the base of the mast. Ancho released his tight hold on her and scuttled over to Svir. Hedrigs held the whimpering animal and helped the sailor to her feet. She was a bit taller than average, with black hair cut in short bangs. At the moment her face was very pale. "That was a brave thing you did," said Svir. Without doubt, she had saved the animal's life. "You really know how to handle those ropes."

The girl laughed weakly. "Not me. I'm an apprentice proofreader." She spoke in brief, anguished spurts. Her mind knew she was safe now, but her body did not. "That's the first time I ever climbed them. Oh God! Every time I looked down, I wanted to throw up. Everything looked so far away and hard."

She sat back down on the deck. She was shaking as much as Ancho. Svir put his hand on her shoulder.

"I like to come up here on my lunch time," she said.

"Your pet came running across the deck like his tail was on fire. He just grabbed that ladder and started up. I could tell he didn't like climbing, but he was terrified of whatever was chasing him. Every few rungs, he'd stop and try to come down. I—I just had to do something."

As she spoke these words, Grimm arrived on the mast deck. Tatja ran over and inspected Ancho with a careful, expert eye.

She didn't say anything for several seconds, though she favored the girl with a long, calculating glance. *Could Tatja be jealous?* thought Svir, surprised. The girl scrambled to her feet and bowed slightly to the Science Editor. Finally Tatja turned to Hedrigs and smiled. "Svir Hedrigs, be introduced to Apprentice Proofreader Coronadas Ascuasenya. Coronadas Ascuasenya, Parallax Astronomer Svir Hedrigs."

"Pleased." The girl bowed again and smiled hesitantly.

"Tatja, Coronadas climbed almost to the top of the mast to save Ancho."

"Yes, we saw from down below. That was a brave rescue." She petted Ancho. "I just hope we haven't wrecked the dorfox. We were fools to take him along this morning." She looked up at the sun, which was just past the zenith. "We might as well get some dinner. It's too late to start any training. We can begin this evening." She picked up Ancho and they all descended to the lower decks.

The sun was three hours down before they began. The night was clear and Seraph's light brought a bluish sheen to the sea. Tatja had used paperboard partitions to simulate a hallway within Benesh's Keep. She had constructed the mockup on a portion of the deck out of the wind and hidden from the view of other ships.

"I'll admit it's pretty crude, Svir, but for the first trials we don't need anything elaborate. The dimensions are the same as inside the castle. You can see there are a couple of side passages opening off the main one." Hedrigs moved to the entrance of the maze. It certainly wasn't very convincing. The ceiling of the passage was purple sky. Posted at regular intervals down the forty-foot passage were company sailors simulating Royal Guardsmen. They didn't seem too certain just what was expected of them.

Tatja petted Ancho gently. "We want Ancho to hallucinate these 'Guardsmen.' It's going to take some training, but I want Ancho to convince whoever he points those pretty ears at, that you and he constitute an authority figure."

Svir was surprised. "Is that possible? Ancho isn't very smart, you know. It seems to me that in order to generate a detailed illusion, Ancho would have to be humanly intelligent."

Tatja shook her head and grinned. "Nope. The intellience of the victim provides all the background detail. I've spent several months on Dorfox Island, and I know things like that are possible. C'mon, let's start, or we'll still be at it when we pull into Bayfast."

Ancho was sometimes sleepy during night wake periods, but he perked up noticeably when Tatja had a large bowl of rehydrated klig leaves brought on deck. He strained against Hedrigs' hands, but the astronomer wouldn't let him at the leaves. The dorfox was going to have to earn his treats. Svir's father had often played games like this with Ancho, and had managed to teach the animal a number of tricks.

Svir stood up and put the dorfox on his shoulder. The "guardsmen" had assumed their posts in the passageway. The only woman among them was Cor Ascuasenya, who stood at the far end of the mockup. Tatja stood behind Hedrigs. In this position, she could watch what happened with relative immunity, since Ancho was not likely to turn around and broadcast in her direction.

"All right, Svir, give it a walk-through. We'll see if Ancho will give us a demonstration," said Tatja.

Hedrigs walked slowly through the mockup. Every-

thing seemed quite normal. But then, Ancho rarely aimed
his hallucinations at his master.

When he was through, Tatja asked the first sailor what
he had seen.

The fellow looked at her a little blankly. "What do you
mean? When are you going to start the test?" The others
were similarly confused. None of them had been conscious of Svir or Ancho as they walked down the hall.
Tatja unfastened the lid on the klig bowl.

"That was a good performance," she said. "Ancho
managed to scan every person as you walked past. Now
we have to make him try his other effects, till he produces
exactly what we're looking for." She fed Ancho two
leaves. The little mammal sucked on them greedily, momentarily enraptured. When he was done he reached out
for more, but Tatja had already relocked the basket. He
had done well, but a larger award must await an even
better performance.

Svir petted the dorfox. Ancho appeared to enjoy the
game. "You know, Tatja, Ancho is really dependable
with that I'm-not-here signal. And he can scan a lot of
people at once. Why don't you settle for that, without
trying for something more sophisticated?"

"It's not enough, Svir. You're going to have to go all
the way to the center of the Keep—to the vault where the
most precious sacrifices are kept. With Ancho's I'm-not-
here, you *probably* could steal the Guards' keys. But
what if some of the doors have combination locks? You
need more than the Guards' passive acceptance. They
must actively help you. And there are more than ten
thousand volumes in the *Fantasie* collection. That comes
to at least two tons. You're going to need help getting
them out." She picked up her noteboard and pen. "Let's
try it again."

And again. And again.

Ancho soon learned that anything he tried would earn
him some reward, but that if he repeated a previous performance, the prize was smaller. So he tried to come up

with a new effect on each try. They soon exhausted the natural dorfox responses—the instinctive responses which served so well on the dorfox's native island. Some of these could drive predators away, or dull their senses. Others attracted insects and lulled their suspicions.

Ancho also tried the tricks he had been taught since arriving in civilization. On one pass, all the crewmen in the passage broke into fits of hysterical laughter. Ascuasenya had the giggles fifteen minutes after Ancho came by. What they saw was hilariously funny, though they couldn't explain to Tatja and Svir just why.

And though Tatja did her best to pace the work, the project became a grind. The sailors were especially tired. Ancho had put them through an emotional wringer. In one twenty-minute period, he made them laugh and cry. The dorfox had responded eagerly to all the attention showered upon him, but now was beginning to lose interest.

For the hundredth time, Svir started down the mock passageway. He was surprised at the degree of respect and obedience these sailors showed Tatja. She must have more authority on the Barge than her title indicated. When she made a suggestion in her low pleasant voice, people jumped. It was evidence how the best people rose to the top in any organization. What had he done to deserve her?

But it was beginning to look as though she was wrong about Ancho. Apparently this was one trick the dorfox couldn't do. Maybe it was just as well. Hedrigs wasn't really eager to stick his nose into the business of Tar Benesh.

"Damn it, man, stand up straight when you walk!" It took Svir an astonished second to realize that Tatja was speaking to him. "Come back and start over. How can you expect the dorfox to cast an illusion of authority if you drag about like an addled triform student?"

Hedrigs bit back a sharp reply. He walked to the beginning and started over. He almost swaggered down the passageway, imitating the gait of a Crownesse Bureaucrat he had once seen at a university dinner in Krirsarque. The effect was subtle. Suddenly Svir was no longer pretending. He actually felt important and powerful—the way he had always imagined politicians and generals feel. It seemed only natural that the sailors should snap to attention as he passed them. He returned their brace with an informal salute. The feeling of power disappeared when he came to the end of the passage.

Tatja smiled. "Wow! All right, Miss Ascuasenya, just what did you see when Svir walked by you?"

Cor looked confused. She glanced from Tatja to Svir and back again. "When I first looked at him coming down the hall, I could have sworn it was my father—but my family is in the Llerenito Archipelagate! As he got closer I saw that it was Jespen Tarulle. I mean, I knew it was Svir—it had to be. But it was Jespen Tarulle at the same time. Even now when I look at him, I see Tarulle —and yet I can see Svir, too." Hedrigs glanced at Ancho's ears. They weren't pointing at Cor. The hallucination persisted even after the dorfox stopped radiating.

Tatja didn't say anything for a second. She made a couple of notes in her book and looked up. "Can you see Ancho sitting on Hedrigs' shoulder?"

Ascasenya squinted. "No. All I see is that queer double image I just described."

The others had similar reactions. About half saw Hedrigs as Tatja. These people were especially confused, since they now saw two Tatja Grimms. Every one of them realized that Ancho's trickery was involved, and all but two could see Hedrigs behind the hallucination.

Svir's shoulders sagged. All that work, and the best they could come up with was a halfbaked illusion that wasn't even uniform. It would never fool the Royal Guards.

But Tatja seemed to feel otherwise. She finished writing in the notebook, and looked up, smiling. "Well, we've done it. The illusion is one of the strongest I've ever seen.

It persists even in the face of contradiction-to-fact situations. See, Svir, all you have to do is *act* confident. Ancho knows you and will radiate the same thing. I really didn't mean to jump on you."

Hedrigs nodded, still blushing from the unexpected attack. Her technique worked, but it was shocking.

Grimm continued, "We'd better knock off now. Ancho's beginning to lose interest. By now he's crammed full of klig leaves. And most of you look pretty dragged out. Let's have another session after lunch."

During the rest of the voyage to Bayfast they had four hours of practice in every wake period. In the end, Ancho was able to broadcast the authority signal even better than he could the I'm-not-here. He also grew fat on the klig leaves, assuming an almost spherical configuration. Tatja had him perform his new trick under every conceivable condition—even in the dark, down in one of the holds. They found that if a single authority figure were suggested to all the victims, then they all saw that same person. It took Ancho only a fraction of a second to set up the illusion in the human mind, and it persisted without booster treatment for almost ten minutes. Ancho could detect people hiding behind bulkheads, and could even project the authority illusion through several feet of stone. Tatja tried several times to make the dorfox generate the illusion for her, but Ancho just purred when she held him.

One experiment was a mystery to Svir. Tatja produced a flat balsir box and strapped it to the dorfox's back. Ancho didn't seem to mind. The box was light and apparently the straps didn't chafe. The contraption looked vaguely like an oversize cookie cutter—its profile was an irregular set of semi-circles and lines. From either side of the box projected stubby cylinders of glass and wood. On top was a little hole—like the keyhole in a spring-powered clock. And the device clicked almost like a clock when it was mounted on Ancho's back.

Tatja refused to reveal the exact purpose of the contraption. She said it was a last precaution, one whose usefulness would be impaired if Hedrigs knew its purpose. Hedrigs couldn't imagine what sort of precaution would have such properties, but he accepted her explanation. Perhaps it was empty—a placebo to give him the false confidence necessary to trigger Ancho's authority signal. But whatever it was, it was for the best—Tatja wanted it.

The Drag kept Grimm busy—even busier than the general run of the crew. Besides their practice sessions, he was with her only two or three hours out of every wake period. He saw almost as much of the proofreader, Coronadas Ascuasenya. It was surprising how often he found her eating at the same time and in the same meal hall as he. Hedrigs came to enjoy those meals more and more. Cor was no competition for Tatja, but she was pretty and intelligent and nice to be with.

Hedrigs spent the rest of his free time in the Barge library, where Tatja's influence had opened some otherwise locked doors. Only fifteen or twenty people out of the thousand on board were allowed access to the library, but once inside there was no restriction on the use of materials. Here Tarulle kept specimen copies of all available issues of magazines published by the company. That amounted to about one hundred thousand volumes. Jespen Tarulle was in the printing business to make money, but he had a sense of history too, and the Barge library was the most luxurious part of the craft that Svir had yet seen. Here was none of the cramped stuffiness of the lower decks. Virtually none of the sea or ship noises were audible through the thick glass windows. Deep carpets covered the floor. During the night wake periods, well-tended algae pots supplemented Seraph's light.

To a confirmed *Fantasie* addict, it was heaven. The Tarulle collection was nearly three-quarters complete— more than seven thousand issues. That was better than any of the libraries Svir had seen on the Islands. They even had several copies of the First Issue, printed just forty years after the invention of moveable type. In those years the magazine was sold in two yard-square sheets, folded into quarters. Only rarely was a story illustrated and then it was with crude woodcuts. But that was part of the enchantment. On that single barque—the predecessor of the Barge—they had printed such stories as *Delennor's Doom,* and *Search for the Last Kingdom*—novels that after seven hundred years were still studied by poets and read with enjoyment by near-illiterates. The genius which showed through those smudged pages transcended the. vehicle that had brought it across time to the present.

That original barque had been owned by an ambitious trading family, distantly related to the present publisher, Tarulle. At first, they confined their trade to the major islands of the Osterlei group—and at the same time provided regular and vital communication between those islands. As the business became more profitable, the family gave up their other trading operations, and visited islands further and further asea. The islands beyond the horizon provided even more enchanting themes and original authors. *Fantasie* readers were the first (and for a long time the only) cosmopolitans on the planet.

The magazine's success was not without social repercussions. The effects of the first interplanetary fantasy were shattering both for the magazine and for the rulers of the Llerenito Archipelagate. *Migration,* by Ti Liso, forecast the rise of contrivance fiction. Liso's hero discovered a species of flying fish which, during the winter season in the northern hemisphere, migrated to the southern hemisphere of Seraph. The hero captured several of the vicious creatures and taught them to pull his sailing boat. After a two-week flight, the fish deposited him half-starved on the south polar continent of Seraph. The story went on to describe the civilization he found there. It was an unfortunate coincidence that his Seraphian government was an absurd dictatorship founded on Tu-worship —for the tyrannical government of the Llerenitos was just such a farce in reverse. In plain fact the story had not been intended as satire. It had been written as straight adventure—Liso was a native of the Osterleis and he had honestly conceived the most ridiculous autarchy imaginable. The Seraphiles of the Llerenitos did not take it as a joke, and for the next fifty years, until the fall of their religion, Llerenito waters were forbidden to the barque. This was an especial hardship, since the technique for sailing to windward was not fully developed at that time. Avoiding the Llerenitos cost many months' sailing time.

Each day brought Hedrigs closer to the coast of The Continent, closer to Bayfast. Back in Krirsarque, the prospect of invading the Crownesse Keep had seemed a faraway adventure. But Svir was coming to realize that it was a reality which he personally would have to face. He spent more and more of his time in the library, taking refuge in *Fantasie*. Sometimes he could avoid thinking of his own problems for hours at a time. He enjoyed the recent stories most. Especially contrivance fiction. The straight fantasy themes had been handled in every conceivable way in the past seven hundred years. It was only in the last two hundred that the idea of physical progress had emerged—the idea that there could be mechanical means of achieving fantastic ends. In the last fifteen years nearly half of *Fantasie*'s output had been c.f.

Hedrigs read straight through Tsumish Kats' new serial. Kats was a biologist in the Tsanart Archipelagate. His science was usually strong and this novel was no exception. Like many authors, he postulated the discovery of large metallic deposits on The Continent. Such deposits made possible the construction of huge metal machines —machines powered by the same (as yet unexplained) mechanism which made the sun shine. As far as Svir could tell, this story contained a genuinely original idea —one that Hedrigs wished he had thought of first. Instead of going directly to Seraph in his metal "ships of space," Kats set up way-stations, tiny artificial moons.

The ultimate landing on Seraph produced deadly peril.

Kats populated the other planet with a race of intelligent germs. Hedrigs choked—this fellow was supposed to be a biologist? But on the next few pages the author actually justified the alien existence in a manner quite as logical and novel as his space-island idea. Hedrigs found himself following the story more and more avidly as the human race fought to protect itself from the menace brought back aboard the landing ship. The struggle against the microscopic invaders was one of the most suspenseful he had ever read. Things looked hopeless for humankind. Hedrigs turned the page.

The dirty bastard! Hedrigs' comfortable shell of illusion burst. Kats had actually let the human race fall before the invaders! Hedrigs suppressed a desire to rip the magazine up into small pieces. The shock was like finding a snake in a schnafel pastry. Wasn't there enough hell in the real world? He had seen far too many stories of this type lately. Feeling quite betrayed to reality by Kats, the young astronomer stood up and stomped out of the library.

Hedrigs halted on the terrace-deck near his cabin. It was past midday. Far above him, the wind whistled through the empty rigging and mastwork. Just two miles away, the brown and gray cliffs of Somnai rose abruptly from the ocean, hiding Bayfast from view. Where the surf smashed into the base of Somnai the concentrated coastal plankton formed a glistening green band. In this longitude, Seraph hung almost thirty degrees above the horizon, its bluish-green crescent wraithlike against the bright blue sky.

The scene didn't appeal. Svir cupped his chin in palm and morosely inspected the pitted guard-railing he leaned against. For all practical purposes they had reached Bayfast. Right now Kederichi Maccioso was treating with the Port Commander for landing clearance. Apparently there was some problem about getting pier space at this time, but this would be cleared up, and this afternoon they would be sailing right past the Regent's Keep into the

Hidden Harbor. And tonight he, Svir Hedrigs, would be risking his life to save the *Fantasie* collection. Could he go through with it?

He didn't notice her until she was at the railing beside him.

"Hi, Cor."

"Hi." She smiled. They stood for a moment silently, watching the sparkling sea. Then she said hesitantly, "It's tonight, isn't it?"

"Yeah."

"Svir . . . don't go through with it."

"Huh?" Hedrigs looked at her in some confusion. "Why not?"

"Those magazines aren't worth dying for. And I think you *would* die. Crownesse is the most powerful country in the world. When we move into the port, we'll pass Hangman's Row. They play awfully rough here."

She was voicing the fears that had transformed these last few days into hell. Now if only she could convince him that it was honorable to back out. "I agreed to do it, Cor. And I owe it to Tatja."

Ascuasenya mumbled something.

"What's that?"

She took a deep breath and started over. "That second is no reason at all. Tatja Grimm is . . . not a very nice person. She came aboard Tarulle only five years ago, as the Barge was passing through the Eastern Crownesse ports. She was an apprentice proofreader like me. Now she is probably the most powerful person in the entire Tarulle Company—Jespen Tarulle included. She has some sort of leverage with every important person on the Barge. Some guys love her, I think. With others it's blackmail. Many people are just afraid of her. And no one knows what she's really after."

Hedrigs scowled. "You can't expect me to believe that. I've watched the crew working with her. She gets more wholehearted cooperation and respect from them than most officers." Svir felt the same hostility toward Ascuasenya that he would feel toward an outsider who slandered a member of his personal family.

Cor looked tired. "That just proves she's a brilliant leader. I don't deny that. And she's at least as talented when it comes to mechanical matters, smarter than anyone I've ever seen. She designed the power trains they use in printing. She also developed some of the special sailing rigs we have on our hydrofoils."

Hedrigs grunted, remembering a certain conversation several days earlier. But this thought was not reflected in the manner of his next question. "Just what brings you to spread this outrageous libel?"

Ascuasenya paled slightly. "I . . . I don't want you hurt, Svir. And I know that if it would further her ends, she'd put your life in jeopardy. Besides, I . . . want you myself." Her voice dropped almost to a whisper.

Hedrigs felt himself soften. The things Cor had said became more understandable and more excusable. "I'm sorry, Cor. I didn't know you felt that way. But you're wrong. Tatja is wonderful. And I love her."

"No!" The response was violent. "Just let me show you. Can Ancho still broadcast that I'm-not-here signal?"

"Yeah." Hedrigs petted the animal sitting on his shoulder. Ancho had seemed almost to enjoy the voyage during the last couple of days. "If he knows that something is expected of him and yet I don't pull that confidence act, he'll generally broadcast the I'm-not-here."

"Fine. Let's use him to do a little eavesdropping. I'll give you odds of five-to-one Grimm will be doing something you'd find out of character."

Svir was shocked by the vehemence of her assertion. Spying on others was an activity he had never condoned. He temporized. "It's kind of late, you know. She's probably asleep."

"Sleep? Sometimes I wonder if she ever does that." She caught his arm. "C'mon."

With an ugly sense of betrayal, Hedrigs followed the apprentice proofreader. Cor led him fifty yards aft and down a couple of flights. They were well into the day sleep period, and hardly anyone was about. The mast watch could detect any hostiles approaching the vessel, but they were not well-placed for observing the deck itself.

Finally Hedrigs and Ascuasenya stood below the balcony of Grimm's office. Hedrigs cuddled Ancho. "Stay close to me up there, Cor, and you'll be inside the illusion, too." He boosted her up to the balcony, then hauled himself up. They had overextended themselves: it was just conceivable that people outside the illusion might be aware of them. But he was committed now.

They crawled to the office window and peeked over the sill. Svir was unprepared for the luxury of that room. It was almost as large as the library. The floor was carpeted with Lockspur jaguar pelts and the furniture inlaid with designs of worked silver—or that rarest of metals, aluminum.

Tatja sat at her desk, her face in profile. She was slumped over, studying a large sheet of paper on her desk. Svir had never seen her look quite so unhappy. Her eyes were wide and staring, and a tear glistened on her cheek. Hedrigs leaned closer against the window. What was she reading that could be so depressing? The paper on her desk was a detailed engineering diagram of— what? Then he recognized it as one of the Osterlei plans for a steam-driven turbine. The engine was ingenious and quite workable—but several thousand ounces of iron were necessary for its construction. Attempts to make boilers of nonmetallic materials had been comical, and occasionally disastrous, failures. How could an engineering diagram cause someone to cry?

Grimm looked up suddenly, not at the window, but at the door to her office. Apparently someone was asking admittance, though it was virtually impossible to hear anything through the thick glass. Tatja moved with amazing speed to cover the diagram and compose her features.

In a matter of seconds, she appeared completely self-possessed.

The visitor was Brailly Tounse. Hedrigs pressed his ear against the glass, forgetting any scruples he had had about eavesdropping. What was said within was barely audible.

Tounse was saying, "Your people took fifteen ounces . . . steel. My steel! Why?"

"I needed it." Her expression was almost haughty.

But Tounse was not put off. "So? I . . . too. We can't run the presses without *some* metals, you . . ."

"Tough. We're . . . lee of the Somnai now, so it doesn't matter . . . return it after we leave Bayfast . . . need it to rescue . . . *Fantasie* collection."

This last promise seemed to mollify Tounse somewhat, but he still asked, ". . . really think . . . will go through with it?"

Tatja laughed. "I can persuade that fatuous idiot to . . . anything—you should know that." Tounse's face went red.

Hedrigs drew back from the window, shocked. Were they talking about *him?* He looked at Cor and she returned his gaze levelly.

"Let's go," Svir muttered. He moved to the edge of the balcony and jumped to the deck below—almost on top of a crewman wearing editorial insignia. The fellow stared at him for a long moment and then continued his walk—apparently Ancho had stopped broadcasting. What if Tatja heard about this? The idea was chilling.

This line of thought was cut short as Cor came over the railing. They walked back toward the crew quarters. He stopped a few feet from the entrance to his own cabin.

Cor looked at him. "Well?"

"I don't know, Cor. Perhaps if I knew more, what we saw wouldn't be incriminating. I'm all confused."

"When do you have to make up your mind?"

"Sometime this evening. I'm going to have a final brief-

ing before lunch in the night wake period. I don't know
how long after that I'd be leaving."

"Don't go—at least think about what I said and what
we saw." She looked at him. "Please."

Svir laughed harshly, "Girl, that's one thing you can be
absolutely sure of!"

Ascuasenya touched his hand briefly, then turned and
walked away.

Svir didn't get much sleep that afternoon. He lay on his
bunk in the shuttered cabin, and stared into the darkness.
What was Tatja Grimm? To him she had been a miracu-
lous discovery, an escape from loneliness. And until now
he had never doubted her sincerity. To the crew she was
an immensely popular leader, one who could solve any
problem. To the top officers on the Barge she was a harsh
and arbitrary tyrant, a seductive genius, a bitch-goddess.
Where did that leave the Tatja Grimm who sat silently,
crying over an engineer's diagram?

In any case, Tatja was not what he had imagined. And
that revelation put the present situation in a new light.

Though it was past sunset, he didn't go down for
breakfast, but paced tensely back and forth in the little
cabin. On the bed Ancho chirped and croaked miserably.

Svir had agreed to do a job. Only now did he realize
just how much he had been influenced by Tatja. He saw
that the rescue of the *Fantasie* collection was an extremely important project—but without the spell Tatja's
personality had cast upon him, he felt no interest in com-
mitting his own skin to the undertaking. Art was art, but
life was sacred—especially his life. If he went through
with the plan, Svir Hedrigs would probably die tonight.
And that death would not be the adventurous, romantic
death of a hero, but a sick, empty, final thing. Just thinking about it gave him the chills. How close he had come
to sacrificing himself for—nothing. If it hadn't been for
Cor he would have, too. Ascuasenya was as true as
Grimm was false. He had found out just in time.

He would turn Tatja down—the most she could get him for was his passage. Grimm would have to find another sucker and another dorfox. Hedrigs would see the Doomsday astronomer and get that situation cleared up. And perhaps—no, certainly—he would see Cor again, and ask her to leave Tarulle and come back to the Chainpearls with him.

Svir fed the dorfox a luscious meal, then went down to the main chow hall. He didn't see Cor. That was unusual, but not surprising. They were still working extra shifts, processing material. He would see her later in the evening, after he confronted Tatja. Svir whistled as he bounded up the steps, thinking of the look on Grimm's face when he told her he wasn't going to help her.

The Barge was entering Bayfast Harbor now. That entrance was a narrow gorge cutting through the Somnai cliffs. Seraph was nearly full and its brilliant blue light transformed the normally brown cliffs into shimmery curtains of stone. Svir had to crane his neck to see the top, where the Bayfast naval guns were mounted, pointing down at him. The Tarulle Barge was almost half as wide as the entrance.

Hedrigs' stride broke as he noticed a small lighter pulling away from the Barge. That girl, with the helmet of short black hair—she looked like Coronadas Ascuasenya. Svir rushed to the terrace rail. She was more than fifty yards away and not facing him—but he was almost sure it was Cor. On her lap she carried a small suitcase. What was going on? He ran along the rail, shouting her name. But the wind, channeled by the gorge, was loud, and she was already far away. The boat rounded the curve of the gorge, disappeared.

Perhaps it wasn't Cor after all; but the old *Fantasie* motto came to mind—"Things are not as they seem."

His mood was considerably subdued by the time he reached the executive decks. He confronted one of Tatja's secretaries and was ushered into the Science Editor's office.

Grimm smiled faintly as Svir advanced to her desk. "Have a seat, Svir. Ready to begin the briefing?"

Hedrigs didn't accept the proffered chair. He stood awkwardly before the desk. Tatja's physical presence almost made him disregard what he had seen that afternoon, and suddenly it was difficult to say the speech he had been planning. "Tatja—Miss Grimm, I've been thinking, uh, about this . . . project. I know it's important to you—to everyone here. But I, uh, I don't think that I'm the right, uh . . ."

Tatja picked a crystal letter-cutter from her desk. She flashed him a broad smile. "To make a long story short, you've decided you would rather not go through with it. You're willing to pay for your passage, but you feel no obligation to risk your neck on this scheme. Is that what you are trying to say?"

"Why, yes," Svir said, relieved. "I'm glad you see my point of view."

Tatja didn't say anything. She inspected the letter-cutter, tossed it into the air in a glittering whirl, and caught it just before it would have slammed into the hardwood desk. A strange gurgly sound came from her lips. Svir realized she was laughing.

"You know, Hedrigs, you are the most gullible person I ever met. Correction: the second most gullible. You're a provincial, overgrown adolescent, and how you thought you could fool anyone into thinking you had ever been off the Islands is beyond me. I need that dorfox. Did you honestly believe that our encounter on Krirsarque was an accident? I've been studying those animals a long time. If I had you killed, I'm certain I could become Ancho's new master. Only my high moral character prevents me from taking that course."

She smiled again. It was almost a sneer, revealing a hostility that seemed to transcend the subject at hand. "If I had known Ascuasenya could be such a nuisance, I would have kept her out of your way. Yes, I heard about your activities this afternoon. No matter. For my plans to succeed I now need some new form of leverage. Poor little Ascuasenya is perfect for my purposes."

Grimm sat back and relaxed. "I said you were the second most gullible person in my experience. Coronadas Ascuasenya is the first. She believed me when I told her that you had already left the Barge for Bayfast. She believed me when I told her that our spies had discovered new information which you had to have to avoid disaster. She believed me when I said that with the proper credentials she could get into the Keep and warn you. And she *will* get rather far into the castle—those credentials are very good counterfeits. When she is finally discovered, the Regent's men will believe they have foiled a serious espionage attempt."

Hedrigs stepped back from the desk, as shocked by her hostility as by what she was saying. For an instant she didn't seem human. Everything Cor had said was true. Grimm was a creature sitting at the center of an infinite complex of scheme and counter-scheme, plot and counter-plot—her ultimate goal beyond human understanding. Every detail of the last ten days had pushed him according to her whim. Even as she spoke now, she was trying to maneuver him into some new trap.

"Do you know what Tar Benesh does with spies, Svir Hedrigs?"

The astronomer shook his head dumbly. Grimm told him.

"And when they get done, the spy is generally burned alive," she added. "So, Svir my love, run back to your cabin, get Ancho, and come back here. The briefing's going to take a while, and I want you off the Barge well before midnight."

Hedrigs had never before wanted to kill anybody. He wanted to now—very much. This creature had imperiled the two lives he valued most. Svir told her so in words he had never used with a woman.

Tatja just laughed. "You may be a good astronomer, dear, but you're weak on biology. Do as I say. And don't

get any ideas of taking off on your own to save Cor. You
will find when I brief you that the only way you can help
her is to save the *Fantasie* collection in the process."

Six hours later, Svir Hedrigs emerged from the offices
of the Tarulle executive deck, and descended to the de-
barkation levels. He wore an old, baggy suit and carried a
light balsir cage disguised as a suitcase. Ancho sat comfortably within the cage. He wore the mysterious clicker
on his back.

The Barge had reached its pier space and was already
so firmly tied in that it was difficult to tell where Barge
ended and pier began. Gibbous Seraph cast a bright,
cheerful twilight across Bayfast. The clashing, bright col-
ors of the city were transformed into pastels. Here and
there those pastels were highlighted by yellow and green
sparkles where people uncovered their evening lamps.
This shimmery, glowing pattern stretched up toward the
edge of the seaward cliffs and around the bay to the in-
land cliffs, which cut off the Monsoonal Drag and made
Bayfast one of the few placid spots on The Continent at
this time of year.

Svir left the Barge and walked along the waterfront.
The Festival of the Ostentatious Consumption was not
due to begin for another six hours, but the citizens of
Bayfast were already competing with one another for the
best sites along the waterfront from which they could
watch the events on Sacrifice Island out in the bay. Hedrigs knew he looked strange walking so seriously among
the happy people. His severe costume contrasted sharply
with the plaids and monochromes of the Bayfastlings. But
Svir had his special reason for not wearing the costume
Tatja had suggested.

The people of Crownesse were happy, confident, and
nationalistic. Originally they had been colonists from the
Chainpearl and other Archipelagates. The hardships of
The Continent had forced an optimistic dynamism on
them. In the thousand years since they declared their

independence from the sea, it had often been remarked that they showed the most initiative and intelligence of any people on Tu. They had developed their bureaucratic system to heights existing nowhere else in the world. Their Bureaucracy was talented, flexible and, above all, devoted to the Crown. In the last two centuries the Reaches of Crownesse had grown threefold. The country already stretched most of the way across the southern coast of The Continent, and steady inroads were being made into the Interior. But the spiritual evolution of Crownesse had ended abruptly twenty years ago, when the strange and implacable Tar Benesh appeared in the King's Court. The King had died and Tar Benesh had become the Regent. Shortly after, the King's children had disappeared in a sea-wreck.

Since those days twenty years before, Tar Benesh's rule had been a study in expanding tyranny. He had, with the faithful help of the Bureaucracy, transformed the open competitive spirit of the Bayfastlings into an aggressive barbarism which could worship the destruction involved in the Ostentatious Consumption, and which could desire world conquest.

Hedrigs was walking east, toward the Keep. That enormous semi-dodecahedron loomed black over the warehouse roofs. Even the ingenious Bayfastlings had needed seventy years to build this ultimate protection for the Crown. Nothing short of a year-long artillery bombardment could breach that artificial mountain—and the Keep had plenty of its own armament. Just ventilating the structure required the services of twenty draft animals.

Svir stopped before he reached the two-hundred-foot open space surrounding the Keep. He slipped into the entranceway of a closed shop and covertly inspected the castle port through which he must pass. Once more the horrible fear rose in him, making his every movement slow and clumsy. He knew he was going to die.

A figure dressed in the uniform of a Guard captain walked across the open area toward the port. That was the signal to begin. The "captain" was a Tarulle agent whose job it was to warn the Guardsmen at the door to look sharp, since the Crown's Inspector General was expected momentarily. In truth, The Crown's I.G. was supposed to visit the Keep at this time, but he was being detained by other Tarulle agents. In any case, the two Guardsmen at the door should now be prepared to assume that the next authority figure they saw was the Inspector General.

Hedrigs fumbled the suitcase open and lifted Ancho out. The animal responded nervously to the human's obvious anxiety. Svir tried to reassure him. He depressed the tiny button on the side of the box strapped to the dorfox's back. The contraption immediately began making a *click-clock-click* sound.

What if the device were a bomb hooked up to a clock, timed to blow up after they were within the Keep? He debated for a moment whether to rip the machine off Ancho's back. But there was no explosive which could possibly be fitted into a package this small and still do any damage to the castle. Tatja had no motive for tagging him with a clock bomb. And since his survival was necessary for the recovery of the *Fantasie* collection, the device probably had some beneficial—though certainly mysterious—role.

He stood up, put the dorfox on his shoulder, and petted him. The animal began radiating immediately. His first target was a middle-aged merchant—one of the few people who were not yet at the waterfront. As the man passed Svir and Ancho, his eyes widened and he performed the nodding bow reserved for members of the Bureaucracy. Svir smiled and walked onto the open area before the Keep. In some peculiar way, when Ancho used the effect on others, it made Svir feel confident, competent. And this feeling of authority actually seemed to feed back to the animal, making him perform even more effectively. Hedrigs strolled briskly across the grassy plain.

The two Guardsmen came rigidly to attention as he ap-

proached. One of them saluted. Svir offhandedly returned
the salute. He passed his credentials to the Guardsman.
At the same time, he spoke the ritual words. "The
Crown's agent to inventory the Prizes."

The senior Guardsman looked up from the papers.
"Very good, sir." Both men wore ridiculously orna-
mented dress uniforms, but there was nothing ornamental
about their weapons. In a single glance, the Guardsman
gave Svir a thorough once-over. His alert and active mind
checked for the minor details that would give an impostor
away. Unfortunately for the Guardsman, his own mind
made him see the details he was looking for. If questioned later, both Guards would swear they saw the
Crown's Inspector General entering the building, and not
Svir Hedrigs.

The fellow returned Svir his papers, and turned to an
inconspicuous speaking tube that emerged from the black
stone of the castle wall. Except for the words "Inspector
General," Svir couldn't hear what was said. But that was
enough. He had passed the second hurdle. At each checkpoint, the word would be passed back as to who he was
supposed to be. With a greased sliding sound, a thirty-ton
cube of stone lifted into the ceiling of the entrance. Beyond was darkness.

Svir walked in, striving not to look up at the mass of
stone above him, or back at the colorful city which would
soon be blocked from his view. The stone cube slid
smoothly down. Svir stood in the dark for almost five seconds. Ancho chirped nervously, and the device on his
back continued to *clock-click-clock*. Hedrigs rubbed the
little animal's neck, and the dorfox began radiating again,
none too soon. A second block of stone was lifting. Al-
gae-generated light flooded the chamber. He stepped into
the hallway and handed his papers to the Guardsmen
standing there. Two of them were right by the entrance,
while a third stood on a crenelated balcony near the ceiling. All three were dressed in loose, comfortable suits of
Bureaucratic black. They weren't nearly as formal as the

fellows outside, but they showed obvious respect—and they were just as alert and competent as the dudes outside. Hedrigs' identity was passed by speaking tube to the next checkpoint.

Svir walked on confidently. The hall was well lighted and ventilated, even though it was within a mass of stone almost six hundred feet high. In some places the cold black stone was covered by wood paneling and cabinets filled with the Arms of Early Kings. He passed through three more checkpoints, each with its own door system. Whenever he had a choice of routes he took the middle one—he was following a radius straight to the center of the Keep, to the Crown Room vault. Some of the outer passages were almost crowded. Bureaucrats were making final arrangements for the evening's events. Svir walked aloof from these groups, and hoped that none of them compared notes on exactly who they thought he was. As he approached the center, however, there were fewer and fewer people. Besides the Guards, he encountered only an occasional, very high-ranking Bureaucrat.

Here the identification procedures became more complex. The walls were uniformly panelled and the floors heavily carpeted. Svir wondered at this strange luxuriousness in the most secret part of the Keep. Besides the usual paintings and displays, there were small glass windows at regular intervals. Beyond that glass, Svir could see only darkness. Probably there was someone back there watching what went on—guarding the guards. Svir was suddenly very glad that Tatja had had Ancho practice at deluding hidden observers. Now he knew the reason for the luxurious trappings. Besides hiding the observation posts, they probably concealed a variety of weapons and deadfalls.

Finally he reached the last checkpoint—the doorway to the Crown Room itself. It was conceivable that at this moment, only the Inspector General and Tar Benesh himself had authority to enter that storeroom of the nation's greatest treasures and most secret documents. Here the clearance process was especially difficult. For a few uncomfortable moments, Svir thought they were going to take his fingerprints and run a comparison right there. Would the illusion extend to fingerprints? But apparently that procedure was used in special cases only, and Svir was not subjected to it.

As they opened the outer vault door, Hedrigs casually turned to the officer in charge. "Captain, I have instructions to move some of the Prizes out to Sacrifice Island right away. I'd like to have a couple of squads ready when I finish the general inventory."

"Very good, sir," she answered. "We have about twenty people with the proper clearance for just that job. I can have them here in fifteen minutes." She handed Svir an algae lamp. "Don't forget this, sir."

"Why, thanks." Hedrigs accepted the lamp uncertainly. "If everything's in order, my inventory should take about forty minutes—if not, it could be longer." *A lot longer,* thought Svir to himself.

Hedrigs turned and walked quickly into the lock area between the double doors. The outer door slid shut, the inner door lifted open, and he stepped into the Crown Room.

The vault was a disappointment. The room was large and without ornamentation. Svir's lamp provided the only illumination. Over all hung a musty smell, which the tiny vault ventilator shafts could not dissipate. The treasures were not heaped in a spectacular pile, but were neatly catalogued on racks that filled most of the room. Each object had its own classification tag. A row of cabinets along one wall housed the personal records of the Royal Family. Svir walked along the racks. (He almost didn't notice the Crown Jewels and the nine-hundred-thirty-carat Shamerest cut diamond. In the dim light everything looked dull.) Finally he reached the red-tag area—the prime sacrifices for the Festival.

And there it was—the *Fantasie* collection. Its sheer bulk was impressive. The ten thousand volumes were stacked on seven close-set racks. The entire mass rested on a dolly for easy handling. Obviously Benesh thought of *Fantasie* as an article of portable wealth rather than a source of philosophical and romantic pleasure. But—as Tatja so cynically pointed out—that massive collection was also the vehicle of Cor's salvation. Even in this dim light, he could read some of the binding titles. Why, there was the last *obra* of Ti Liso's Time Travel Series! For the last three centuries, the Chainpearl experts had been trying to find that issue. The series had been illustrated by Inmar Ellis—probably the greatest artist of all time. Svir noticed all this in passing. No matter how valuable this collection, its physical dimensions were much more important to him now. There was indeed enough room between the third and fourth racks to hide a human body.

Now he had to find the correct passage to the prison tier. If Tatja had lied about that—

The vault doors were so well constructed that Hedrigs did not know he had been discovered until the inner door lifted and he heard the raging voice of—

Tar Benesh.

The Regent advanced into the room. A look of astounded shock came to his face as he saw Hedrigs. Svir wondered briefly what authority figure the dictator saw in Ancho's illusion. Benesh was less than five feet tall. He weighed more than two hundred pounds. Once that weight had been slablike muscle, but now he was as soft as the velvet and flutter-feather costume he wore.

The Regent shakily raised his arm and pointed at Hedrigs. "Take that—man," he choked. The black-uniformed Guardsmen swarmed toward Svir, their momentary confusion replaced by cool professionalism. Svir felt only confidence as they approached. He was in trouble, true, but he could work his way out of it.

The confidence vanished. As the Guardmen grabbed him, Svir collapsed into the quivering apathy of total fear. He felt a burning needle thrust into the base of his neck, and simultaneously his entire body became a single charlie-horse. He couldn't move, he could hardly breathe, and what he saw and heard seemed to be far away, observed through a curtain of pain. He felt his person being searched, and dimly heard Benesh say, "A dorfox, that's the creature you saw."

"But, M'lord Regent, that's a mythological creature."

"Obviously not! Search the Crown Room." An unprecedented order. "No one enters or leaves this vault till we find—" he paused, realizing that this was impractical. It would tie up the Guard situation in the whole Keep. "No, belay that. But I want that creature, and I want it alive." There was a lustfulness in his voice. "Check everyone and everything that passes through these doors."

Svir felt himself picked up, moved swiftly toward the door. And of all the humans in the room, he was the only one who noticed the dorfox seated on the shoulder of Tar Benesh.

As they rushed him through the Keep passageways, Svir vaguely wondered what had given him away—though he really didn't care now. Nothing could save him and Cor. And soon this paralysis would be replaced by the ultimate agony of interrogation.

Finally his captors stopped. There was a dull creaking sound. Then he was sailing through the air. His hip struck the hard stone floor. His head and shoulders were resting in a pile of straw. He smelled rot and blood. The heavy door swung shut and he was in darkness.

There was a shuffling sound, and someone was holding him. Cor! She pressed her body tight against his and whispered in his ear what seemed a complete irrelevancy. "I'm so sorry, Svir! I tried to warn you but they got me." She was silent for a second, waiting for some response. He longed to put his arms around her. "Svir?" she whispered. "Are you all right? Svir!" But Hedrigs was so thoroughly paralyzed, he couldn't even croak.

"—realize we're sitting beneath the Keep artillery. To get out, we'd have to go around the peninsula past the entrance guns. And now you want me to send twenty people on a diversionary raid! If Benesh ever connects us with this scheme, we'll be blown out of the water—if we're lucky!" Kederichi Maccioso slammed his broad fist down on Tatja's desk, jarring her aluminum drinking carafe half an inch into the air.

"Relax, Ked, we aren't suspected of anything yet. It's still a state secret that the collection is one of the sacrifices. There's—" She broke off and motioned Maccioso to be silent. Even over the thrumming crowd sounds outside, they could both hear a scratching against the office window.

Tatja Grimm pushed the window open and pulled a shivering, croaking Ancho into the room. She held him close and comforted him with low, gentle sounds. Maccioso sat down abruptly and stared at them, shocked.

"The—dorfox wouldn't come back alone unless Hedrigs had been taken," he stuttered.

Tatja smiled. "That's right. Svir never had a chance—though he lasted longer than I thought he would."

"But this means Benesh knows. We've got to get a—" Then he seemed to realize what Grimm had just said. *"What did you say?* You knew all along he would fail?" His voice rose to an astonishing volume, rattled the window. "We're all going to die because of you, you—"

"Shut up, Ked," Tatja said pleasantly. "You're disturbing Ancho. Do you really think I would do anything to jeopardize my own life?" She set Ancho on her desk. "You know," she said with apparent irrelevance, "I've studied dorfoxes. If they were just a little smarter or a little more mobile, they could take over the world. As it is though, I can manipulate them. With Hedrigs out of the way, I think Ancho will accept me as his new master." She undid the clicker and set it carefully on her desk. "Hand me that bottle of lacquer, will you?" She accepted the bottle and screwed an atomizer onto its cap. Then she inserted the nozzle into the clicker's keyhole and puffed the volatile lacquer into the box. In spite of himself,

Kederichi Maccioso leaned over the table to watch this mysterious ritual. Ancho moved over to the corner of the table and munched the klig leaves that Tatja had thoughtfully provided.

"That should fix it." She undid the hidden catches and lifted the top off the box. "You know that picture-maker we've been using in our latest issues? I've made some refinements on the invention."

Maccioso looked at the machine's innards. It resembled only vaguely the picture-maker Tarulle used. In that device, light was focused on a special cellulose plate coated with very fine algae powder. Wherever light fell on the plate, the cellulose became charged and repelled the greenish powder from its surface. If the plate were properly coated with lacquer, a permanent picture resulted.

Tatja pointed. "See, this clock movement pulls the reel of cellulose tape through the central area. Once every two seconds, this shutter takes an exposure. On alternate seconds, the shutter on the other side of the box takes a picture. So we now have a pictorial record covering nearly three hundred degrees. A picture every second, for nearly ten minutes." She pulled the reel out of the clicker and began to examine it under a large magnifying glass. Maccioso had a clear, though distorted, view of the pictures through the same lens.

The first thirty pictures covered Hedrigs' approach to the Keep. Every other picture was reversed since it had been made on the opposite side of the cellulose. In spite of this, and the fact that the pictures were considerably less clear than ones made with simpler, one-shot devices, the sequence gave Maccioso the unreal sensation that he was sitting on Hedrigs' shoulder. On every second frame, Svir's head blocked out part of the picture.

Tatja carefully inspected each picture, but it was obvious that she didn't expect anything strange this early in the sequence. She became increasingly excited as the pictures showed the interior of the Keep. Here the exposure she had chosen was much more effective and the pictures sharper. "See, that paneling and those paintings—they weren't in any of the reports. And here, I'll bet this is what snagged dear Hedrigs."

Maccioso squinted at the tiny picture. It looked no different from the three or four previous. Then Tatja pointed out the rectangular patch of darkness on the passage wall. "That's not a painting. It's some kind of window. My guess is that the Guards have heard of the poison gases developed in the Sutherseas. That little window is one end of a periscope, and the observer is in another room, protected from the gas—and apparently beyond Ancho's range." They looked at the rest of the pictures, but most were badly fogged. As the exposure had been made, more and more algae powder had been sent into a colloidal suspension in the clicker. An equilibrium state had been reached, where as much green was being deposited as was being dissipated by the exposures. Those last pictures showed vague green blurs. They saw something of the interior of the Crown Room. And in one of the pictures, Tatja claimed she saw a group of men.

Grimm set the film aside and picked up a pair of dividers. "We discovered that Ancho can broadcast through almost twenty feet of porphyry." She made some rapid measurements of relative sizes on the film. "That periscope window is about three inches by three." She sat back and her eyes unfocused for a moment. "Now assuming their optics are no better than elsewhere, that periscope can't have a resolution higher than half an inch." She looked up and flashed Maccioso a dazzling smile. "I'm all set! Svir has served his purpose."

Tatja got up and began to take her clothes off. Maccioso stood up too. He was a big man, an experienced man, a leader. But he appeared to be none of these now. His face bore a peculiar mixture of hatred, surprise, and confusion. As Grimm laid her shirt on the chair, he reached out a huge hand, grabbed her by the shoulder, drew her face close to his.

"You never intended this plan to save *Fantasie*, did you?"

Tatja shrugged. "You know the saying, Ked, 'Things are not as they seem.'"

"What are you after then, damn you?" He shook her violently, but received no answer. "Well, if you think I'm going to risk any more Tarulle people for your pleasure, you're crazy."

"Poor Ked," Tatja said gently. Her hand moved softly up his arm, found a nerve in his elbow. As he jerked back, she slipped away. "I see that I've almost driven you beyond logic and self-interest. Almost." She reached into an alcove and drew out a suit of black armor. The Crown's Inspector General was about her height, but the armor had been designed for a male. In places it chafed, but she managed to get it on.

She slipped the épée into its sheath and picked Ancho up from the desk. At the door she turned back to face Maccioso. "But I know you will go through with that attack. You know that whatever my plan is, it's the only chance you have of getting out of this alive, now that Benesh has Ascuasenya and Hedrigs. Right?"

Kederichi Maccioso glowered at her for a moment, then slowly nodded his head. "That's right, you . . . bitch."

Seraph was in its last quarter, and the evening wake period was ending. Nearly a million people—the entire population of the capital—were crowded along watersedge. In the waning blue light, the crowd was a mosaic carpet covering the streets and stretching up over the roofs of the lower buildings. The Festival was at its noisiest as the Bayfastlings cheered the first sacrifices being towed into the bay. These were the secondary sacrifices —the appetizers. The tiny barges formed a continuous train out to Sacrifice Island. Each barge was stacked high with worked jade, optical devices, paintings. Hanging from the stern of each barge, an algae-water sphere lit the sacrifices.

A twisted smile crossed Tatja's lips as she regarded the scene.

She descended to one of the sub-pier passageways reserved for official use, and five minutes later emerged on the city side of the crowd. Here were the stragglers, the individuals without initiative enough to push into the crowd. She petted Ancho, spoke quietly to him. This was a critical test. According to theory, Ancho should accept her as his new master, but Tatja had to be sure. She couldn't tell whether he was radiating or not. Certainly the signal was having no effect on her. Then she noticed that people came to attention as she walked past. Good Ancho.

She reached the Keep without incident. The Guardsmen looked her over very carefully, this being the second Inspector General they had seen that day. But they let her through. As she stood in the darkness between the two doors, Grimm moved the dorfox to her waist. The armor plates gave him good purchase, and now he was below the view of the periscopes.

At last she came to the doors of the Crown Room. Tatja spoke in a low masculine voice, to fool any listening devices. Even with her visor up, she knew that wearing the I.G.'s armor would deceive the hidden observers. And of course the Guardsmen in the hall didn't have a chance. With Ancho's help, even her fingerprints passed inspection.

Once in the Crown Room she moved quickly to the royal records. She lifted out the drawer she wanted, thumbed through it, and pulled out a single sheet of vellum. Good. It was the same form as had been publicly displayed at the Assignation of the Regency. From her pouch she drew a seemingly identical paper, smudges and all, and slipped it into the file.

Then she left, ignoring the puzzled Guards. They had expected the I.G. to supervise the removal of the prizes.

Tatja found the stairway to the Conciliar Facet unguarded. This was unexpected good fortune. Perhaps Maccioso's diversion had been more effective than she had hoped.

She removed the black resin armor and set the outfit on one of the display racks which lined the base of the stairwell. This was the most perilous part of her plan. If she were discovered in the next three or four minutes, there'd be real trouble. From a gray cloth pouch she drew a white dress and jeweled sandals. She slipped them on, put Ancho on her shoulder and ran up the stairs. This stairway wasn't often used since it was a single spiral ascending six hundred feet. Most people preferred to go by stages. Even so, Tatja kept the heavy épée. Except for that, and the dorfox clutching her shoulder, she might have been an island girl at a communion picnic.

She took the steps three at a time, so fast that she had to lean toward the center of the spiral in order to keep her balance. When she had first conceived this scheme, she had spent three years in Bayfast studying the people and especially the Keep. Tar Benesh had created the Festival of the Ostentatious Consumption in order to draw attention from a much more solemn event that took place every five years at the same time. The top people in the Bureaucracy were scrupulously honest, but if she were even five minutes late, she would have to wait five years —or possibly forever. Taking the back way should save her from Benesh's Special Men, but if she were wrong about the Bureaucratic esprit of the rest, then she would die—though death could make her failure no worse. If she couldn't succeed, life wasn't worth living.

Tatja took the six-hundred-foot stairway in a single sprint. At the top of that long flight was an entrance to the Conciliar Facet, the pentagonal amphitheater on the very top of the enormous dodecahedron that was the Keep. Beyond this next door was the final test. She slid the door open and crept out into the uppermost tier of the amphitheater. There was a faint cool breeze and Seraph-blue covered everything. From the city came crowd-sounds.

Less than a third of the seats in the Facet were filled and those were down in the center, by the podium and reading lamp. Virtually everyone present was dressed in Bureaucratic black. An important exception was the gross and colorful bulk of Tar Benesh, sitting in the first row before the podium.

Tatja glanced around the Facet. Maccioso's diversion must have worked. Few of the Guards appeared to be Benesh's bully boys. There were only fifteen or twenty armed men present. Of course one of them might still be rotten, but that was a chance she must take. She noticed one man just five feet from her hiding place. The fellow leaned unprofessionally against the edge of the tier, blocking her entrance. She reversed the hilt of the épée and moved swiftly forward, ramming the pommel into the base of the man's neck. He collapsed quietly into her arms. She dragged him back, at the same time watching for signs that someone below had noticed the incident.

The speaker's voice came clearly to her. She knew there were about five minutes until the ceremony reached its critical point. She looked at her épée. It was no longer an asset. Without putting herself in silhouette, she reached up and slid the weapon over the parapet. There came a faint sound of scrape and clatter as the épée slid slowly down the side of the hundred-foot facet. Tatja sat Ancho on the edge of the tier and petted him. They waited.

In the center of the amphitheater, the ceremony was nearing its end. On the podium stood the Lord High Minister to the Crown—the highest Bureaucratic officer of Crownesse. The man was old, but his body was lean, and his voice was clear and strong as he read from the curling parchment. He had the air of a man who is for the thousandth time repeating a fervent and sincere prayer, a prayer that has so often been fruitless that it has almost become perfunctory.

"And so in the Year of the Discovery Nine Hundred and Seven did the Crown Prince Evard II and his sister, Princess Marget, take themselves aboard the Royal Yacht *Avante* to tour the western reaches of their Dominions.

"And on the fifth day of their voyage a great storm sent their yacht upon the Rocks of the South—for so we have the word of the ship's captain and those crewmen who survived the tragedy."

Tatja stood up slowly, out of their view. She fluffed out her full skirt and waited quietly for the moment that would come.

"The Royal Children were never found. So it is that the Regent continues to govern in their stead until such time as our rulers are recovered. On this twenty-fifth anniversary of that storm, and by order of the Regent, I ask that anyone with knowledge of the Royal Family step forth." The Lord High Minister glanced about moodily. The ceremony was almost a legal fiction. It had been fifteen years since anyone had dared Tar Benesh's revenge with a story of the lost children. It was not surprising that the Minister almost fell off the stand when a clear, vibrant voice answered his call.

"I, Marget of Sandros, do claim the Crown and my Dominions." Tatja stood boldly on the uppermost tier, her arms akimbo. Behind her, and invisible to those below, sat a small animal with large ears. The startled Bureaucrats stared at Tatja. Then their eyes turned to the Regent. How would he accept this challenge? The gaily-dressed dictator advanced six ominous steps toward Tatja. His pale eyes reflected hatred and complete disbelief. For twenty years he had ruled the most powerful country on Tu—and now a female was challenging him at the very center of his power. Benesh gestured angrily to the Guardsmen—the sleek professionals with thousands of hours of target and tactical experience, the deadliest individuals in the world.

"Kill the imposter," he ordered.

When they came, Svir was ready.

He and Cor had lain quietly in the darkness, telling each other their stories in frightened whispers. As Cor massaged the numbness from his arms, Svir told her of his one backstop against Grimm's treachery. Tounse, who hated Tatja as much as Hedrigs did, had provided the astronomer with five pounds of Michelle-Rasche powder. Now that powder lay in the heavy fiber weave of his clothing.

"It's perfectly safe until the cloth gets twisted into a constricted volume," he whispered to Cor. "But then almost any extra friction will set it off."

He struggled out of his overjacket. Cor helped him wedge the fabric into the door crack. Though only a small portion of the jacket could be jammed in, it would be enough to set off the rest of the powder. Then they retreated to the far corner of the cell. There was nothing more they could do. He hadn't said so to Cor, but the best they could hope for was a quick death. If they weren't killed in the explosion or by the Guards—then the next stop was the torture chambers. Their present cell was a carefully contrived filth-pit, designed to prepare prisoners psychologically for what was to come. Somehow the prospect of torture and death no longer provoked absolute terror in him. Cor was the reason. He wanted to hide his fear from her—and to protect her from her own fears.

He put his arm around Cor's waist and drew her to him. "You came out here to save me, Cor."

"You did the same for me, Svir."

"I'd do it all over again, too."

Her reply was clear and firm. "So would I."

When they came, there was plenty of warning. It sounded like a whole squad. The heavy footsteps stopped, and when they began again, it sounded like only two or three men. Svir and Cor slid under the filthy straw. The footsteps stopped at the door. Svir heard the key turn, but he never heard the door open. For that matter, he never actually *heard* the explosion. He felt it through his whole body. The floor rose up and smashed him.

Hedrigs forced himself to his feet, and pulled Cor up. The doorway was a dim patch of light through the dust and vapor that the explosion had driven into the air. They gasped futilely and ran toward the opening. Svir was aware of blood flowing down his jaw from his ear.

The blast had destroyed the bottom hinges on the door and blown the whole mass into the ceiling. In the hallway lay the two Guardsmen. Both were alive, but in much worse shape than the prisoners. One, with a severe scalp cut, tried ineffectually to wipe the blood from his eyes. Svir and Cor stepped over them and ran down the hall. Then they saw the men at the end of the passage—the back-up section. The two prisoners came to a sudden halt and started to turn in the other direction.

A Guardsman smiled faintly and twisted a lever mounted in the wall. A weighted net fell from the ceiling onto the two escapees. As the Guard approached, Svir lashed out at his legs, hoping to provoke lethal retaliation. The Guard easily avoided the extended hand, and grabbed it with his own. "You know, fella, for someone whose life we're supposed to protect, you're making things damn difficult."

Svir looked back blankly. He couldn't make sense of the words spoken. The net was removed, and the Guards marched Svir and Cor down the hall. The proofreader and the astronomer looked at each other in complete confusion. They weren't even treated to the paralysis the Guards had used before. It was a long uphill walk, and the Guards had to help Cor the last part. Svir wondered if he had gone crazy with fear and was seeing only what he hoped to see. They came to the final door. The Guard captain went through. They could hear him through the open doorway.

"Marget, the individuals you requested are here."

"Fine," came a familiar voice. "Send them out, I want to talk to them alone."

"Begging your pardon, Marget, but they have repeatedly offered us violence. We could not guarantee the safety of your person if you interview them alone."

"Mister, I told you what I wanted," the voice said in a tone that brooked no argument. "Now jump!"

"Yes, Marget, immediately!" The captain appeared at the door. He gestured courteously to Svir and Cor. "Sir and madam, you have been granted an interview with the Queen."

"The—Queen?" Cor asked incredulously. She got no answer. They were pushed past the door and found themselves standing on the top tier of the Conciliar Facet. By the light of waning Seraph they saw a beautiful girl in a full-skirted dress.

Tatja turned to them. "You two look like hell," she said.

Hedrigs started angrily toward her. All his fright and pain was transformed into hate for this monster who pretended to be human. There was a scuttling sound on the floor, then a tugging at Svir's clothing. A soft wet nose nuzzled his neck. Ancho! Svir's hands reached up and petted the trembling animal.

"Marget?" asked Coronadas. "Queen? Are you really the Lost Princess of Crownesse?"

"Since you were in on part of the scheme, I suppose you might as well know the truth. You can't do anything about it. I was no more Marget of Sandros than you. But now I am incontrovertibly the Queen. My fingerprints match those of the Princess which are kept in the Crown Room. You should have seen the look on Benesh's face when the Lord High Minister announced that I was heir to the Crown. The Regent had the Royal Children murdered twenty years ago. The job was bobbled and he couldn't produce bodies that would pass an autopsy. He *knew* I was a fraud but there was no way he could prove it without revealing that he was guilty of regicide."

Svir looked out over the curving dome of the Keep toward the city. The crowd sounds came clear and faint through the air. The crowd had moved away from the waterfront. There would be no sacrifices tonight—the people had been told that the Crown had been claimed. Crownesse had a Queen—that called for the largest of festivals, a celebration that would go on for many days. Hedrigs turned to Tatja Grimm. "You had to lie and cheat and steal and—probably—murder to do it, but you certainly got what you wanted. You control the most powerful country in the world. I've wondered so many times what could make you as vicious as you are. Now I know. The hidden motive that mystified me so much was simple megalomania. Female 'Tar Benesh' has taken over from male. Is this the end of your appetites," said Svir, putting as much derision and hate into his voice as he could, "or will you one day rule all Tu?"

Tatja smiled at Cor and Svir—the same scornful, bitter smile they had seen so often before. "You never were very bright, were you, Svir? It's possible that I'll take over the world. As a matter of fact I probably will. It will be a by-product of my other plans. I chose Crownesse very carefully. The country has immense physical resources. If there are large heavy-metal deposits anywhere, they are in Crownesse. The government is talented and dedicated. Most administrative posts are awarded on the basis of civil-service tests. And the entire Bureaucracy is fanatically dedicated to one person—the legal holder of the Crown. They served Tar Benesh and his evil for twenty years, and they will serve me just as faithfully. I will not be bothered with coups and elections, as I might if I took over one of the archipelagates.

"We've reached a very critical point in the development of civilization—in case you don't realize it. In the past century there have been a number of really basic scientific discoveries made in all parts of the world. The pharmacists of the Tsanart Islands are very close to immortality drugs. A physicist in the Osterlei Archipelagate developed that picture-maker we use. All over the world, revolutionary advances are being made. Sometimes I think that organizations like Tarulle are responsible for this. For centuries they spread ideas from island to island until finally scientists stopped thinking of them as fantasy and actually invented what writers described. I'm making a gift of that *Fantasie* collection to Tarulle, by the way."

"That's big of you," snapped Svir. Grimm ignored him.

"All these inventions and techniques are going to have effects far beyond what is obvious. Just think what that picture-taker will do for parallax astronomy. You'll be able to make pictures of all observations. If these inventions were brought together and worked over intensively, the changes would be even more spectacular. But you people out in the islands are too lazy to do that. The people of Crownesse are not. They've had to work awfully hard just to stay alive here on The Continent. They will take your inventions and use them and develop more inventions—until they control the entire planet."

Tatja looked up into the sky, at Seraph and the bright star Prok. "You know, there is a very common legend among the Wildmen at the center of The Continent. The legend says that man originally came from the stars, that he landed on The Continent and lost his magical arts to the storm and wind. Sounds like a *Fantasie* story, doesn't it? But imagine—if it is true, then the races of men live among the stars, their empires so vast that they can 'forget' whole planetary systems. They may have colonized Seraph at the same time as Tu. We are not alone." As she spoke to them, Tatja's voice changed, lost its authority and its spite. Now she spoke softly, sadly. Her shoulders slumped. For a moment she wasn't the master of events, but a young girl, very much alone, and very lonely. "No, Svir, ruling this world does not interest me, except for one thing. I've never found anyone I can talk to, anyone that can understand the things I often want to say. When I call you stupid—I mean it, even though you're of above-average intelligence, and even though I just say it to make you angry." She turned to look at Svir and Cor. Her eyes were soft, and her lower lip almost seemed to tremble. Her vast intelligence had crippled her, just as surely as if she had had no arms. In point of fact there was no person on Tu who was her equal. Svir suddenly understood the meaning of her scornful, hostile smile. It was the bitter, hopeless envy of a woman seeing well-adjusted people all around her and not being one herself.

"And that is why I am going to turn this world upside down, and regain the ancient arts that mythology said we once had. For somewhere in this universe there *must* be what I need most . . . a man." The fallen goddess turned away from the parapet and the gay crowds. She didn't look up as she walked slowly away.

James Sallis, 23, is a Southerner educated at Tulane. Until recently he lived in rural Iowa with his wife, a painter and medical illustrator, and their son Dylan, 3. At present he is living in London, where he is fiction editor of New Worlds. *With Thomas M. Disch and Samuel R. Delany, he typifies the emerging new generation of science fiction writers.*

Almost to a man, the writers of "new wave" science fiction deny that there is any such thing as a new or old wave; they say there are only good stories and bad ones. Nevertheless, the new writers form a distinctive group. They are trained in the arts, particularly in poetry and music, rather than in science or engineering, and it shows in their work. (Some of the older writers majored in English, but went ahead and wrote pulp just the same.

Like Disch and Delany, Sallis uses all the resources of English, not just those few that have trickled down our side channel in the last forty years. "A Few Last Words" is an end-of-civilization story, if you like, but it owes much more to Eliot than to Wells or Wyndham. Its domain is not the great out-there of conventional science fiction, but the poetic intensity of right-here, right-now:

Is this how it feels, the instant of desertion?

A FEW LAST WORDS

By James Sallis

> What is the silence
>   a. As though it had a right to more
> —W. S. Merwin

Again: the dreams.

He was eating stained glass and vomiting rainbows. He felt he was being watched and looked up and there was the clock moving toward him, grinning, arms raised in a shout of triumph over its head. The clock advanced; he smelled decay; he was strangled to death by the hands of time . . . The scene changed. He was in a red room. The hands of the clock knocked knocked knocked without entering . . . And changed again. And the hours had faces, worse than the hands. He choked it was all so quiet quiet only the ticking the faces were coming closer closer he gagged screamed once and—

Sat on the edge of the bed. The hall clock was ticking loudly, a sound like dried peas dropping into a pail. This was the third night.

The pumpkin-color moon was arrested in motion, dangling deep in the third quadrant of the cross-paned window about three-quarters out along the diagonal. Periodically clouds would touch the surface and partly fill with color, keeping it whole. Dust and streaks on the window, a tiny bubble of air, blurred its landscape; yellow drapes beside it took on a new hue.

He had watched it for hours (must have been hours). Its only motion was a kind of visual dopplering. It sped out into serene depths, skipped back in a rush to paste itself against the backside of the glass, looking like a spot of wax. Apogee to perigee to apogee, and no pause between. Rapid vacillation, losing his eyes in intermediate distances, making him blink and squint, glimmering in the pale overcast. And other than that, it hadn't moved. Abscissa +, ordinate +. Stasis. This was the third night.

His wife stirred faintly and reached to touch his pillow, eyelids fluttering. Hoover quickly put out his hand and laid it across her fingers. Visibly, she settled back into blankets. In the hall, the clock ticked like a leaking faucet. The moon was in its pelagic phase, going out.

The third night of the dreams. The third night that lying in bed he was overcome by: Presence. In the dark it would grow around him, crowding his eyes open, bunching his breath, constricting—at last driving him from the bed, the room. He would pace the rugs and floors, turn back and away again on the stairs, wondering. He would drink liquor, then coffee, unsure which effect he wanted, uneasy at conclusions—certain only of this sense of cramping, of imposition. In the dark he was ambushed, inhabited, attacked again from within.

His wife turned in bed, whispering against sheets, taking her fingers away.

Hoover lifted his head to the dresser, chinoiserie chair, sculpt lame valet, to glazed chintz that hid the second, curiously small window. A simple room, sparse, clean, a room with no waste of motion. And a familiar room, intimate and informal as the back of his hand, yet his eyes moving through it now encountered a strangeness, a distortion. He cast his vision about the room, tracing the strangeness back to its source at the window: to pale plastic light that slipped in there and took his furniture away into distances. It occurred to him that he was annoyed by this intrusion, this elusive division of himself from his things. He watched the moon and it stared back, unblinking.

Hoover fixed his chin between his fists, propped elbows on knees, and became a sculpture. His face turned again to see the window, head rolling in his hands, ball-in-socket.

A cave, he thought: that was the effect. Gloom, and

moonlight sinking through cracks: pitch and glimmer. A skiagraphy of the near and foreign. Quarantine and communion, solitude and confederation. A cave, shaped in this strange light . . .

And bruising the light's influence, he walked to the chair and stared down at the suit he'd draped over one arm—looked at the hall clock—ten minutes ago. It was happening faster now . . .

The suit was pale, stale-olive green and it shined in a stronger light. The coat barely concealed the jutting, saddlelike bones of his hips; his wrists dangled helplessly away from the sleeve ends like bones out of a drumstick —and Cass hated it. Regardless of fit, though, it *felt* right: he was comfortable in it, was himself.

He took the coat from the chair, held it a minute, and put it back. Somehow, tonight, it seemed inappropriate, like the man-shaped valet that no one used. As with the room, the furniture, it had been taken away from him.

He turned and shuffled across the rug to search through the crow-black corner closet behind the creaking, always-open door, discovering a western shirt, with a yoke of roses across its breast and trying it on, then jeans, belting them tightly, and boots. The clothes were loose, looser than he remembered, but they felt good, felt right.

Stepping full into light at the door, he shattered strangeness, and looking back saw that the moon was now cockeyed in the corner of the pane.

Ticking of a clock, sound of feet down stairs.

He assassinated death with the cold steel rush of his breathing . . .

The night was pellucid, a crystal of blackness; hermetic with darkness. He moved within a hollow black crystal and up there was another, an orange separate crystal, bubble in a bubble . . . And quiet, so quiet so still, only the ticking of his feet, the whisper of breath. He pocketed his hands and wished for the coat he'd left behind.

Hoover turned onto the walk, heels clacking (another death: to silence).

A sepulchral feeling, he thought, to the thin wash of light overlaying this abyss of street. A counterpoint, castrati and bass. Peel away the light and you: Plunge. Downward. Forever.

Another thought . . . you can tell a lot by the way a person listens to silence.

(Sunday. It was evening all day. Over late coffee and oranges, the old words begin again. The speech too much used, and no doors from this logic of love. We go together like rain and melancholy, blue and morning . . .)

At the corner, turn; and on down this new abyss. Breath pedaling, stabbing into the air like a silent cough, feet killing quiet—

I am intruding.

Darkness is avenging itself on my back.

(And I, guilty realist, dabbler at verses, saying: There is no sign for isolation but a broken spring, no image for time but a ticking heart, nothing for death but stillness . . .)

Light glinted off bare windows. Most of the houses were marooned now in a moat of grass and ascending weed. Driveways and porches and garages all open and empty, dumbly grinning.

(Evening all day. World out the window like a painting slowly turning under glass in a dusty frame. Rain in the sky, but shy about falling. The words: they peak at ten, pace by noon, run out to the end of their taut line . . .)

The shells have names, had them. Martin, Heslep, Rose. Walking past them now, he remembered times they were lit up like pumpkins, orange-yellow light pouring richly out the windows; cars, cycle-strewn yards, newspapers on steps. The casual intimacy of a person inside looking out, waving.

(And I remember your hair among leaves, your body in breaking dew, moonlight that slipped through trees and

windows to put its palm against your face, your waist;
bright and shadow fighting there . . .)

Darkness. It moves aside to let you pass. Closes, im-
passable, behind you.

(Four times: you came to bed, got up, came back to
bed. You turned three times, you threw the pillows off
the bed. Michael, never born, who had two months to
live, was stirring in you and stirring you awake.

Your hair was on the bed like golden threads. The
moon had pushed your face up into the window and hidden your hands in shadow. You were yellow yellow on
the linen bed, and opened your eyes.

—If I weren't afraid, I could leave and never look
back.

You say that, sitting in a hollow of bed, knees tucked
to your flanneled breasts, arms around yourself.

—Would you follow, would you call me back?

I watch your steps track down the walk to the black,
inviting street. And later, when I open the door, you're
there, grinning, coming back; coming back to make coffee
and wait for morning. And another night, another day,
saved from whatever it is that threatens at these
times . . .)

Hoover looked at the streetlight shelled in rainbow and
it was ahead, above, behind, remembered. Darkness
shouldered itself back in around him. Snow hung in the
air, waiting to fall. The dead houses regarded him as he
passed, still, unspeaking.

(October, time of winds and high doubt. It comes
around us like the shutting of a light: the same thing is
happening to others. And the people are going away, the
time has come for going away . . . It all boils up in a
man, and overflows. His birthright of freedom, it's the
freedom to be left alone, that's what he wants most, just
to be left alone, just to draw circles around himself and
shut the world out. Every man's an island, why deny it,
why tread water. So people let go . . .)

Hoover picked the moving shape out of the alley and

was down in a crouch, whistling, almost before the dog saw him. It raised its nose from the ground and walked bashfully toward him, sideways, tail banging at a drum, whining.

"Folks leave you, fella?" A brown shepherd with a heavy silver-studded collar; he didn't bother to look at the jangling nametags. "Take you home with me then, okay?" The shepherd whimpered its agreement. Hoover rummaging in his pockets.

"Sorry, fella, nothing to give you." Showing empty hands, which the dog filled with licks and nuzzles, snuffling.

"Bribery, eh. Sorry, still no food." He stroked his hand into the dog's pelt, found warmth underneath. It sat looking up at him, waiting, expecting, its tail swishing across pavement.

When he erected himself to full height, the dog jumped away and crouched low, ready to run. Hoover walked toward it and put out a hand to its broad, ridged head.

"It's okay, fellow. Tell you what. Come along with me to see a friend, then I'll take you right home and see about getting you something to eat. Think you can wait?"

They punctured the night together, down the walk, heels clacking, claws ticking. Hoover kept his hand on the dog's head as they walked. The nametags threw bells out into the silence.

"Or maybe he'll have something for you there, come to think of it."

Click, clack, click. Staccato tattooed on the ponderous night. The sky is still ambiguous.

(Remembering a night we sat talking, drinking half-cups of coffee as we watched stars sprinkle and throb and fade, then saw dawn all blood and whispered thunder. I remember how your eyes were, pink like shrimp, pink like the sky when it caught the first slanting rays and held them to its chest. And as morning opened around us we were talking of Thoreau and men who sailed the soul, of ways and reasons to change, the old orders, and of why

things break up. Outside our window it was growing between them, people were letting go, were wanting their
Waldens, their Innisfrees, their Arcadias, they were falling away from the town like leaves, like scaling paint, by
twos, by ones. Even in our house, our hearts, it moves
between us. Between us. We feel it turning, feel it touching. But we care, we love, we can't let go . . .)

Hoover drew up short, listening. The shepherd beside
him cocked its ears, trembled happily.

It happens like this . . .

A drone, far off. Closer. Becomes an engine. Then a
swelling of light blocks away. Then a rush and churning
and soon two lashing white eyes. Loudest, chased by a
dog. A roar and past, racing. A thrown thing. Neil's car
. . . and silence again.

And minutes later, the shepherd's body went limp and
its head fell back onto his lap. Hoover took it in his arms
and walked out of the road, its head rolling softly along
the outside of his elbow. In the streetlight his face glistened where the dog had licked it.

Crossing the walk, kicking open a gate that wind had
shut, Hoover surrendered his burden into the lawn. Ten
steps away he looked back and saw that the dog's body
was hidden in deep grass, secret as any Easter egg.

Three hundred and some-odd steps. Two turns. Five
places where cement has split its seams, heaved up, and
grass is growing in the cracks. Pacing this map . . .

(The sea grew tired one day of swinging in harness,
ticking in its box of beach. One spark in the flannel sea,
possessed of fury, gathering slime like a seeded pearl,
thinks of legs and comes onto a rock, lies there in the sun
drying. It seeps, it slushes, it creeps, it crawls; it bakes to
hardness and walks . . . All to the end: that I am walking on two feet down this corridor of black steel and my
hand is turning like a key at this found door . . .)

The door collapse-returned. He looked around. A single light cut into the cafe through a porthole of glass in

the kitchen door; powdery twilight caught in the mirror. In the dim alley before him, neon signs circled and fell, rose and blinked across their boxes like tiny traffic signals. Profound, ponderous grayness, like the very stuff of thought . . .

Decision failed him; he had turned to go when he heard the door and saw light swell.

"Dr. Hoover . . ."

He turned back.

"Didn't know for sure you were still around." Nervously. "About the last ones, I guess."

Hoover nodded. "Any food, Doug?"

"Just coffee, sorry. Coffee's on, though. Made a pot for myself, plenty left." He stepped behind the counter and knocked the corner off a cube of stacked cups, burn scars on his hands rippling in mirror-bemused light.

"Sugar, cream?" Sliding the cup onto crisp pink formica.

Hoover waved them both off. "Black's the best way."

"Yeah . . . No one been in here for a week or more. I ain't bothered to keep the stuff out like I ought to."

Hoover sat down by the cup, noticing that Doug had moved back away from the counter. "Like you say, I guess. Last ones."

Doug scratched at his stomach where it depended out over the apron. Large hands going into pockets, rumpling the starched white.

"Reckon I *could* get you a sandwich. Or some toast— then it don't matter if the bread's a little stale."

"Coffee's fine. Don't bother."

"You sure? Wouldn't be any trouble."

Hoover smiled and shook his head. "Forget it, just coffee. But thanks anyway."

Doug looked down at the cup. "Don't mind, I'll have one with you." His penciled monobrow flexed at the middle, pointed down. It was like the one-stroke bird that children are taught to draw; the upper part of a stylized heart. "Get my cup." Over his shoulder: "Be right back."

Light rose as the kitchen door opened; died back down, leaving Hoover alone. He turned his eyes to buff-flecked white tiles; let them carry his interest across the floor, swiveling his chair to keep up. Light picked out tiny blades of gleam on the gold bands that edged formica-and-naugahyde. A few pygmy neons hopscotched high on the walls. The booths were empty as shells, humming with shadow; above them (showing against homogenized paint, rich yellow, creamy tan; sprinkled among windows) were small dark shapes he knew as free-painted anchors.

(All this shut in a small cafe, sculpt in shades of gray. Change one letter, you have cave again . . .)

Doug came back (light reached, retreated), poured steaming coffee. He squeezed around the end of the counter and sat two seats away.

"Neil left today."

"Yeah, I saw him up the street on the way here."

"So that's whose car it was. Wasn't sure, heard it going by. Going like a bat out of hell from the sound." He drank, made a face. "Too hot. Wonder what kept him? Said he was going to take off this morning." He blew across the mouth of his cup, as though he might be trying to whistle, instead breathing vapor. He tried another taste. "Will came through, you know . . ."

Hoover's own cup was sweating, oils were sliding over the surface. It was a tan cup; the lip was chipped. They weren't looking at each other.

"That big cabin up on the cape. His grandfather built it for a place to get away and do his writing, way the hell away from everything. Now it's his."

"I know. My sister called me up last week to say good-bye, told me about it, they thought it was coming through. Wonder when *she's* leaving?"

Doug looked up sharply, then dropped his head. "Thought you knew. She left about three, four days ago." Doug belched, lightly.

"Oh. I guess she went up early to get things ready, he'll meet her there. You know women."

"Yeah. Yeah, that's probably it." He went for more coffee, poured for them both. "Coffee's the last thing I need."

"You too."

"Yeah—lot worse for some, though. Been over a week for me, lost about twenty pounds. Catnap some . . . Thing you wonder about is, where'd they find a lawyer? For the papers and all. Didn't, maybe, guess it don't make much difference anymore, stuff like that. Anyhow, they're gone."

(And the wall's a wedge. Shove it between two people and they come apart, like all the rest . . .)

Hoover shrugged his shoulders, putting an elbow on the counter and steepling fingers against his forehead.

"Almost brought a friend, Doug . . ."

The big man straightened in his chair. His mouth made "Friend?" sit on his lips unspoken.

"But he was indisposed, disposed, at the last minute."

Doug was staring at him strangely.

"A dog. Neil hit it. I was going to see if I could talk you out of some food for it."

"Oh! Yeah, there's some stuff, meat and all I'm just gonna have to throw out anyway. What isn't spoiled already's getting that way fast. Didn't know there were dogs still around, though? Whose is it?"

"There aren't now. I hadn't seen it before. *Was* it: it's dead." Extinct.

"Oh. Yeah, Neil *was* going pretty fast. Dog probably wandered in from someplace else anyway, looking for food after they left him." Gazing into the bottom of his cup Doug swirled what coffee was left against the grounds, making new patterns, like tiny cinders after a rain. "Always been a cat man myself. Couldn't keep one, though, haven't since I was a kid. Sarah's asthma, you know."

"You do have to be careful. Used to have hay fever

myself, fall come around I couldn't breathe. Took an al-
lergy test and they cleared it up."

"Yeah, we tried that. Tried about everything. You
oughta see our income tax for the last few years, reads
like a medical directory. Sarah got so many holes poked
in her, the asthma should have leaked right out. Wasn't
any of it seemed to help, though."

"How's Sarah doing? Haven't seen her for quite a
while. She's usually running around in here helping you,
shooing you back to the kitchen, making you change your
apron, talking to customers. Brightens the place up a lot."

Doug tilted the cup to drain an extra ounce of cold
coffee off the grounds.

"Not much business lately," he said. "Boy I had working for me just kind of up and left three-four months ago
and I never got around to looking for help, no need of it,
specially now."

"She's well, though? Doing okay."

Doug put his cup down, rattling it against the saucer.

"Yeah, she's okay. She—" He stood and made his way
around the counter. "She went away awhile. To get some
rest." He dipped under the counter and came up with a
huge stainless steel bowl. "Think I'll make another pot.
This one's getting stale. Better anyhow if you use the stuff
regularly, easier on it, works better—like getting a car
out on the road to clean her out."

He started working at the urn, opening valves, sloshing
dark coffee down into the bowl. Hoover watched Doug's
reflection in the shady mirror and a dimmer image of
himself lying out across the smooth formica.

So Doug's wife had gone away too; Sarah had gone to
get some rest . . . Hoover remembered a song he'd heard
at one of the faculty parties: Went to see my Sally Gray,
Went to see my Sally Gray, Went to see my Sally Gray,
Said my Sally's gone away—only this time Sally Gray had
taken everybody else with her . . .

Doug was chuckling at the urn.

"You know I gotta make twenty cups just to get two

for us, I mean that's the least this monster here'll handle. Ask him for forty-fifty cups, he'll give it to you in a minute. But you ask him for two, just two little cups of coffee, and he'll blow his stack, or a gasket or something." He went back to clanging at the urn. "Reckon you can handle ten of 'em?" He started fixing the filter, folding it in half twice, tearing off a tiny piece at one corner. "Hell, there ain't enough people left in town to drink twenty cups of coffee if I was giving it away and they was dying of thirst. Or anywhere around here."

He bowed the filter into a cone between his hands, climbed a chair to install it, then came down and drew a glass of water, putting it in front of Hoover.

"That's for while you wait."

"I need to be going anyway, Doug. Have to get some sleep sooner or later."

Doug reached and retrieved Hoover's cup, staring at the sludge settling against the bottom. "One last cup."

"All right. One more."

One for the road . . .

Doug bent and rinsed the cup, then got another from the stack and put it on the counter. He stood looking at the clean, empty cup, wiping his hands against the apron. He lit a cigarette, nodding to himself, and the glowing red tip echoed one of the skipping neon signs on the wall behind him. He put the package on the counter and smiled, softly.

"You know, you could've sat right here and watched the whole thing happening. I mean, at first there'd be the usual group, but they were . . . nervous. You know: jumpy. They'd sort of scatter themselves out and every now and then the talk would die down and there'd be this quiet, like everybody was listening for something, waiting for something. Then a lot of them stopped coming, and the rest would sit all around the room, talking across to each other, then just sitting there quiet for a long time by themselves. Wasn't long before the regulars didn't come anymore—and you knew what was going on, you knew they were draining out of town like someone had pulled the plug.

"That was when the others started showing up. They'd come in with funny looks on their faces, all anxious to talk. And when you tried to talk to 'em, they'd be looking behind you and around the room and every once in a while they'd get up and go look out the window. And then they'd leave and you'd never see them again."

Hoover sat with his legs locked back, toes on the floor, regarding the glass of water (the bubbles had nearly vanished). He nodded: he knew, he understood.

"For a while I got some of the ones that were coming through. I'd be in the back and I'd hear the door and come out, and there'd be this guy standing there, shuffling his feet, looking at the floor. He'd pay and take his coffee over in the corner, then the next time I looked around, he'd be gone—lot of them would just take it with them, to go. Then even that stopped."

(The people: they drip, trickle, run, pour, flood from the cities. They don't look back. And the ones who stay, try to fight it—they feel it growing in them worse than before. Turning in them, touching them, and they care they love they can't let go. But the harder they fight, the worse it is, like going down in quicksand, and the wall's a wedge: shove it between two people and they come apart, like all the rest, like all the rest of the world . . .)

Doug found something on the counter to watch.

"One time during the War, the ship I was on went down on the other side and a sub picked us up. I still remember how it felt, being in that sub, all the people packed in like sardines, stuffed into spaces between controls and motors. You'd think it would be full of noise, movement. But there was something about being under all that water, being closed in, something about the light —anyway, something that made you feel alone, made you want to whisper. I'd just sit in it and listen. Feel. And pretty soon I'd start wanting them all to really go away, to leave me alone . . ."

Doug stood looking for a moment out one of the small round windows past Hoover's shoulder.

"Yeah. Yeah, that's the way it is all right." Then his eyes switched back to Hoover's cup. "I better go get that coffee, just take it a minute to perk."

He picked up his cup and walked down the counter toward the kitchen, running his hand along the formica. The door swung back in, wobbled, stopped (light had reached, retreated).

Hoover felt suddenly hollow; empty; squeezed. He looked around. The room was a cave again.

Out in the kitchen, Doug moved among his stainless steel and aluminum. Hoover heard him banging pots on pans, opening doors, sliding things on shelves out of his way. Then the texture of sound changed, sank to quiet, became a silence that stretched and stretched. And seconds later broke: the back door creaked open and shut with a hiss of air along its spring, clicking shut.

(So now the quicksand's got Doug too, for all his fighting. Now he's gone with the rest, gone with Sally Gray . . .)

Outside in the alley angling along and behind the cafe, Doug's Harley-Davidson pumped and caught, coughed a couple of times and whined away, one cylinder banging.

Hoover sat looking at the abandoned cup as silence came in to fill his ears. Then he heard the buzzing of electric wires.

The last grasping and their fingers had slipped.

The wedge was driven in, and they'd come apart . . .

He stood, digging for a dime and finding he'd forgotten to fill his pockets, then walked to the register and punched a key. "No Sale" came up under the glass. There were two nickels and some pennies.

He fed the coins in (ping! ping!), dialed, and waited. The phone rang twice and something came on, breathing into the wires.

"Cass?"

Breathing.

Again: "Cass?" Louder.

Breathing.

"Cass, is that you?"

Silence.

"Who is this? Please. Cass?"

A small, quiet voice. "I'm afraid you have the wrong number."

A click and buzzing . . .

After a while, he reached up and flipped out the change tray. As the lid slid away, a tarnished gray eye showed there: someone had left a dime behind.

Nine rings. Cass' voice in the lifted phone. Sleepy; low and smooth; pâté, ready for spreading.

"Cass?"

"Is that you, Bob? Where are you?"

"Doug's place. Be right home." The space of a breath. "Honey . . ."

"Yes?"

"Get your bags packed, we're leaving tonight."

"Leaving?" She was coming awake. "Where—"

"I don't know. South maybe, climate's better. But maybe that's what everyone will think—anyway, we'll decide. Just get your things ready, just what you absolutely have to have. We can always pick up things we need in towns. There's a big box in the bottom of the utility closet, some of my stuff, some tools and so on I got together awhile back. Put that with the rest—there's some room left in it you can use. I'll be right home. Everything else we'll need is already in the car."

"Bob . . ."

"Just do it Cass. Please. I'll be right back, to help."

"Bob, are you sure—"

"Yes."

She paused. "I'll be ready."

He hung up and walked into the kitchen, came out again with a ten-pound sack of coffee under one arm. He started over the tiles toward the door, then turned back and picked up the cigarettes lying on the counter. He stood by the door, looking back down the dim alley: stood at the mouth of the cave, looking into distances (he'd seen a stereopticon once; it was much the same effect).

The tiny neons skipped and blinked dumbly in their boxes; the kitchen light glared against the window, fell softly along the mirror. Shadows came in to fill the cafe; sat at tables, slumped in booths, stood awry on the floor; watching, waiting. At the end of the counter, the blank tan cup silently surrendered.

He turned and switched the knob. Went through the door. Shut it behind him. The click of the lock ran away into the still air and died; he was locked into silence . . .

Cautiously he assaulted the street's independence, heels ticking parameters for the darkness, the motive, the town. The sky hung low above his head.

(I walk alone. Alone. Men don't run in packs, but they run . . . Death at the wheel expects his spin. Dark seeps in around the edges, winds rise in the caves of our Aeolian skulls, five fingers reach to take winter into our hearts, the winter of all our hearts)

And they came now in the darkness, they loomed and squatted about him, all the furnished tombs: this dim garden of rock and wood.

(Bars of silence. Score: four bars of silence, end on the seventh. See how they show on my white shirt among the roses. Bars and barristers of silence)

The quick blue spurt of a struck match. A cigarette flames, then glows, moving down the street into darkness.

(There is no sign for isolation but a broken spring, no image for time but a ticking heart, nothing for death but stillness . . . and the wall, the wedge, is splitting deeper but we'll hold, for a while we'll hold on, you and I)

He stood still in the stillness that flowed around him and listened to the hum of insects calling through the black flannel. As if in answer, clouds came lower.

(At the mouth of caves, turning. We can't see out far, in deep, but the time has come for going away the time

has come for becoming . . . At the mouth of caves, turning, and time now to enter the calm, the old orders. At
the mouth of caves. Turning)

He walked on and his heels talked and the night came
in to hush him.

He hollered out into the dark, screamed once out into
silence—and it entered his heart.

He passed a pearl-gray streetlight, passed a graveyard
lawn.

("Sudden and swift and light as that the ties gave, and
we learned of finalities besides the grave." Is this how it
feels, the instant of desertion—a vague epiphany of epo-
chal stillness, primal quiet?)

Around him, scarcely sounding his echo, stood the
shells of houses, like trees awaiting the return of dryads
who had lost their way.

(The instant of desertion, the instance of silence)

The cigarette arced into the street and fell there, glowing blankly.

He bent his head and began to hurry.

And with a flourish, the snows began.